"A clever, ou

✻ ✻ ✻

"I think we could've planned this one better."

Jake sighed. "Just like a woman. Always got 20/20 hindsight."

"This is not about 20/20 hindsight," I said. "It's about you letting the damned gate swing shut because you were in too much of a hurry to check behind yourself."

"It was wide open," Jake protested. "We disabled it."

"Well, it's shut now," I said. "Hold on." I punched the accelerator.

"Stella, no!" Jake yelled. "Don't hurt my truck!"

I heard gunfire behind us and mashed the accelerator pedal to the floor. "Brace yourself!"

Dear Reader,

What do you plan to accomplish in 2005? Let Silhouette Bombshell jump-start your year with this month's fast-paced lineup of stories featuring amazing women who will entertain you, energize you and inspire you to get out there and get things done!

Author Nancy Bartholomew brings on the heat with *Stella, Get Your Man*. P.I. Stella Valocchi is on a missing-persons case—but with a lying client, a drug lord gunning for her and a new partner who thinks he's the boss, Stella's got her hands full staying cool under fire.

The pressure rises as our popular twelve-book ATHENA FORCE continuity series continues with *Deceived*, by Carla Cassidy, in which a computer whiz with special, supersecret talents discovers that she's on the FBI's Most Wanted list and her entire life may be a lie.

Reality isn't what it seems in the mystic thriller *Always Look Twice* by Sheri WhiteFeather. Heroine Olivia Whirlwind has a unique gift, but delving into the minds of crime victims will bring her ever closer to a ruthless killer and will make everyone a suspect—including those she loves.

And finally, travel to Romania with Crystal Green's *The Huntress*, as an heiress with an attitude becomes a vampire hunter on a mission for vengeance after her lover is captured by those mysterious creatures of the night.

Enjoy all four, and when you're finished, please send your comments to me c/o Silhouette Books, 233 Broadway, Suite 1001, New York, NY 10279.

Sincerely,

Natashya Wilson

Natashya Wilson
Associate Senior Editor, Silhouette Bombshell

Please address questions and book requests to:
Silhouette Reader Service
U.S.: 3010 Walden Ave., P.O. Box 1325, Buffalo, NY 14269
Canadian: P.O. Box 609, Fort Erie, Ont. L2A 5X3

Stella, Get Your Man

NANCY BARTHOLOMEW

Published by Silhouette Books

America's Publisher of Contemporary Romance

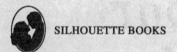

SILHOUETTE BOOKS

ISBN 0-373-51339-9

STELLA, GET YOUR MAN

NANCY BARTHOLOMEW

didn't seem like the Bombshell type at first. Sure, she grew up in Philadelphia, but she was a gentle minister's daughter. Sometimes, though, true wildness simmers just below the surface. Nancy started singing country music in biker bars before she graduated from high school. And yes, Dad was there, sitting in the front row, watching over his little girl! She graduated from college with a degree in psychology and promptly moved into the inner city, where she found work dragging addicted inner-city teenagers into drug and alcohol rehabilitation. She then moved south to Atlanta and worked as the director of a substance abuse treatment program for court-ordered offenders.

When the criminal life became less of a challenge, Nancy turned to the final frontier—parenthood. This drove her to writing. Nancy lives in North Carolina, rides with the police on a regular basis, raises two hooligan teenage boys and tries to keep up with her writing, her psychotherapy practice and her garden. She hopes you'll love her third "child," Stella Valocchi, and thanks you from the bottom of her heart for reading this book!

For Martha,
who taught Stella how to be a true Bombshell!

Chapter 1

It was 3:00 a.m. and freezing. I was lying next to my partner, Jake, belly deep in pig shit and trying to remind myself that repo is an art form. A good repossession requires creativity and ingenuity. Repo, like art, is not always comfortable or warm. It is messy. Artists are, by their very nature, required to suffer. I took a deep whiff of Mama Pig and knew I was truly suffering. But it wasn't the agony that bothered me really, it was my karma. This job could ruin my karma for all time. You see, we were robbing Santa Claus.

Jake hates it when I say that, but it's true. Okay, so it's not *exactly* true, but try to tell that to any good Italian-American in Glenn Ford and see where it gets you. We were huddled up inside Santa's pigpen, waiting for our Golden Moment, the time when the coast was clear and Jake could bring the tow truck up the driveway.

"Nothin' good is gonna come of this," I muttered.

"Stella, you were a cop. 'Santa,' as you so lovingly refer

to him, is a crook. He's a dope dealer. He didn't pay for the sleigh, despite having the cash, so we're taking it back. Clear and simple. It's a job, Stella, nothing more."

I stared up at the moon and shuddered. Joey "Smack" Spagnazi, aka "Santa," did have a bad reputation. He hadn't served time. He hadn't even been convicted, but every man, woman and child in tiny Glenn Ford knew he was "connected," in a mafioso sort of way. Everyone thought he was Chester County, Pennsylvania's, drug kingpin, but so far, the police hadn't been able to catch him. He was just too slick. But Joey Smack had his good side, too.

"Maybe he used the payment money to send more kids to that summer camp of his," I offered.

Jake snorted, ever the cynic. "Yeah, right, save kids with cancer so you can later introduce them to a lifetime cocaine habit. Stella, I don't get you. Usually you're the one giving me the soft-heart lecture."

"All's I'm saying is, Joey Smack doesn't mind copping to running numbers, loan-sharking or an assorted list of criminal activities as long as your arm, but he says drugs aren't his thing. What if he's telling the truth and we're robbing Santa Claus?"

"Jesus." Jake moaned. "Listen, we took the job, let's just do it. If Joey Smack wants a sleigh so bad, let him pay for it. We don't have a dog in this fight, all right? We work for Lifetime Novelty. We are not the judge and jury for Joey Smack!"

I studied my partner. Good-looking, in a tall, dark and handsome sort of way. Smart, on most occasions, and resourceful when smarts failed. Why was he so stupid about humanity?

I mentally slapped myself. He was, after all, a man, wasn't he?

Jake was staring back at me, the impatience leaving his face as something else replaced it, something smoldering hot and, up until now, unrealized between the two of us, unfinished business that had been on the back burner for years. Yep, Jake was a man all right, the kind of man that makes you tingle all over and slowly come to a steady, about-to-boil-over-if-you-touch-me simmer that I found frankly maddening.

"Go get the truck," I said. "Let's get this over with."

I rolled away from him, coming up into a low crouch that startled Mama Pig and her babies. In the darkness I heard Jake chuckle as he moved off toward the road. I forced myself to focus on the job at hand. Joey Smack's farmhouse sat on a slight rise, hundreds of yards from the road, protected by a wrought-iron electrified fence, which we'd disabled.

In the middle of the huge expanse of pasture he called a lawn sat a huge Christmas panorama. Joey Smack was famous for this. On one side of the field, the Baby Jesus had just been born, surrounded by his entourage, every piece hand-painted and lit up to be visible from the road. On the right, Frosty the Snowman looked on a fake pond filled with magnetic figures that swirled and skated to cheery Christmas music. But it was in the center of the field, most prominently displayed, that Joey Smack had finally outdone himself.

An electronic Santa sat in an illuminated sleigh, hooked up to nine sizable and well-lit reindeer. As you watched, Santa waved and slowly doffed his hat. Every piece of the display used the appropriately colored lights. It was wired into a panel that insured a visual feast for the hundreds of cars that drove by each evening in a long slow snake that snarled traffic for hours every night from mid-November until January. The entire showcase probably compromised the electrical power banks that fed the eastern seaboard, but this didn't worry old Joey Smack.

No, the affable host, dressed as Santa, would wander to the roadside every night, all smiles and good cheer. He'd hand each innocent child a sucker and ask earnestly, "What do you want for Christmas?" Joey seemed to believe he really was

Santa Claus and the new sleigh just added fuel to his delusional fire. It was a custom-made, larger-than-life sleigh and
Joey was often spotted from the road, maniacally polishing
its brass frame, or sitting up on the bench, shoving the wire-
mesh Santa to one side as he cracked the whip over poor Rudolph's head.

The word on the street was that Joey slipped his regulars
rocks of crack when they pulled up in front of the estate for
the grand nighttime viewing, but again, there was no proof of
this. The other myth about Joey Smack was easier to verify.
If he knew of an Italian-American family in Glenn Ford who
was in need or without at Christmastime, Joey took care of
them, with presents and food and an envelope stuffed with
cash to tide them over "until there's better times."

Was it any wonder Joey Smack never had to worry about
prosecution? Who would testify against a saint like that? Further, who in their right mind would attempt to repo Santa's
sled from Santa Claus? We were risking the wrath of hundreds
of children, dozens of Joey's minions, and probably risking
our own lives as well, and for what, a few lousy hundred dollars? What was the big deal about eating and paying the rent?
Was that really so important? Was this really a viable career
choice?

I crept slowly toward the darkened display, looking for the
panel to disconnect the wires before Jake arrived with the
truck. Repo is all about speed. We had to load old Santa, his
vehicle and the nine tiny reindeer before someone woke up
and realized what was going on. No amount of Yankee ingenuity or artistic license would make Joey Smack decide to let
Santa go without a fight. Stealth was our middle name, repossession was our game.

I was half swaggering now, buying into my own propa-
ganda. Jake and I were pros. This was a cakewalk for us.
After all, he was a former Delta Force Army Ranger, while I

was a veritable killing machine, a former cop with every bit of specialized training I could absorb. What could be easier than a simple repossession? In fact, maybe that was the real problem; I just wasn't challenged by my newfound profession.

When Jake came chugging up the driveway, I was ready for him.

"They're unhooked. Let's do Santa and the sleigh first and then stuff the reindeer around them."

He nodded and we flew into action, moving as quickly and quietly as possible. We were easily a hundred yards from the house, but every move sounded like a shotgun and the diesel's engine seem to roar louder and louder as we scrambled to load old Saint Nick.

The true shotgun blast was almost a relief.

It thundered into the still night air, turning baseless apprehension into fully grounded reality. We were busted. Rudolph stood alone on the snowy ground where he waited to join his imprisoned but unsecured buddies on the flatbed of the truck. As far as I was concerned, he could stay there, too. The Lifetime Novelty Company would just have to make do with the haul we had on the back of the truck. I was not battling shotgun fire to reclaim one red-nosed reindeer. Not me.

"Drive!" I yelled, diving for the passenger-side door.

The gun roared again.

"Jake, damn it! Let's go!"

I could hear voices now, men calling out as they ran toward the pasture.

I screamed his name one more time, but knew even before I looked, that Jake had been hit.

I flew out of the truck, ducked low behind the flatbed and yelled, "Repossession! Hold your fire!"

This was met with another blast from the shotgun, this time over my head. They didn't care who I was. They were protecting their property and would say that when the police came to investigate our murders. Shit!

"Stella!" Jake's voice, weak, came from the rear of the flat-bed. I found him, struggling to stand, and went to him. I grabbed his arm, slipped my hand around his waist and felt sticky liquid coat my fingers. My heart clutched in my throat and for a heartbeat I found I couldn't move.

"Okay, babe, hold on," I whispered.

A blast of gunfire blew out the windshield and back window of the truck. With strength I didn't know I had, I pulled Jake forward, throwing him onto the floorboard of the truck as I dived over him to slide behind the wheel.

I heard Jake moan as I pulled my Glock out of its holster and slammed the truck into gear. We were moving.

Jake squirmed, trying to pull his door shut as he, too, reached for his weapon.

"I got it!" I said. "Just lie still. You're bleeding!"

I was driving hell for leather toward the front gate. Behind us, Joey Smack's security guards fired again. As I watched in the rearview mirror, a set of headlights swung out from behind the farmhouse and began following us. I glanced at Jake, saw the color drain from his face and knew we were in trouble.

My chest tightened with feelings I didn't want to acknowledge, not to myself and certainly not to Jake. I was scared, but not about Joey Smack or his men. I was scared because it was Jake lying there, bleeding, and because I knew with a deep certainty that he mattered to me, really mattered.

"This is so not good," I muttered.

"What?"

I didn't answer him immediately. It wouldn't do for Jake to see me scared, or worse, concerned. Any sign of emotion from me would be a dead giveaway. Around Jake I was as cool as a cucumber. I forced myself to take a deep breath before I spoke.

"Oh, nothing," I said. "I just think we could've planned this one better, that's all."

Jake sighed, a half moan that sounded like raw pain. "Just like a woman," he gasped. "Always got twenty-twenty hind-sight, always gotta process the problems in the relationship."

I looked out in front of us, squinting as the cold night air hit my eyes.

"No, this is not about twenty-twenty hindsight," I said. "It is about you letting the damn gate swing shut because you were in too much of a hurry to check behind yourself. Admit it, you were in a big hurry to score Santa and you let the gate swing shut!"

"It was wide open," Jake protested, starting to sound like a querulous child. "I knew we'd be leaving in a hurry. Remember? We disabled it."

I stared at the eight-foot wrought-iron fence up ahead. It was closed and locked. I took a deep breath.

"Well, it's shut now," I said. "Hold on!"

I punched the accelerator and gripped the steering wheel with both hands.

"Don't hurt my truck!" Jake yelled. "It's all I got left of the shop!"

I ignored him. Jake's truck was dispensable, we were not. His shop might've been blown to bits by a maniac, and he might love his truck, but I had to believe our lives were worth a lot more.

"Stella!"

We hit the fence dead-on. The shock of the impact threw me against the steering wheel and wedged Jake tighter beneath the glove compartment. The F–350 bent the metal bars like green tree limbs, but they refused to break. I shook the impact off, fastened my seat belt and shot a look in the rear-view mirror as I backed up and got ready to try again. The headlights were gaining on us.

"Stella, no!" Jake screamed.

I ignored him and yelled. "Brace yourself!"

I mashed the accelerator pedal to the floor, held my left foot on the brake and then, just as I felt certain the engine would blow, released the brake pedal. We slammed into the fence, the lock gave, and we were through.

"My truck!" Jake moaned.

"Your ass," I said, wincing as I tried to turn my neck and look into the rearview mirror. "I saved your ass and all you can think about is a few cosmetic repairs to your grillwork?"

I heard gunfire behind us, close behind us, and saw Joey Smack's people on our tail.

"You still got your gun?" I asked.

Jake pulled himself up onto the front seat, SIG-Sauer in hand, panting with the pain and exertion.

"Out the back window," I said.

Another gunshot and the left rearview mirror bit the dust.

"Goddamnit! That does it!" Jake cried. He sprang up, aimed, and then lowered the pistol. "I can't see a fucking thing! The damn sleigh's in the way. I can't get a shot off."

I veered left, then right, hoping to keep the car from pulling up alongside us. I looked in the rearview mirror again just as Santa took matters into his own hands. As I watched, the robotic Santa seemed to sway, his arms spinning wildly as he careened out of the sleigh and almost toppled off the back of the flatbed. He lay like a swimmer, poised to dive, wobbling.

"Jake?"

"What now?"

"You didn't have time to tie Santa down, did you?"

Jake rose to look out the back window frame.

Santa began to move, sailing off the flatbed in slow-motion perfection, and crashing down onto the hood of our pursuers. There was a loud sound of tires screeching. The car bobbled across the highway and off into the woods. The last

image I had was of a black sedan crashing into a tree and exploding into a fireball.

"Damn!" Jake murmured. "I think they're dead."

I ignored him and drove. There was nothing I could do
about that right now. Saving our lives and taking care of Jake
was my only focus. I had no idea how badly he'd been
wounded. My chest hurt with the effort to keep from screaming. I wouldn't allow myself to even consider the possibility
of Jake's injuries being life-threatening. I couldn't go there
and still function. It was all business or Stella blows a gasket,
and I just couldn't afford the luxury of emotion. I had to make
sure Jake was safe and on the mend before I gave in to my
feelings.

Along the way to the hospital we lost a couple of reindeer,
but considering we'd managed to survive, I viewed the loss
more as casualties of war and not shrinkage of the merchan-
dise. I planned to charge Lifetime Novelty a hazard fee, too,
for pain and suffering. By the time we actually reached the
medical center, I'd managed to parlay our near disaster into
a right hefty invoice, due upon receipt.

"You know," I said as we pulled up to the emergency-room
loading dock, "it wasn't such a bad night after all! We got
what we came for, nobody on our team died and we're going
to make a lot of money!"

When Jake didn't answer, I turned to look at him. He was
slumped against the passenger-side window, unconscious.

Chapter 2

Eventually, the entire team assembled in the emergency-room waiting area. I call us a team, but that's really for lack of a better term. A few months ago, after my career and love life went ka-plooie in one short night, I'd returned home to my old hometown, hoping to lick my wounds and regroup. What's that old saying? We make plans and God laughs? Three months later I was still here, only now I was in business with most of my extended family and a man who'd once left me standing at the altar.

If I'd seen another option, believe me, I would've hopped on it like ugly on an ape, but my uncle was dead, my aunt needed me, and my cousin was too much of a fruitcake to hold down a regular nine-to-five job. Besides, she was in love with the former assistant D.A. for Chester County. That kind of hookup comes in real handy when you're starting a one-stop-does-it-all private investigation agency.

Jake won his ticket into the deal by helping me find my uncle's killer. My aunt was along for the ride because she is one of our country's brightest chemists, and because of that, she requires almost constant protection. Where better place to be protected than in an agency specializing in detection, protection and repossession?

So when Jake got shot, it was only natural that they all showed up to show their support. We might not have a plan, and on any given day one or more of us has at least one screw loose, but we are loyal, and my aunt loves Jake for reasons I may never really understand. There was no stopping them from coming, and to tell the truth, I was relieved. I looked around the waiting room, saw them sitting there, and felt somehow better about everything, even Jake.

My aunt Lucy, her gray hair still in pink rollers, her butterball body encased in a solid black dress with black sensible shoes, sat next to my bizarre cousin, Nina. My aunt was frowning and clutching her black purse to her ample bosom.

Nina, despite the early hour, looked the same as she always did, disheveled. She sat next to Spike Montgomery, Chester County's former assistant D.A., and her girlfriend. Nina was wearing wrinkled khakis, a T-shirt under a wrinkled man's cotton dress shirt and open-weave, thick-soled sandals. Her short, spiky blond hair stood out all over her head, its pink tips glowing like traffic cones in a work zone out on I–95. Sometimes I wondered how Spike, the seeming counterculture opposite to Nina, had ever fallen in love with such an oddball.

Spike was the only one of us who seemed unperturbed by a 4:00 a.m. wake-up call to the emergency room. Her long brown hair was pulled back into a simple, conservative ponytail. Her jeans were Tommy Hilfiger, dark denim, and very much unwrinkled. Her turtleneck sweater was unblemished beige, and matched her skin tone and flawless complexion. She wore stiletto heels, even at this hour, when it was all I could do to balance myself in sneakers. But that was Spike, performance artist and former D.A. With her, nothing was truly as it seemed. She was like a tiny Christmas present in a huge, well-wrapped box.

Of course, Lloyd wasn't allowed in despite my aunt's protests that he was really my uncle Benny reincarnated. He was, after all, an Australian sheepdog. My dog. Instead, Lloyd was relegated to Aunt Lucy's ancient Buick, where he sat behind the wheel, with one paw on the gearshift, waiting for updates. Nina had tried to smuggle him in to no avail, and I could tell she wasn't going to let the issue die an easy death.

As if reading my thoughts, Nina got up and decided to revisit the issue with the powers that watched over the emergency room. She walked across the room, shoulders squared, head held high. Spike watched, following Nina's progress with a benevolent smile.

"The Western world so discriminates against Eastern philosophy," Nina told the security guard at the E.R. entrance. "I mean, like, in China, Border collies would be a part of the family. They wouldn't have to wait in cars."

"Yeah, but that's on account of the family don't want nobody eating their backup stash," the guard said. "Here we just say leave the animals outside where they belong."

"You are such a bigot!" Nina sputtered.

That was when Aunt Lucy decided to get into the fray. "You are talking about my husband, sir," she snapped. "And I do not appreciate your attitude! Benito should be with Jake."

The security guard wasn't sure what to do with this turn of events. He took the cigar stump out of his mouth and stared, slack-jawed, at my aunt.

"Excuse me?" he said.

Nina stepped in between the two. "My uncle died a few months ago. Aunt Lucy says the dog is him, reincarnated." She glared at the guard. "And who's to say he isn't?" she finished, daring the man to disagree.

The security guard cocked his head to one side. "Is this uncle related to the patient?" he asked.

"No," Aunt Lucy answered. "But we look out for each other."

The guard gave her a patronizing smile. "Well, then," he said, "if he ain't family, he ain't coming in anyway, so he can park his canine butt in the lot like all the other dogs!"

That's when Spike took over dragging the two women inside while I took a detour back into Jake's examining room. I was family on account of I'd told the admitting clerk that I was Jake's wife. I figured they might get sticky on the policies and procedures, so I took care of the red tape early on.

After all, Jake had been unconscious. It was up to me to ensure his safety and overall well-being. We were partners now and even if I had mixed feelings about the guy in real life, it wouldn't do to act that way when the chips were down. It just wouldn't be professional. Actually, I was about to lose my mind worrying about him. I was having a great deal of trouble stuffing my feelings back into a neat little box. I couldn't stand thinking he might be critically wounded.

"Relax," the resident told me. "It's just a flesh wound with a lot of blood loss. The bullet went clean through his side. Other than a couple of little scars, he should be fine. Just give him a few days' rest and go easy on the, um, physical activities."

It must've been the late hour. I stared at the doctor, not comprehending what he was trying to tell me.

"He means no sex for a couple of days, honey," Jake said, leering at me from the exam table. "He doesn't want you wearing your old husband out and possibly busting something open." Jake chuckled. "Like I told you, Doc, she's a feisty one, that wife of mine!"

The young doctor had the decency to blush, but Jake merely looked pleased with himself.

"I was only looking out for your best interests, Jake!"

"Don't worry, baby," Jake said. "I won't let you get too frustrated."

I crossed the room to the stretcher, bent down close to Jake's ear and whispered. "You just wait until I get you out of here, then we'll see who gets frustrated. You're lucky I don't rip those stitches out here and now, sport."

Jake moaned and the doctor worked to conceal a smirk. I turned around just as he reached to hand me Jake's discharge instructions.

"It's really not at all like it seems," I said. "He's been like this since high school. See, I turned him down and he just hasn't gotten over the shock. And by the way, we're not really married. I just said that so the guard dogs out there would let me in. We work together."

The doctor smirked harder. "Sure," he said. "Happens all the time." He stepped closer and peered into my eyes. "Were you injured at all? I mean, like a blow on the head maybe?"

I spun around just in time to see Jake behind me, making circular motions around his ear and then motioning to me, trying to indicate that I was the crazy one and the doc should humor me.

"Listen here, you," I told Jake. "Don't try me, buddy. It's never too late to be seriously wounded."

Jake laughed.

The doctor turned back to me. "I want you to close your eyes, then stand on one foot and touch your nose with the tip of your left index finger."

"Oh, bite me!" I said. "Are you coming, Jake?"

"Not yet," he said, grinning. "I'm running a little slow. Maybe if you talk dirty…"

"It's probably the pain-medication talking," the doctor said, still peering intently into my eyes. "Now, I really would like to check you out."

"Wouldn't we all?" Jake leered.

The doctor handed me a bottle of pills. "Give these to him every four hours, as needed."

I gripped the bottle and looked back at my new victim. "Hear that, big boy? I'm to give these to you for pain, so I'd suggest you behave."

I turned and glowered at the doctor who was approaching me with a blood-pressure cuff. "Back off, Shorty. I told you, I'm fine!"

The doctor blanched and practically ran from the room. I watched the door swing shut behind him and turned my attention back to Jake Carpenter. I was about to take him to task for everything, from leaving me at the altar my senior year of high school to making my life a living hell, but we were interrupted before I could launch my lecture.

"How you talk, Stella! I could hear every word you said to that nice doctor. What a disgrace. And then, to turn on this one when he is wounded and half out of his mind with the pain."

Aunt Lucy stood in the doorway, glaring at me then smiling at Jake.

"He's hurt! This is how you treat someone who saves you from God knows what kind of madman? I thought you said it was just going to be a routine side job?"

Aunt Lucy was taking no prisoners, but she had the facts all wrong.

"First off, he didn't save me. I saved him! Secondly, it was supposed to be routine, but repos can go down easy or they can turn into your worst nightmare. This was just one of those times."

Aunt Lucy ignored me, walking instead to the gurney where Jake sat, attempting to put on his shirt.

"Don't move!" she groused. "Here." With a deft hand, Aunt Lucy began buttoning Jake's work shirt, all the while issuing orders. "You need rest and someone to look after you." She shot a menacing look in my direction. "You are coming home with us."

"Oh, Mrs. Valocchi, you don't need to do that," Jake protested.

It was as obvious he didn't mean a bit of what he was saying. He let the words slip out slowly, as if he was feeling uncertain and weak. When Aunt Lucy patted his arm, Jake, man of stone, actually faked a wince. I could've thrown up. What a con!

"Yeah, Aunt Lucy," I said. "Jake's gonna be fine. Besides, where would you put him anyhow? All the bedrooms are taken with me and Nina and Spike there. I'll look in on him at his apartment. It's just a flesh wound. He'll be fine."

Wrong. I would've been better off taking a two-by-four and hitting myself in the head. Now I had incurred the wrath of Aunt Lucy.

"Stella Luna Valocchi!" she cried. Then she lapsed into Italian, which was unusual considering she was born and raised in the United States and learned Italian in college while also completing her Ph.D. in chemistry. But whatever the source of her rich vocabulary of Italian curses, the results were going to be the same. Jake was coming home with us, whether Jake liked it or not.

To add insult to further injury, the police, in the form of one very pissed-off and familiar female detective, materialized just as Aunt Lucy had Jake leaning on her arm and hobbling toward the exit.

Detective Poltrone, a bleached blonde with a brain deficiency, stood blocking our exit, notepad in hand and smug satisfaction written all over her face.

"Not so fast, kids," she said. "I've got a report of a gunshot wound here and I'm thinking that somehow it has something to do with a burned-out sedan smoldering out off Route 322. How's about we talk awhile?"

Aunt Lucy was incensed. "Can't you see this man's in pain?" she sputtered. "He can't talk to you now. They gave him medicine. He won't know what he's saying!"

Jake's eyes were a bit glassy, I thought, looking at him, and he had a goofy smirk on his face. Was it the pain medicine, or was he just enjoying himself too much?

Aunt Lucy didn't wait for an answer. Instead, she offered me up like a sacrificial lamb.

"Stella was there. She'll be glad to answer all your questions, won't you?" Before I could open my mouth, Aunt Lucy went on. "I'm taking Mr. Carpenter home to my house. You can call tomorrow and I'll let you know if he's up to speaking. In the meantime, good night!"

The two of them left me at the mercy of the dragon lady, without so much as a backward glance.

I turned back to her with a resigned sigh. "Let's get this over with."

Detective Poltrone smiled. "This could take quite some time," she said.

"Dead bodies usually do," I muttered.

"Dead bodies?" Poltrone blurted. "What dead bodies?"

I stared at her. Surely the two men in the car had died, hadn't they?

"Nothing. I thought you were talking about a burned-out car. I just figured…"

Poltrone was waiting for me to stick my foot all the way down my throat, and I had been about to oblige her.

"Nothing. Now about this shooting. You see, it was a simple repossession gone wrong…"

I started talking and Detective Poltrone began writing in her slow, laborious scrawl. I knew without a doubt we'd be stuck like this for another hour, and then what did I have to look forward to? Jake Carpenter would be asleep, most certainly given my bed in the guest room, and I'd be the one sleeping on Uncle Benny's old couch in the basement.

In reality, it was worse. Not only did I return home at dawn to catch a few hours of shut-eye in the dank basement, but I was also the one who got elected to carry trays up to the wounded warrior all day and wait on him hand and foot while my aunt glowered at me for being "unappreciative."

"There's plenty of room, Stella," Jake whispered, patting the vacant side of the bed. "You don't have to sleep in that cold, drafty basement. I'll be a perfect gentleman." He patted his bandaged side gently and smiled up at me. "After all, you heard what the doc said, no strenuous physical activity."

"Oh, yeah, like you would listen to someone else's instructions," I said. "I know you, Jake Carpenter. I wouldn't be in this bed two seconds before you made a move."

Jake smiled and gave me that look that made my stomach dive into a free fall. "Well," he said, "it wouldn't be strenuous physical activity if you were the one on top."

I didn't dignify that with an answer. I spun on my heel and tromped back down the stairs to the kitchen, planning my revenge on Jake Carpenter and then revising it to include more forms of slow torture.

My cousin, Nina, was waiting for me. She was sitting at the kitchen table, a deep frown furrowing lines across her forehead as she stared at a blank piece of white paper. When I slammed Jake's tray down onto the countertop she jumped, her pen skidded and a long, jagged black line snaked its way across the clean, unblemished surface of the paper.

"See?" she cried. "That's just what I was trying to tell you! If you don't have a goal, your life lacks direction. You become just like the line on this paper."

I looked around, thinking maybe she was talking to Spike and I hadn't seen her.

"You talking to me?" I asked.

Nina looked around the empty kitchen. "You see anybody else standing here? Of course I'm talking to you! Who else would I be talking to?" She sighed, took up her pen again and frowned at me. "Jake got shot because you didn't have a plan."

Oh, right, another country heard from.

"Nina, Jake got shot because Joey Smack's people had guns."

Nina shook her head and smiled like I was stupid.

"No, he didn't. He got shot because you thought we should pool our talents into an agency that helps people in trouble, only you wound up taking a repo job on account of you didn't have a mission statement."

"No, Jake got shot on account of they had guns and Jake wasn't expecting them."

Nina smiled as if I'd made her point for her. "Bingo!" she cried. "If we'd all planned what this agency was about and what kinds of jobs we wanted to take on, then we would've been prepared. You wouldn't go fix a faucet without a wrench or something, would you?"

As she spoke, I saw Spike appear in the doorway, her head cocked to one side as she listened. I turned to appeal to her.

"So do you think it's my fault Jake got shot, too?" I asked.

Spike shrugged and walked over to the table.

"I think Nina has a point." She spoke slowly, as if weighing her words. "I mean, granted, we've all got skills in the same area. I'm a lawyer and you used to be a cop. Jake's former Special Ops and Nina's... Well, Nina's..." She paused and smiled at her girlfriend. "Nina's just Nina. Now, while it was a good idea to decide to go to work together, we haven't really talked about it since then. All we did was rent office space. You and Jake started taking on freelance investigative work and repos, but Nina's right, we do need to think about where we're headed."

"Yeah," Nina said. "I answer the phone. I mean, that is so bogus! What a waste of my talent!"

Once again I had no idea what Nina meant. The only talent she had that I was aware of was mud wrestling, and where could you go with that?

"I've been giving this a lot of thought," Nina continued. "I think I have a calling and I think I ought to follow it."

The phone rang, startling us all. Spike and I stared at it, then looked at Nina, who sat smiling like the Cheshire cat.

"So are you people going to get that, or must I do everything?" Aunt Lucy came in from the back porch, followed by Lloyd, and grabbed the receiver off the hook.

"Hello?" There was a brief pause as Aunt Lucy listened. "Who? Private investigators? Hold on a minute." She turned to glare at me. "So now you got clients calling the house?"

I was already halfway across the room, reaching my hand out for the phone, but she jerked it back, insisting on an answer.

"Actually," I said, "I believe you can blame this one on old Jake. He had the calls forwarded to his apartment after business hours. I suppose he had them sent here after you insisted that he recover over here instead of in his own bed in his own apartment!"

I snatched the phone from her, listened to a muttered diatribe in Italian, and ducked into the kitchen pantry where I could attempt to hear.

"This is Stella Valocchi, may I help you?"

The answering voice on the other end of the line was female and muffled, intentionally muffled, I thought.

"Yes, I need to make an appointment, as soon as possible. Is Mr. Carpenter available?"

It was starting to steam me, the way everyone was assuming that Jake ran the business, rescued damsels in distress and took a bullet to save my hide, when in fact, the reverse was true. What had he been telling people?

"Actually," I said, "he's a little under the weather, so he's not taking any appointments today. However, you're in luck. I'm Stella Valocchi. I own the agency and Jake works for me. I've had a cancellation in today's schedule and could work you in around four o'clock. Is that soon enough?"

There was a brief hesitation on the other end of the line. "I suppose," she said, sounding just like a whiny kid who had to settle for vegetables instead of candy. "But I really wanted Jake."

I sighed. "Take a number," I muttered.

"Excuse me?"

"I said, 'Do you know where the office is? Four Wallace Avenue, second floor?'"

"I'm sure I can find it," she snapped.

"I'm sure we'll be able to handle your case without any difficulty. Trust me."

"Oh, all right!" she said, and hung up.

I looked over and saw the others hanging on my every word. "Of course, you do know that we charge a thousand dollars a day, plus expenses?" I asked the empty line.

Nina's eyes widened into saucers.

"And we will need a week's deposit in advance."

The line began to hum.

"Fine then, I'll see you at four."

I hung up and turned back to the assembled group at the kitchen table. "Now, what was this about a mission statement?"

Chapter 3

Just once I'd like to have a plan go my way. Just one time. Was that too much to ask? I stood in what had been my bedroom, clutching my towel and clean clothes to my chest, watching as Jake rolled off the bed, fully dressed, and proceeded to search for his shoes. He should have been fast asleep.

"She asked for me. I'm going."

I adjusted my towel turban, tightened my hold on the jeans that were wrapped around my underwear and bra, and gave him the no-shit-I-mean-business stare.

"You are mortally wounded, remember?" I said. "That's how you scammed your way into Aunt Lucy's house and my bed, isn't it? You've been gut shot. You need my aunt to tend to your every need. You can't go see clients in the office. I'll handle it and you can hear about the job later."

Jake found his lizard-skin boots, pulled them on slowly and gave me a look of his own. I was working on becoming immune to the way he looked at me, but so far I found myself weak-kneed every time.

"What's the matter, Stella? Afraid I'll be tougher than you? Afraid you can't keep up?"

He stood and took two steps toward me.

"Be careful. Remember, you're wounded."

Jake smiled. "Funny, it hardly hurts at all." He reached me, his hands reaching to grip the sides of my arms.

"Jake, you're out of your mind on pain medicine. You don't know what you're doing."

I felt my grip go weak on the clothes I held in front of me and clutched tighter to keep my towel wrapped securely around my body. He stepped closer, towering over me, his breath hot on the side of my neck.

"Why, Stella, you're not afraid of me, are you?"

"I'm not scared of you, Jake." My voice cracked into a squeak that told him I was lying, only believe me, I wasn't really afraid of him, just a little…apprehensive maybe? I actually had come in only because I'd forgotten to bring a change of clothes into the bathroom. If I'd known he was awake, I would have asked my aunt to get them.

Jake ran the index finger of his right hand down the side of my face, the work-roughened skin exciting every nerve ending as it moved.

"I think you're scared, Stella," he whispered, cupping my chin with the crook of his finger. "I think you're very scared."

He bent his head toward me. My stomach pitched and his lips met mine. Finally.

The clothes hit the floor. The towel followed. I heard his foot kick the door shut behind us as I pressed into him. The rough fabric of his denim shirt brushed across the tips of my nipples and they hardened, begging for his touch.

Jake sighed. His tongue searched my mouth and mine answered him. In an entire lifetime of fantasizing, nothing could have matched the reality of Jake Carpenter's kiss.

The turban holding my damp hair slid to the floor. Jake's fingers raked my scalp, pulling my head back to better meet his inquisitive lips. He stroked the back of my neck in one long fluid movement that seemed to pulse with energy and heat. How long had I waited for this?

Since high school? Since the day he'd run off, too scared to elope, leaving the mousy little nerd to explain all to her aunt and uncle? Had I still been secretly waiting for him when I ran off to reinvent myself? Because I know I'd been waiting for this moment ever since my return to tiny Glenn Ford, Pennsylvania. But did I really want Jake, or did I just want him to want me so I could be the one to walk away?

His fingers slipped down my back, circled my waist and moved up toward my breasts. His hot mouth bruised my lips as I answered him with a passion I didn't know myself capable of feeling. I felt him harden against me and knew I had Jake Carpenter in the palm of my hand. I could finally pay him back for every moment of agony he'd put me through eleven long years ago.

So why then didn't I break it off and leave him there, wanting me and never being able to have me? Why was I lingering when I owed the son of a bitch a good and final payback? I mean, it wasn't as if he was really my type, now, was he?

Jake's thumb and forefinger found my left nipple, squeezed softly, and then pinched harder as I moaned and my knees went weak.

Okay. What was the better revenge, really? To leave him all worked up, or to get my needs met and leave him wanting?

Oh, definitely the latter. I mean, after sleeping in the cold, dank basement on Uncle Benny's couch, didn't I deserve a little satisfaction?

I felt his left hand moving down my side, felt him guiding

us toward the bed, and knew I was going for all I could get before I rolled away and said, "There, that's what you get for jilting me and humiliating me in high school!"

We half fell backward onto the bed and Jake only winced once as he rolled onto his left side and shifted to find a comfortable position. Once he'd settled in, his hands began to explore every tender, responsive inch of my body. When his fingers slipped between my legs, I stopped breathing. Oh, yes, this was definitely the good part. Oh, please hurry, I begged silently.

I grabbed the waistband of his jeans and fumbled with the button. Might as well do some exploring of my own, I figured.

"I'm not hurting you, am I?" I whispered.

I felt the button give, tugged at the zipper, and was rewarded with a gasp from Jake as my fingers found smooth, hardened skin.

Jake rose up onto one elbow and stared into my eyes. His fingers moved closer and closer and if he didn't touch me soon I was going to have to beg. Without a word, he read my mind, and I felt his fingers plunge deep inside me.

Oh, yes, I was going to enjoy this. I was going to…

"Stella! You in there?" Nina banged on the door. "Hey! We need to leave! It's almost three-thirty. Isn't she coming at four?" More banging.

I jumped off the bed, snatched my towel off the floor and wrapped it tightly around my torso. What in the hell had I been thinking?

"Yeah," I called. "I'm coming!"

"Does Jake need anything before we go?" she asked.

I looked at the man lying on my bed. He'd fallen back against the pillows, eyes shut, his facial expression the perfect picture of frustration. Revenge was sweet, but so unfulfilling!

I struggled into my clothes, danced around the floor on one

leg as I pulled my almost too-tight jeans up and quickly zipped them.

"No, he doesn't need a thing," I called to her.

Jake opened one eye and frowned. I stood, topless, at the end of the bed and let him suffer as I slowly, very slowly, pulled on my bra and fastened it.

"He's not in pain, is he?" Nina asked. "Aunt Lucy says he can have another pain pill now."

I looked at the bulge in Jake's pants and smiled. "He may be a little uncomfortable," I said, "but he'll manage. He's a tough guy."

I smirked, pulled my black turtleneck sweater on over my head and turned to open the door.

"Wait," he gasped, pushing himself up into a sitting position. "I'm coming."

I looked at his crotch, then at his darkened eyes. "No, you most certainly are not," I answered.

I opened the door and Nina half fell into the tiny bedroom. She took one look at me, glanced over my shoulder at Jake and started laughing.

"You didn't… I mean, you weren't…" She gasped.

"No!" we both answered.

Nina's grin broadened. "Oh, man, wait until I tell Spike!"

I glowered at her, sure that behind me, Jake was doing the same. "Nina, let's just get going, all right?"

Nina looked miffed. "Well, don't take it out on me!" she huffed. "I'm not the one who said she'd be at the office in an hour!"

She spun on her heel and headed down the steps, leaving me to dash off after her. When Jake didn't follow us, I was both relieved and disappointed. He needed to stay home. After all, a gunshot wound was nothing to fool around with, even if it had been superficial.

I raced Nina to my Camaro, slid behind the wheel, cranked

the engine and looked at my watch. Ten minutes. We'd make it with five to spare, even with it being rush hour. Of course, rush hour in Glenn Ford meant a four-minute commute across town instead of the usual two.

"What's that red light mean?" Nina asked, breaking her pout.

I looked at the instrument panel.

"Damn! We need oil."

Nina sighed. "Oh, that's nothing! One time I drove my car with the oil light on for two weeks."

I looked over at my pink-haired cousin. "And then?"

"Oh, well, it died forever, but that wasn't because of the oil light. The engine block froze."

"Nina," I said, rolling my eyes mentally, "that's what happens if you don't get oil!"

Nina stared at me. "You're kidding, right?"

I started down the driveway. "No. We have to stop."

"But we'll be late. You told her four and she's paying a thousand dollars a day."

"She'll wait."

"This is so totally why you need a mission statement," she muttered.

I failed to see the connection between stopping to put oil in my car and a corporate mission statement, but I kept my mouth shut. I drove to Sheeler's Garage, ran inside to grab two quarts of oil, and figured at most, we'd be five minutes late.

That was before Joey Smack's representatives, in the form of a long, black sedan with dark, tinted windows saw fit to stop by Sheeler's and give me a personal season's greeting from their boss, aka Santa Claus, aka The Man Voted Most Pissed Off About Having His Sled Repo'ed.

I had the hood popped and was about to insert the funnel, when the car rolled to a stop beside us. The right-side passenger window slowly slid down, just far enough for an arm and a hand to emerge. The arm was wearing a charcoal-gray suit jacket and a light blue cotton shirt with cuff links. The hand was holding a gun.

"Merry Christmas!" the arm's owner called, and started shooting.

Nina screamed and ducked down in her seat. I hopped behind the car, wedged between the pumps and the Camaro and wished like hell I'd worn a holster instead of leaving the Glock wedged down beneath the driver's seat.

The bullets hit the right front tire, the right rear tire and the back window, before the driver of the sedan hit the accelerator and tore off out of the lot.

I heard the squeal of tires and cautiously popped my head up over the open hood and watched the getaway.

"Nina, you all right?" I called.

Nina slowly rose up from the front passenger-side floorboards and gave me a nasty look.

"We could've been killed!" she stormed. "Don't you take precautions? Why didn't you shoot them?"

"My gun was in the car," I said.

Nina nodded an I-told-you-so nod. "See? No planning. No mission statement. That's how you wind up in situations like this. You need to be prepared!"

"I'm sorry, honey," I said, realizing how scared she was.

Nina shook her head. "It's not just that they shot at us," she said softly. "I'm used to that by now, I mean, ever since you started chasing bad guys and all, but we could've been better prepared, Stella, that's all."

Of course, that wasn't all. Nina was right, as usual. I hadn't been prepared. I hadn't figured Joey Smack would go so far, but he had and we hadn't been ready.

"You ladies okay?" The shaken garage attendant popped his head out of the door. "I called the cops, they're on the way."

Needless to say, we were late for the client meeting.

We pulled into the parking lot at 4:20 p.m. Nina practically flew out of the car in her rush to unlock the front door and open up the office. "Office" is a euphemistic term here. Our temporary quarters were over a print shop in what had been a long-vacant apartment in major need of renovation and cosmetic improvement.

When Nina slid her key into the door leading to the steps up to the second floor, she turned, her eyes widening.

"It's not locked," she whispered. "I think somebody's up there!"

I walked back to the car, stuck my hand through the now-missing back window and pulled my Glock out from its resting place beneath my seat.

"Wait here," I told her. "I'll go check."

"But what if he shoots you?"

I rolled my eyes. "Well, you could start by calling 911. If I'm dead, bury me in my jeans. I don't see the sense in getting all dressed up and uncomfortable just to be buried."

"Stella!"

"Okay, okay! Just call 911 if you hear gunshots, and stay out of the way!"

I handed her my cell phone, gently pushed open the front door and started up the stairs. I kept the gun low by my side, careful to step on the outside edges of the old stairs, and slowly moved toward the second-floor office.

I hated coming in this way. Approaching a possible bad situation from the ground floor was potential cop suicide and I knew it. If someone heard me, if they were waiting for me, I was a sitting duck.

I crawled the steps, flattened against the wall, and reached the landing. So far, so good. I paused, listening, and was rewarded with the sound of muffled voices, male and female, coming from the upstairs office.

You'd think burglars would be quieter. I snuck up three

more steps, my head rising just above the hall floor. I peeked around. Nothing. I trained my gun on every possible hiding place and still saw no sign of illegal entry or Joey Smack's people. As I listened, I heard the impossible.

Jake Carpenter's unmistakable rumble echoed out into the hallway. He laughed and I knew for certain he was inside. When a woman's high-pitched giggle erupted, I knew the score. Jake had beaten us to the punch. He was sitting in my office, in my high-backed desk chair, talking to our client as if I didn't exist. Damn him!

Someone tapped me on the shoulder. I jumped, spinning around to face Nina, who'd managed to sneak up the steps behind me.

"What are you doing?"

"I thought I told you to wait!" I whispered loudly.

Nina grinned and brandished the Camaro's tire iron. "Yeah," she replied, "you did, but now I'm armed. I can help."

Nina cocked her head and listened intently for a moment. "Besides," she said, brushing past me, "it's only Jake anyhow."

Leaving me to follow in her wake, Nina sailed through the office waiting room and on into the inner sanctum where Jake held court with our new client.

"Maybe we do need a mission statement," I muttered. "Maybe a few people need to know who's in charge around here."

I stiffened my shoulders and walked behind Nina into the office. The new client sat with her back to me. She was so unconcerned with our arrival that she didn't even turn to look over her shoulder as Nina made her entrance.

For some unknown reason this was all about Jake. I knew that much from our brief telephone conversation. She probably assumed, wrongly, that since he was the man, he would handle her investigative matter better than any mere girl. I sighed inwardly, funny how some women were like that.

Jake finally broke his contact with our new client and looked up.

"Well," he said, smiling, "finally. We were beginning to wonder about you."

He rose and indicated the woman sitting across from him. "Stella Valocchi, may I introduce you to Mia Lange?"

Our new client stood and for the first time I got a good look at her. A few inches shorter than my five-eight, closely cropped straight black hair, black leather jacket, short skirt, black stockings, high heels. Dressed to impress, or rather, dressed to seduce. Deep, dark eyes, small, perfect mouth, but the pout said she was not a happy woman.

I noticed something else about her, too. When she turned to me the light went out of her eyes, but when she looked at Jake she lit up like a Christmas tree. She was as phony as they came and I disliked her instantly.

I extended my hand and smiled, figuring two could play this game. "I'm sorry we're late. We got held up."

Her grip on my hand was like iron and she squeezed hard. I figured she wanted to see me wince, so I squeezed back. Was that the merest flicker of pain I saw cross her marble features? I smiled a little wider. Nina broke the moment.

"Held up?" she sputtered. "Well, not exactly, more like shot at by attempted murderers!"

Mia Lange's eyebrows lifted and her mouth dropped into a perfect O of surprise, but her eyes remained coolly detached and I thought she seemed completely indifferent to Nina's news. She released my hand, returned to her seat and dismissed me entirely.

But Nina had Jake's complete attention. He raised his eyebrows. "What happened?"

I smiled frostily. "Don't worry. I took care of it."

Jake nodded, silently agreeing to discuss it later, and started to sit back down in my chair. When he caught the look I gave him, he hastily grabbed one of the spare chairs and pulled it up beside the desk.

"Here," he said, gesturing to my chair. "Why don't you sit here."

I gave him a withering glance, nodded him into the spare seat and took my rightful place behind the desk. Nina was right. We were so going to have an organizational meeting just as soon as our newest client left.

"Ms. Lange."

"Mia," she cooed, her eyes widening and fluttering in his direction.

"Mia," he echoed, "has asked us to find her brother. It seems they lost contact with each other after their parents died and they were adopted out."

I felt the first tiny twinge of remorse for not liking our new client. She'd lost her parents when she was a kid, too. I'd been lucky. I got to finish growing up with my mother's sister, Aunt Lucy, while Mia got stuck with strangers.

"I'm so sorry," I murmured. "How old were you when this happened?"

Mia looked down at her lap. "I was very young," she answered. "I couldn't have been more than four-years-old at the time. My brother was older, I think, but not much, maybe a year or two."

I nodded and gave her a sympathetic look. "How long has it been since you've seen your brother?" I asked politely. "Do you have any idea at all where he might be?"

Mia never looked at me, instead she lifted her head and stared straight into Jake's eyes.

"Like I told you," she said softly. "The investigator I hired a few years back was able to learn that he might have been adopted by a family in Surfside Isle, New Jersey, where we were born. He couldn't find out anything else."

"So you've tried to find him before and couldn't?"

Mia nodded. "I was so young when my parents died, too young to even remember my siblings' names—or even our family name. I have nothing to go on. My adoptive parents gave me the name of the adoption agency, but the agency would only tell the P.I. that my brother grew up in Surfside Isle. The records were sealed and they couldn't give him anything else to go on. The same thing happened with my sister. The agency said she was adopted to an out-of-state family, but wouldn't give us more." Mia shrugged. "I made sure the agency had my name and address. I told them that if my brother or sister ever wanted to find me, they could give out my information, but that's all I could do—wait and hope they come looking for me. I gave up until about a month ago. That's when my sister contacted me." Mia bit her lip and fell silent for a moment.

"I really need to find my brother," she said, her voice tinged with desperation. "You see, he may be my sister's only hope." As I watched, tears formed in her eyes and her lower lip trembled slightly. "She needs a kidney transplant. I would have given her one of mine, but it turns out I'm not a suitable donor. I'd go look for him myself, but my sister's so ill now that I'm afraid to leave her. I would hate to go looking for my brother and have my sister die. I mean, we've only just found each other! That's why I need you." She gazed into Jake's eyes as big tears rolled down her perfect cheeks.

He leaned forward, patted her knee and handed her a tissue. Nina, watching from the edge of the room, bit her lower lip and frowned.

Mia shook her head, brushed away the tears with one elegantly manicured index finger, and seemed to struggle for control of her emotions.

"I'm all right," she said, smiling bravely at Jake. "I just feel so alone in all this. Without my brother, I really have no one I can turn to." She stared into Jake's eyes. "Please tell me you can help me help my sister."

"Don't worry," Jake said. "You're not alone anymore. We'll find your brother."

"Good."

Mia straightened in her chair, her attitude changing from pathetic damsel to businesswoman the instant she heard Jake say he'd help. She reached into her large leather bag, brought out a thick, business-size envelope and handed it to Jake. "I hope this covers my retainer," she murmured.

Jake tossed the envelope onto the desk unopened and said, "I'm sure it's fine."

I was less trusting. I reached for the packet, opened it and almost gasped. There were ten one-thousand-dollar bills inside.

"I'll get you a receipt," I said. "Of course, there will be expenses in addition to our usual daily rate…"

She didn't even let me finish. She dismissed me with a wave of her hand, her eyes never leaving Jake's infatuated face. "Of course, whatever you need. Just let me know and you'll have it." She smiled at Jake.

She reached back into the bag, pulled out a manila envelope and handed it to Jake. "I've heard such good things about you," she said softly. "I just know I can trust you to find him."

Jake beamed, while I took the more paranoid worldview of a cop. How had she heard anything about us? We'd only been in business for a month. So far our biggest coup had been the repossession of Santa's sleigh, and I hardly thought Joey Spagnazi was bragging about what a great job we did.

"I'm glad we come so highly recommended," I said. "Who do we have to thank for sending you to us?"

Mia glanced briefly in my direction.

"My sister. She's a bookkeeper for a local businessman and she gave me your name."

"What's your sister's name? Maybe we can find your brother by tracing your sister back to Surfside Isle."

"Oh, we tried that already."

Jake nodded sympathetically. I was less impressed.

Mia fluttered her eyes in Jake's direction and I wanted to slap her.

"You see, I came to Glenn Ford, hoping against hope that I'd be a match, but it didn't work out."

"Didn't work out?" I echoed.

Mia's head dropped slightly and she stared down at her hands.

"No," she said softly. "I have hepatitis C, so I'm not an option. That's why we're so desperate now. My brother is her only hope."

Before I could ask her anything else, she stood up, this time making eye contact with both of us.

"I only have one request," she said, her voice firm and undeniably hard.

"What's that?" I asked.

"Find him, but don't approach him. Don't tell him about us." She paused, apparently remembering her helpless act, and continued, this time in her little-girl-lost tone. "It might be a shock to him, that's all. I want to be the one to break it to him. I don't want to jeopardize my sister's chances by having a stranger tell him about us." She fluttered her eyes at Jake again. "You do understand, don't you?"

Jake seemed to grow two inches taller. "Of course, Mia," he said, soothing our poor little client. "Don't you worry about a thing."

She reached out and gripped his arm, her eyes pleading. As she did this, I had an instant mental memory of myself standing naked in front of Jake, the same expression mirrored in my own eyes. Now, here I was, the bystander, while Mia Lange, the dark-haired pixie, was the object of Jake's very rapt attention.

"I just knew you'd be the one," she whispered. "I'll be in touch."

Oh, no you won't, I thought, you will so not be touching

this man. He's mine! The thought jumped unbidden into my head and just as quickly I forced it back out.

"How will we reach you, Ms. Lange?" I asked.

"It's all in there," she said, indicating the manila folder she'd given Jake. "All my numbers are in there, my sister's, my cell and my pager."

Jake and I watched Mia Lange turn and walk away. She strode out the door past Nina without so much as a sideways glance. She almost collided with Spike in the hallway.

"Excuse me!" Spike said as Mia practically ran her down.

"Certainly," Mia murmured, apparently oblivious to the sarcastic tone.

Spike stepped into the waiting room, saw the three of us staring after Mia and stopped.

"Who the hell was that?" When no one answered, Spike shook her head. "Important client, huh?"

Nina was the first to snap out of the Mia trance.

"Oh. My. God!" she squealed. "Important? You wanna know what's important? Me and Stella almost got killed at Sheeler's gas station! Some idiots shot at us! Oh. My. God!"

Spike stared at Nina, her face whitening as the news sank in. "Are you all right?" she asked. "Who did this?"

She crossed the room to Nina, put her arm around her shoulders and hugged her. "Honey, are you okay?"

Nina nodded, her eyes huge with remembered fear. "They could've killed us! But don't you worry, I'm ready for them now!" She reached underneath her desk and pulled out the tire iron and a spray can of room deodorizer.

Spike looked at the two objects and frowned. "Okay," she said slowly. "I understand the tire iron, but what about the room freshener?"

Nina grinned, pulled a lighter out from the pocket of her jeans and brandished it in front of us.

"My secret weapon," she said. "The bad guy comes for me.

I try to hit him with the tire iron, but in case it doesn't work, I pull out my spray can. I point it at him, flick my Bic, and push! Instant flamethrower! See?"

She made a move to click the lighter, but Jake was faster, pulling the Bic out of her hand as I grabbed the spray can.

"I believe you!" Jake said. "I just don't want you to miscalculate and torch the office."

Nina rolled her eyes. "I wasn't going to actually do it, stupid. What do you think I am, a pyronaut?"

"Pyromaniac?" I prompted.

"Whatever!" Nina groused. "I'm not stupid, that's all I'm saying."

"Well, of course not, baby," Spike cooed. "No one thinks you're stupid. I think you're very brave."

Nina quit pouting and smiled. "Yeah," she breathed. "Totally. You do?"

Spike nodded.

Jake nudged me, motioning me back inside our office. "Joey Smack, you think?" he murmured.

"Absolutely. I think paybacks are murder and he's pissed. We'll be on his shit list for quite a while."

Jake smiled. "Nothin' we can't handle, especially from New Jersey." Jake plopped back down in my chair, propped his feet up on the desk and turned his thousand-watt attention to me. "Yep, old Joey Smack is gonna have a hard time exacting his revenge when we're in New Jersey and he doesn't have a clue."

"New Jersey?" I echoed stupidly.

"Yeah, I mean, that is where the boy was born and raised. Don't you think we oughta take up the trail there and see where it leads?"

Jake's eyes twinkled as he picked up the envelope stuffed full of cash and tapped it against his open palm.

"Oh, yeah, babe. Me and you. A tiny mom-and-pop motel,

all but vacant for the winter and a missing brother. Oh, yeah. What a life! It could take weeks to find that boy. Imagine."

I kept silent, knowing full well Jake was quite capable of hanging himself without my help.

"Yep," he said, stretching back in the leather chair. "Two people could get to know each other quite well in a situation like that. Intimately, I'd say."

There you go. Give a man enough rope and he'll ruin every opportunity, usually with his mouth.

I leaned in the doorway, arms folded across my chest, the perfect nonverbal picture of the word *no*.

"So, you're looking forward to a little time away, just the two of us?" I purred, enjoying the setup.

Jake gave me the look that flipped my stomach like a pancake, savored the effect, and practically crowed. "Oh, yeah, babe. I've been waiting for this for a lifetime."

"Obviously," I murmured. I let my gaze drift lazily down his body, stopping midway as I licked my lips and only half faked anticipation.

Jake smiled. It was a shame to have to burst his bubble.

"So, Jake?" I cooed.

"Yeah, babe?"

"Has it occurred to you that Joey Smack won't settle for us being out of town and that he'll come after Aunt Lucy and Nina next? Have you forgotten that Aunt Lucy is a very valuable chemist and that you remain under government contract to ensure her safety? Have you completely stopped thinking with the Big Head because the Little Head is currently in charge of your life, thus insuring that I won't come within thirty yards of you, even if you were suddenly the last human being alive and all the vibrators had dead batteries?"

I fired the questions like rifle shots and the effect was worth every word. Jake went from complacently confident of popping me in the sack, to confused and finally, irritated. I had him, all right, right where I wanted him. So why did I still feel disappointed?

"So what are you saying, one of us has to stay here?"

I shrugged. "That's one option, or they could come with us."

Jake exploded. "Oh, now that's a plan, Stella. We pack up two, maybe three cars, with your aunt, your cousin, her girl-friend and Lloyd, then proceed to Surfside Isle, New Jersey, to look for a missing person whom we are to find but not ap-proach. We don't have a name, a description, or any other in-formation, but you want to make this 'easy' case into a family fishing trip. Oh, now *that's* professional. Yeah, the Beverly Hillbillies Private Investigation Company is at your service!"

I straightened and went in for the kill. "At least I wasn't so busy thinking about getting laid that I forgot about Aunt Lucy and the safety of my co-workers!" I snapped. "At least I... Whoo!"

Something cold and wet nuzzled my ass from behind. Lloyd, happy to see me, was demanding my attention.

"Dog!" I screeched. "Get off me!"

Aunt Lucy stepped forward. "Your uncle has something to say."

"By sticking his nose up my ass?"

Aunt Lucy stiffened and raised one imperious eyebrow. "He can't help that he's hampered by his new body," she said. "Reincarnation isn't exactly easy, you know. It's not like the Sears catalog. You can't just pick out your new body and say, I'll take that one! The Lord giveth and the Lord taketh away!" She sniffed. "And I don't think profanity amuses him. It's not exactly like you're on God's A-list, anyway. When was the last time you made confession?"

The conversation was definitely taking a dangerous turn for the worse.

"How do you like the shore?" Jake asked, attempting to rescue me.

Aunt Lucy didn't seem especially thrilled to see him, either.

"What are you doing out of bed?"

"Surfside Isle has some great fishing," he added, completely ignoring the question.

"Surfside Isle has mobsters, too," she retorted. "It's cold. The wind blows in off the ocean and you can feel it in your bones."

Lloyd barked once, a short yip that seemed to mean something to Aunt Lucy. She cocked her head, smiled and said, "Well now, you're right. That was nice."

Lloyd moaned and padded over to investigate the trash can under my desk.

"I suppose," she said, then turned back to us humans. "Your uncle likes to surf fish. Maybe the blues are running." Then she frowned at us. "Of course, you won't have much time for fishing if you're trying to find someone's brother."

Busted. Aunt Lucy, Nina and Spike had obviously overheard every heated morsel of our conversation, not that we were trying to hide anything. I looked over my aunt's shoulder and saw the other two hanging just behind her, obviously curious.

"Okay," I said. "We'd better talk." I looked at Nina. "I think this time it might be a good idea to have a plan."

"We could start by naming ourselves," Nina said. Then she stopped, her forehead creased in thought. "Well, actually, I think we might want to do some team-building exercises first. Maybe a trust walk."

"A trust walk?" Aunt Lucy echoed. "How's about we start with a place to stay? I have a friend who's got a house in Surfside Isle, just one block off the ocean. Why don't we start by asking her if the place is open? Trust walk!"

Nina bristled. "We blindfold partners and walk them around, you know, so they develop a trusting relationship and confidence in their partner's ability to keep them safe."

Spike was standing by the window in the office staring down at the street. She seemed so absorbed in the cars below that I was surprised when she roused herself to speak.

"Well," she began, in her clear, crisp attorney tone, "I think there are more important issues to be addressed first."

The room fell silent.

"Like what?" Nina asked.

Spike glanced out the window again. "Well, we could start with the four men in the car across the street. They've been watching the building for about five minutes, but now another car is pulling up behind them and everyone's getting out and heading our way, and just so you know, I think they all have guns under their overcoats."

The entire room exploded into quick, silent action. There wasn't time for team building, mission statements, or a corporate name that reflected our unique abilities and talents. It was showtime.

Chapter 4

"Wait!" Spike commanded. "Stella, look at this!"

Jake moved with me, taking the side of the window opposite Spike while I stood and watched over Spike's shoulder. We stood where we wouldn't be seen from the street, hidden by the thick, dust-covered velvet drapes that had once been elegant accessories to someone's bedroom.

Below us, on the busy small-town street, stood six men, all wearing overcoats and looking like movie extras in *Scarface*. They were prevented from crossing to our side by what can only be described as a parade float, a flatbed truck covered in thousands of roses sculpted to look like a garden scene. The trailer slowly inched down the main street of Glenn Ford, its loudspeakers blaring "Let Me Call You Sweetheart," as a figure wearing a groundhoglike headpiece and a tuxedo held on to a microphone and swayed in time to the music.

"Okay, okay, okay!" Jake barked. "Let's move it!"

"What is that?" I asked.

Spike met my eyes. "Beats me. Looks like a one-man parade."

"Bring it on!" Nina yelled. "I'm ready to rumble!"

We all jumped, startled. Nina stood in the doorway, her eyes wild with adrenaline, a Bic lighter in one hand and the can of air freshener in the other.

She turned away from us, faced the open waiting-room door and screamed, "I got somethin' for ya! Do you feel lucky?"

"Oh, Jesus," I moaned. "Why me?"

"Nina, come on. There's a time to kick ass and this ain't it. Follow Jake!" I slid my hand behind my back and pulled the Glock out of my waistband. "I'm the tail on this one," I called to Jake. "Get them out of here!"

I wanted to say, "See, I told you so!" but, of course, this was definitely not the time for that. We had six men with guns looking to have a close encounter and the only thing standing between us and annihilation was a one-man parade. I looked back out at the street. The song was ending and the groundhog seemed to be signaling the driver to stop. Who in the hell was this guy? Was it Joey Smack in a new costume or what?

As the truck shuddered to a halt, the groundhog in black tie looked up at the office window and began to speak.

"Lucy, darling, I know you're in there! Let me see your sweet face at yon window!"

He threw his arm up and out toward our office, almost reeling off balance with the force of his movement. I shrank back against the drapes and watched as Joey Smack's boys stared in helpless frustration. A crowd of onlookers was beginning to gather, not a good omen for your run-of-the-mill mafia retaliatory hit. The mob, on the whole, and Joey, aka "Santa" Smack, in particular, liked anonymity when they killed people.

I felt some of the tension begin to ease out of my neck and

shoulders and a smile began to play across my lips. This wasn't Joey Smack, but who in the world was it and how did he know Aunt Lucy was in my office?

"Lucy, dear, I have loved you from afar, and now I come searching for some sweet remembrance of you, some token I might carry close to my heart until you accept me as your soul mate!"

I turned and stared back at Jake. He was herding the others toward the back exit, the door that led downstairs to the employee parking lot. We might not have a mission statement, but we, by God, had an emergency exit to the first floor.

The music started up again outside, accompanied by a chorus of car horns as the trapped motorists voiced their irritation at the prolonged delay.

"Lucy dearest, I must bid you adieu for now. Parting is such sweet sorrow!" the lovesick groundhog cried.

The truck jerked into gear and lurched forward as the quivering flatbed began inching once again down Lancaster Avenue.

"'Tis a far, far better thing I do…" I heard the guy yell, "than I have ever… Oh, dear!"

The microphone clattered to the floor of the truck as its holder grasped frantically at a rose-covered jukebox for balance. Joey Smack's men seemed momentarily undecided about pursuing their mission, and I decided to err on the side of caution. I jumped in front of the window, threw it open and leaned out as far as I could.

"Help! Police! Those men have guns!" I yelled. "I think they're going to rob the bank! Call 911!"

The disbursing crowd stopped, frozen by the new drama.

"Over there!" I yelled, pointing to Joey Smack's elves. "Call the police!"

If there had been any ambivalence on the part of the six men below me, it was now gone as they headed for their two cars, heads down, hat brims pulled low over their Neanderthal brows.

"Yes!" I crowed triumphantly. I flipped open my cell phone, hit number one on the speed dial and waited.

"Done!" I said when Jake answered. "But not for long. Pull into Aunt Lucy's garage, sneak them into the house and tell them to grab whatever essentials they need for a week out of town. And I mean essentials like medicines and dentures, not hair gel and accessories."

Jake chuckled. "That might be a hard sell," he murmured. "You know your aunt. She'll pack half the lab and then start on the kitchen."

"There were six of them," I said. "They weren't looking to play. Jake, I think Joey Smack's mad about more than a sleigh repo. I don't know what's going on, but I don't have a good feeling about it. I think a week away ought to give us enough time to figure out what the hell is going on."

There was a long silence on the other end of the phone. Jake hated anything that seemed like a retreat in the face of enemy combatants, his Delta Force training had made him like that. He hadn't modified his approach to accommodate the civilian business world, where tanks and machine guns didn't grow on trees, and the laws forbid the use of deadly force on a casual basis.

In the background I could hear my aunt's voice explaining something technical, probably to Spike. I shivered. If anything happened to her, or in fact to anyone close to me, I wouldn't be able to forgive myself. What had we been thinking, starting up such a risky business without considering the repercussions?

"Can you get out of there safely?" Jake asked. "Do you need backup?"

I looked out at the street. Joey Smack's men were gone, or at least, out of sight.

"I'm good," I said. "I've got Aunt Lucy's spare car key on my key chain. I'll drive her Buick. I'm not coming near the house unless you need me. I'll head on down to the shore. I'll call you when I get into town and tell you where to meet me."

"Good," he said. There was a brief pause and when he spoke again his voice was soft and husky. "Be very careful."

I smiled in spite of myself. "I will."

I flipped the phone shut, still smiling, and locked up the office. I grabbed the paperwork on Mia's case, pulled up the trapdoor and made my escape through the back exit of the print shop below. Joey Smack's goons were nowhere in sight. Ten minutes later I was on Route 322, leaving town with nobody on my tail and nothing but the highway to keep me company.

I found myself flipping through the radio stations, looking for road music, not listening to any of it because all I could hear was Jake's voice in my head. "Be very careful," he'd said. His tone had been different from anything I'd heard from him before. It wasn't casual; it was full of unspoken emotion. It wasn't Jake tossing off an order; it was Jake invested in the outcome, very invested.

Oh, who was I kidding? Jake didn't really want me. He wanted the thrill of the chase, not a relationship. He wanted to make up for being too scared to follow through with the ceremony during our botched elopement in high school. He didn't really want me; he wanted to polish his tarnished bad-boy crown.

I stabbed at the radio, looking for something to drown out the embarrassing memory of parking in front of a Maryland justice of the peace's house and waiting for hours for Jake to show up so we could get married. I cringed as I remembered that I'd only left after the justice of the peace himself had emerged from his front door and started walking purposefully toward the car.

Bruce Springsteen's voice broke in on the memory singing "Born to Run." I took my finger away from the scan button and let him have his say. It was the perfect music for a trip to Jersey and a stroll down bad-memory lane.

I'd come back to Pennsylvania for all the wrong reasons. I'd come back, tuck-tailed, because I'd caught my boyfriend in bed with my patrol partner. I'd come back to lick my wounds, and yes, I'll admit it, I'd come back seeking revenge on Jake. But, revenge was supposed to be a passing encounter on the street.

I had it all worked out in my fantasies. I'd walk by. He'd stop and scratch his head, thinking, "Hey, wasn't that Stella?" Only, I looked good now and I kicked bad-guy ass for a living. I wasn't some shy nerd with no experience who believed any line of talk a guy gave her. I was the new-and-improved version of the old Stella Valocchi and Jake Carpenter didn't stand a chance with me.

So how was it I wound up trusting him when everyone else thought he'd murdered my uncle? Of course, we'd found the real murderer, but that didn't explain why I'd gone into business with him. And how on earth did I wind up butt naked this afternoon, lying on my bed with his lips dangerously close to providing me with a dose of nirvana I might never be able to forget?

The mere memory of this afternoon's close encounter brought my heart up into my throat. All right, so maybe I wanted the man, but just on a temporary basis, then I'd be over it. One night of torrid lovemaking and I could put Jake Carpenter behind me. One night and I could move on with my life. Hell, maybe we could even be friends one day.

I mulled that one over for a moment, watching the traffic ahead of me as day turned into night and rush hour dispensed millions of cars onto the highway. Jake and I had to work together. It wasn't as if we really had any viable alternatives. His auto-body shop had burnt to the ground in a fire. It would be months before the insurance money came through and he finished rebuilding. He needed money, and repo work was usually a cakewalk.

And what did I have to go back to in Florida? A boyfriend and a partner who'd betrayed me by sleeping together. What kind of life was that? No, my days on the force were a thing of the past. I had to find a new career and take care of my aunt. That meant Jake and I had to work together. Romance mixed with business spelled disaster every time. I was living proof of that.

I sighed and stabbed the scan button again. There was no way I could really sleep with Jake Carpenter. The revenge might be sweet, but the consequences could ruin me. No, it was definitely better not to think about Jake at all, not in that way at least. I felt my heart sink as Aunt Lucy's Buick began to crawl across the Ben Franklin Bridge into New Jersey. I was feeling sorry for myself. I mean, all I wanted was a normal relationship, with a normal guy. Was that so much to ask?

The cell phone chirped and I lunged for it, happy to have the distraction.

"Hello?"

There was a pause, the crackle of static, and then a voice, low and guttural, spoke.

"You took something of mine," it said. "You got exactly twelve hours to return it."

"Mr. Spagnazi," I said, guessing. "We were employed by the Lifetime Novelty Company to repossess your sled. Take it up with them."

"I'm taking it up with you. This don't have nothing to do with them."

The man was a total lunatic.

"It's on their lot," I said patiently. "It's not my problem."

I flipped the cell phone shut and tossed it onto the passenger seat. This was insane. We do a simple repossession and look at the consequences: Jake gets shot and Joey Smack loses his mind. I shook my head to clear it, switched off the radio and forced myself to begin thinking about the business at hand. I made a mental to-do list: find a place to stay, ask around about Mia Lange's brother and get Joey Smack off our backs.

I was winding my way through the lonesome stretch of Jersey Pine Barrens when the cell phone rang again.

"Your aunt talked to her friend with the house in Surfside Isle," Jake said. He was all business, no "hello," no concerned tone. Clearly I'd been hallucinating when I'd talked to him last time, but my stomach lurched all the same at the sound of his voice.

"She left a key with the neighbor. The address is 732 Forty-eighth Street. You got that?"

"No problem," I answered.

"Good. Stop by the local grocery on your way in, too, okay? We're gonna need beer, and coffee for the morning. I figure we can order pizza later. I'm starved."

What was I, his mother? I felt my grip tighten on the cell phone. "Anything else?" I asked, my tone sticky sweet.

The sarcasm was lost on him. "Yeah, if you don't mind, swing in somewhere and pick up a saltwater rig and some tackle. I wanna get some surf fishing in before we leave."

I flipped the phone shut and tossed it over my shoulder into the back seat. Men! What a piece of work!

"I wanna get some surf fishing in," I mimicked. "Yeah, and I want to spend a day at the spa and have my hair and nails done afterward." What a freaking clown.

I looked at the clock on Aunt Lucy's dash and figured I had a half hour left before I hit Surfside Isle. I settled back in the driver's seat and tried to catch a glimpse of the ocean, but it was pitch-dark outside. I tried to remember the last time I'd paid a visit to the Jersey shore and found nothing but a few vague memories from high school.

The Shore was where everyone in Glenn Ford went for Senior Week if they couldn't afford Florida. It was a black-and-white TV, a poor substitute for the living color of Florida with its crystal-blue waters and green palm trees. The Shore was in-your-face action, loud music, the boardwalk and sex.

Where Florida was all talk, Jersey delivered. Jersey didn't make you act nice or talk pretty to get what you wanted; it shoved it at you with one hand and took your money with the other. The Shore fit the Jake I knew from the old days, but it couldn't hold me, not any longer. I wanted something with more passion, more feeling behind it. I wanted something wonderful to remember, not an embarrassing encounter I couldn't forget.

I cruised through Long Beach and thought about summers with my girlfriends, back before I'd known Jake. I remembered a sky-blue bikini with metal star studs, the smell of lemon juice in my hair, and the sting of too many hours spent laughing and playing in the sun. I remembered in flashes a vacation before my parents died, my father laughing and my mother taking pictures. It was good back then.

I sighed and looked past the ghosts, out into the winter's night, and saw the briefest glimpse of moonlight hitting water. It could be good again, I thought. "Good times always follow the bad," I murmured, quoting my uncle Benny.

A few miles later I entered Surfside Isle. Even on a winter's night, with almost everything closed up tight, Surfside Isle demanded attention. The Ferris wheel in the amusement park caught the eye of the moon and glowed like a streetwalker wanting attention. Neon signs winked Vacancy, or worse, Closed for the Season. I slowed the Buick to a crawl, passing shops and restaurants. Row after row of shingled cottages looked bereft without their summer visitors.

I pulled into the parking lot of the only place in town that appeared to serve food and was still open. The sign in the middle of the big glass window said Marti's Café. It was the kind of place that probably got overlooked in the summer. It didn't have the typical beach neon to beckon customers. No plastic swordfish to imply a rich menu of fresh seafood. It was simple, the kind of place locals probably frequent and guard as a jealous secret against the onslaught of tourists. I stepped out of the car and started for the door just as the lone waitress switched the Open sign to Closed.

"Shit!" I swore under my breath. What now?

As if she'd heard me, the woman looked out, saw me, and with a sigh, gestured toward the door. She looked tired, as if it had been a long, slow day. Her pale pink uniform was stained with what looked like spaghetti sauce and coffee. I waited, smiling, as she fumbled to unlock the door. Her wiry red hair fell across her shoulders and she flipped it back impatiently as she struggled with the lock.

"Thanks," I said as the door swung open.

She looked at me, dark circles under her even darker eyes, and attempted a return smile.

"Hey," she said. "I'm the only game in town this time of year and you look worse than I feel. What's another customer, eh? I could use the money, and honey, looking at you, you could use something to eat."

Damn. Was it that bad? I inspected myself in the mirror above the diner counter and thought, well, yeah, I guess it is. My hair lay flat against the sides of my head. I was pale, even more washed-out because my naturally dark hair was still blond due to an unfortunate undercover assignment that had happened months ago in my former cop life. I looked like a tired ghost.

"Coffee?" the woman asked. She'd gone around the counter to grab the pot of ancient brew off its stand.

"Is it safe?"

"Do you really care? Beggars can't be choosers, you know."

"Don't mind her," a male voice interrupted. "She talks to everybody like that, don't you, Marti?"

I'd overlooked the guy at the end of the counter. He was maybe midforties, curly salt-and-pepper hair, tall, wearing jeans and a faded navy T-shirt. From the way he looked at Marti, I figured him for a boyfriend. He looked lovesick. Then I looked at Marti and realized she was completely unaware of his feelings for her. I revised the picture. Maybe he was her husband; marriage is like that sometimes.

"You complaining, Tom?" she asked.

"Not me, babe, never." He turned his attention to me and smiled, but not the way he smiled at Marti. "Get her to heat up the chili. Her chili's like…" He hesitated for a moment. "Like…winning the Super Bowl when the other team was favored to cream you."

Marti actually blushed. I did another mental revision; this was an awakening, a new relationship about to flower.

"Yeah, thanks," I said. "I'll do that. Chili sounds great."

"You want fries with that?" Marti asked.

Behind her, Tom slowly shook his head.

"No, chili's fine."

"You know, I forgot about that corn bread you made," Tom murmured.

I took the hint. "I love homemade corn bread!"

Marti, seeing the setup, smiled at Tom. I settled back on my stool and felt myself begin to relax. Maybe this wasn't going to be such a raw deal after all. Maybe we'd find Mia's brother right away and still have time to spend a few days relaxing.

"Do you live here?"

Tom took a sip from his coffee mug. "Well, I did when I was little, but I moved away. I came back a couple of months ago for a two-week visit and haven't left yet, so I guess you could say I live here."

"Must be a pretty small town in the winter months," I said.

Tom smiled. "Just gives me more time to learn the routine around here before the tourists start coming back and all hell breaks loose."

I tried to drink a sip of my coffee, smelled the acrid scent of burned beans and put the cup back on the counter. Tom's attention was split between entertaining me and being entertained by Marti. He watched every move she made through the open window into the kitchen, but glanced away if she looked up, too shy to be caught and too entranced to stop staring.

"Yeah, Surfside's small but it's grown a lot since I lived here." He swiveled a little on his stool. "What brings you to the beach in the dead of winter?"

"Well, I met a guy who said he lived here. He made the town sound really beautiful. I thought I'd come visit, maybe run into him again."

Tom's attention switched back to me. "He doesn't know you're here?"

I tried to look embarrassed. "Well, no. You see, we met in a park two years ago in…New York, Central Park, and well, somehow we just started talking. He said I should come to Surfside Isle and look him up if I could, but…"

I looked down at my hands and bit the inside of my cheek thinking I should've taken up acting.

"I feel so stupid. See, he gave me his card and I lost it."

Tom laughed, a rich, deep chuckle that made Marti look up from her place behind the window.

"You lost it? So you just came here looking for a guy who lives somewhere in Surfside Isle but you don't know where? What's his name? And why did you wait two years?"

I kept my head down. "I don't know," I murmured. "I can't remember his name. You see, I was dating someone and so I didn't think much of it at the time, but I kept thinking about him, I don't know why, and when Glen and I broke it off, I suppose I…oh, I know, it's stupid!"

Tom almost fell off his chair laughing. Marti slid chili and corn bread up onto the window's counter and walked through the door to join us.

"What's so funny about that?" she asked. "You mean to say you never met somebody, looked into their eyes and felt they could be the one? And then something happens and—" she snapped her fingers "—just like that, they're gone and you never got a chance to see what was there. That never happened to you?"

Tom looked right into Marti's eyes and smiled. "Yes," he said. "And I made a resolution about that kind of thing. I don't waste opportunities anymore."

The force of Tom's intensity seemed to radiate into the room, filling it with feeling and unspoken emotion. If it had been a two-by-four, the realization couldn't have hit Marti any harder. Her eyes widened, her mouth fell open, and she turned bright red.

"Oh," she said. "Oh!"

I watched my chili grow cold in the pass-through window behind her for a long minute as Marti and Tom stood staring at each other, oblivious to anything and everything but their own, newly created world. It was Marti who dropped back into the reality of the moment and realized where she was.

"Your chili!" she said, practically throwing the bowl from shelf to counter.

"Thank you!" I scooted back as the bowl slid toward me, sloshing dangerously.

Marti picked up a rag and began swiping furiously at the counter between us, ignoring Tom.

"You don't remember his name?" she asked.

I shook my head. The chili was hot and deliciously spicy. I'd almost lost interest in Mia Lange and her brother. Almost.

"What's he look like?"

I choked. What the hell did he look like?

"Well, he's about forty, I'd say, and um…well, you know… cute…average height, great eyes."

I shoveled chili into my mouth and avoided eye contact. They had to think I was a total ditz. I couldn't even describe him to them. Fortunately, Marti and Tom were too wrapped up in each other to pay too much attention to me. They tried, but I knew they were just waiting for me to leave so they could talk.

They made a halfhearted attempt to review the café's regulars. By the time I'd finished the corn bread, they agreed that they hadn't seen any "cute" men in their forties who lived year-round in Surfside Isle, but they did know how to direct me to my rental house.

I left with a clear idea of where I was heading, but the sinking feeling that finding Mia Lange's brother would be no easy task.

My cell phone rang as I started the car.

"You buy bait?" Jake asked without preamble.

"No," I answered. "Did you really think anyplace would be open this time of year?"

Jake sighed. "There are no problems," he said, "only solutions. That's why I'm calling. I stopped a while back and took care of it."

In the background I heard Nina yell, "I told him it could wait!"

"Well, you can buy all the bait you want, but you're not fishing until we find our client's brother."

Jake snorted. "How hard can that be? A small beach town can't have too many regulars."

I rolled my eyes and visualized myself punting him like a football out into the surf off Surfside Isle.

"We'll be there soon," he said. "We're just crossing the bridge. How's the house?"

"I don't know. I'm just pulling up in front of it now. You'll see for yourself in about twenty minutes."

I rolled slowly down Forty-eight Street and pulled into the driveway of a small, brown-shingled cottage. The street was desolate. A few houses, including the neighbor to the left of our house, had lights on, but that was it. No one moved in front of the windows, no one walked down the sidewalks, nothing passed under the few lonely street lamps.

"The neighbor on the right has the key," he instructed.

"The neighbor on the left," I said.

Jake sighed. "She said right."

"Depends on how you look at it," I snapped. "See you when you get here." I closed the phone, cut the engine and got out of the car before he could call back.

"Do I look like I need supervision?" I asked the car. "I didn't think so!"

I walked across the short frozen brown grass to the house next door, a large blue-shingled thing that looked more like a series of boxes than someone's cozy beach cottage.

I started up the steps, saw a white envelope with Aunt Lucy's name on it, and stopped. Inside was the key. I looked back up at the house for signs of life, saw none and shrugged.

"That was easy," I muttered. "No muss, no fuss. Guess they didn't want us waking them up." I looked at my watch. It was barely after nine. "Old people," I sighed.

I walked back to the Buick, grabbed my purse, my gun and my keys. I took a long look up and down the deserted street. The sound of the surf pounding the shore behind me and the scent of salt air couldn't override the silent alarm that made the hairs on the back of my neck stand at attention.

I whipped around and thought I saw the slats on the neighbor's blinds drop quickly back into place. I stared hard at the darkened window but saw no further movement.

"You're seeing things," I muttered. "You're like a kid scared of the dark. Get a freakin' grip!"

I walked up the narrow concrete walkway to the house,

climbed the steps to the glass-enclosed front porch and fit the key into the lock. I stopped, listening to the sounds of the vacant house before fumbling for the light switch. Nothing out of the ordinary, just the creaks and squeaks of a windblown beach cottage.

I flipped on the lights, stepped inside and locked the door behind me. I was standing in a cozy, beachside cottage that could've been furnished by my grandparents. Overstuffed recliner, blue tweed couch, braided rag rug and knotty-pine walls. Someone had hung café curtains with cheery, yellow rickrack in the kitchen, and a large rectangular table with mismatched vinyl-covered chairs took up the eat-in area.

"Homey," I said out loud.

Still, I found myself reaching to pat the Glock tucked securely behind my back as I walked through the rest of the house. One bedroom and bath downstairs that would do for Aunt Lucy; no one would hear her snoring if she slept in the back of the house. But this left only two bedrooms upstairs; one with two double beds and one with a queen. Shit. How was that going to work? I couldn't sleep with Aunt Lucy; no one could sleep with snoring that sounded like a jet engine roaring in their ears all night. Spike and Nina were virtually newlyweds, so that left their room out as an option. I was not sleeping in a bedroom with Jake Carpenter. No way.

Of course, the second I told myself I wouldn't, all I could think about was, what if? My imagination went wild. I thought about it, pictured us starting out in two separate beds, then somehow, overcome with either revenge or lust, ending up in one bed, and then, well, I didn't let myself go there, at least, not for long. Okay, so I thought about the two of us, horizontal and naked. Thought about it so hard and long that when I heard the front door open, I jumped up, grabbed the Glock, and might've shot somebody from sheer frustration.

"It's freezing in here!" I heard Nina complain. "She didn't turn on the heat yet?"

"Where are you?" Jake called.

I darted out of the bedroom.

"You guys made good time," I called, sticking the gun back in my waistband.

Heavy footsteps sounded on the stairs. Jake materialized on the landing and gave me a lopsided grin. "You said time was of the essence, didn't you?" He looked at me, maybe noting the flush on my cheeks, and said, "What's going on?"

"Nothing. I just got here myself. I was just checking out the bedrooms—I mean, looking around, you know."

Oh, he knew all right. I had the feeling he could look right past my face and into the most hidden recesses of my mind. What in the hell was wrong with me?

I started down the steps, intending to brush past him, but he stopped me, his hand firm on the crook of my arm.

"We need to talk," he whispered. "Without the others. Later."

I raised an eyebrow. "Is it about the—"

"What are you two doing?" Nina stood at the bottom of the steps watching, a knowing smirk playing across her features.

"Nothing!" I said. "I was just telling Jake about the house. It's a relic."

"Uh-huh," Nina said. "I bet."

I moved away from Jake, trotted down the steps and joined the others. Aunt Lucy was inspecting the kitchen cabinets, pulling each door open, studying the contents and sighing, clearly not pleased.

Lloyd followed her, sniffing at her heels, now and then looking up and around. If I didn't miss my guess, he was feeling as wary as I had. Something about the small house just didn't sit right. I couldn't put my finger on it, and apparently Lloyd couldn't either, but we both had that feeling.

Spike wandered out into the family room, coming from the

direction of the downstairs bedroom, and stood staring up the stairway to the second floor.

"Couldn't you just see this place as the setting for a slasher movie?" she asked quietly.

"Oh, my God!" Nina gasped. "That is totally not good for my serenity. I am so not going to sleep with that on my mind!" She stopped, dropped into a lotus position in the middle of the room, closed her eyes and inhaled deeply. "Cleansing breaths," she whispered to herself.

This fascinated Lloyd. He watched for a moment, and then wandered over to stand right in front of her.

"Umm…" Nina intoned solemnly.

Lloyd cocked his head to the side, his tongue lolling out as he began to smile. Obviously Nina was inviting him to play some new game.

"Umm…" she moaned again.

Without hesitation, Lloyd leaned forward and licked her face ardently.

"Eww! Dog breath! Spike, do something! Oh, God! You dog!"

Nina's eyes popped wide open and she reached out to push Lloyd away, but he ducked down and under her arms, bounding into her chest with a leap that sent Nina sprawling backward onto the floor.

"Help!" she sputtered.

"Oh, Nina, now honestly. Your uncle was only trying to reassure you," Aunt Lucy said. "Benito!" she called. "Enough! She is a grown girl. If she wants to sit on the floor and moan, so be it!"

Lloyd, who had answered to my uncle's name ever since he learned that it usually resulted in people food, stopped licking Nina immediately and trotted to my aunt's side. She smiled and bent down to pat his head softly. "I brought pepperoni," she murmured.

Jake crossed the room to stand beside me. "You see why I wanted to fish?" he whispered. "Your family is nuts."

I rocked back with one heel and planted it squarely on the toes of his left foot. With steady pressure I transferred all my weight onto his defenseless foot.

"All right, all right!" he cried softly. "But you got to admit—" He broke off as I ground my heel in harder.

Spike offered Nina her hand and pulled the distraught girl to her feet. "Come on, honey," she said. "Let's go look upstairs. Maybe there's a more appropriate place for you to meditate."

Nina smiled up at her. "You wanna meditate, too?" she asked slyly.

Spike tilted her head, looked around the room at the rest of us, and shrugged her shoulders. "You never know," she murmured.

Damn those two! They made it look so easy, not to mention special and intimate. Oh, well, some days you get the bear and some days, your love life just sucks. I wouldn't let myself look at Jake. I knew he was watching me. The damn man was always watching me! Too bad he didn't have a romantic bone in his muscle-bound body.

Aunt Lucy was unpacking groceries, setting bottles and boxes on empty shelves and muttering to herself.

"I know it's a bit rustic," I said, "but it's only for a few days, just until I get a handle on Joey Smack."

Aunt Lucy looked up, giving me one of her cut-the-crap glares. "I need to be in the lab," she said. "The Household Shopping Show booked me back next week and I need product."

So that was the problem. It wasn't that she missed her kitchen and cooking homemade Italian specialties for us. My aunt had discovered a new forum for her inventions and she just couldn't wait to go on the air again.

"Hey," Jake said. "My grandmother saw you on there last

week. She said you're a natural. She said you had them eating out of your hand with that little-old-grandma act of yours."

Aunt Lucy feigned shock. "Jake Carpenter, I never act. All I did was show the people how my homemade cleaner works on all surfaces." Without even realizing it, Aunt Lucy had swung into gear, staring out at us as if we were the audience, smiling sweetly and gesturing to a bottle she brought out from one of her many bags.

"I thought I told you not to let her pack," I muttered.

"It was that or face her digging in her heels and refusing to come," he answered.

"I can't disappoint my people," she snapped. "I'm wasting valuable time here."

I tried changing the subject. "So the guy on the float today, who was that?"

That stopped her in her tracks. "What guy?" she asked.

"She didn't see him," Jake reminded me. "We went out the back."

I didn't care. I was just happy for the working distraction. I told her all about the groundhog, about his float, the song and the way he'd danced across the platform. I was rewarded with the most unexpected reaction. Aunt Lucy's eyes widened, and for a moment I thought I saw all-out panic.

"Huh!" she said, and turned her back to us. She started fumbling with the empty grocery bags next, carefully folding them, but having difficulty with the creases. Her hands shook ever so slightly. Aunt Lucy's hands never shook.

"Did I say something to upset you?" I asked.

Aunt Lucy opened the refrigerator door and stuck her head almost all the way inside it. I felt Jake go still beside me, watching.

"No, Stella, what makes you think a foolish thing like that?"

"Well, if you're not upset, then why didn't you answer me? Who is that guy? Don't you know him?"

Aunt Lucy threw her hand up, waving it like a flag. "Don't be so melodramatic, Stella Luna. He probably saw me on the shopping show and decided he needed a girlfriend. I don't have time for that sort of nonsense. I have work to do."

She still wouldn't look at us, but I thought I knew why. She missed Uncle Benny and was embarrassed to be so publicly wooed. It was too soon, and frankly, I doubted there would ever be room for another man in her life. That's why she insisted Lloyd was my uncle reincarnated. She couldn't stand the thought of Uncle Benny really being gone. A dog was a safe enough way to keep suitors away. After all, men don't want crazy women.

Jake touched my arm and gestured toward the front door. "Let's go for a walk," he murmured.

"But I don't want to…"

"Yeah, you do," he whispered.

Lloyd squirmed into the space between us, seizing on the word *walk,* and agreeing vigorously with the suggestion.

I rolled my eyes at Lloyd and grabbed my coat. "It's freezing out there."

Jake smiled. "It's not so bad. Might go up to fifty tomorrow. Great fishing weather."

He held open the door, waiting patiently while I wrapped a long furry scarf around my neck, tucked my hair up into a knit cap and pulled on wool gloves. Lloyd shot past him and ran down the steps, ready to explore his new turf.

When the door closed behind us, I was surprised that Jake didn't move. He stood on the stairs, staring up at the sky, slowly surveying his surroundings with what seemed to be satisfaction.

"It's beautiful out here, isn't it?" he said. "The sky's so clear you can see every star, and the moon's got a ring around it. Now, how often do you see that?"

I stamped my feet to keep them from going numb and

wrapped my scarf a bit tighter around my neck. "Have you lost your mind? It's gotta be twenty degrees out here!"

Jake sighed. "It's all in how you perceive it, Stella."

"I perceive it as freaking freezing!"

Jake wasn't listening. His attention was caught by something lying on the ground next to the house.

"Would ya look at this," he said. "Somebody must've left it behind. It's a nice one."

Jake inspected the rod. "Even left a nice lure on it, too. Wonder how that happened."

He turned, holding a fishing rod in his hand. A silver bauble dangled from its tip, catching the moonlight as it twirled. Whatever agenda Jake had was forgotten as he started off at a brisk pace, walking straight toward the ocean.

"Come on," he called over his shoulder. "It'll warm you up to walk."

No, snuggling down under an electric blanket would warm me up, I thought. Walking along the beach at midnight in December would only cause pneumonia.

"The doctor said you should take it easy. I think you should go back inside and rest."

Lloyd ran back and forth, covering the distance between us like a relay racer, barking his excited pleasure in Jake's choice of direction.

Jake paused, waiting for me to catch up, and when I did, slung one arm across my shoulders. I started to shrug him off, but he held fast.

"I'm just keeping you warm, Stella. Relax."

"Doesn't your side hurt?"

He smiled. "Pain is all in the perception," he answered.

"I guess that shotgun blast was a hallucination then."

Jake shook his head, still smiling. "You need to work on your negativity."

"Negative? I am not negative!"

Jake chuckled and began walking at a slower pace, his arm still holding me close to his side.

"You prefer paranoid?" he asked.

I couldn't think up a snappy comeback. It was too late and too cold. Besides, Jake was close to being right about me. I was negative, especially when it came to men and romance, but look at my track record. I had a right to be skeptical. Too bad I couldn't cut my heart out and survive.

I walked beside Jake, feeling the strength of his arm around me and rehearsing what I'd say next. It was going to be all business, no matter how hard he tried. I was a no-nonsense woman with a job to do. The sooner we all accepted that, the better off we'd all be. Right?

I lowered my head, ducking the stiff breeze that numbed my skin. Who was I kidding? The only one who needed to quit living in a fantasy world was me. I still had feelings for a man I hadn't known since high school. I was living in the past, fantasizing that by some small miracle Jake Carpenter had suddenly morphed into Prince Charming. When was I ever going to grow up?

Chapter 5

Jake led us right past the boardwalk, down the steps and onto the beach. It was clear he wasn't planning to discuss anything with me until he'd planted himself along the surf's edge and had that stupid silver bauble immersed in saltwater. He wasn't the only idiot on the beach, either. I counted at least four others, spaced maybe ten feet apart, all watching the surf for signs of action. What kind of shared craziness brought them out on a frigid night to stand waiting patiently for the hit of a lifetime?

Probably the same strain of insanity made women believe in Prince Charming.

I waited on Jake, stewing with the timeless frustration that had gone on for generations before me and would continue long after Jake and I were distant, past memories. Men fish. They fish for no reason, for endless amounts of time, and often return with whopping lies about their missed opportunities. Women know this; I just don't see why they persist in putting up with it. It had to tie in with that Prince Charming thing somewhere.

Jake brought his arm up over his head, rod in hand, and cast his line far out into the surf. With slow precision, he reeled the line back in and repeated the process, over and over again. Five minutes passed without a word while I slowly became an ice cube. When I couldn't feel my toes any longer, I lost my patience.

"Listen, if you don't have anything important to say, Lloyd and I are leaving." I turned away and started walking. Lloyd, the disloyal, raced off in the opposite direction, trotting up to investigate the other fishermen, leaving me to make my last stand alone.

"Stella, damn it! Wait!"

Jake shoved the butt of his rod down into the sand and caught my arm.

"Come on, honey, I was just trying the thing out!"

"Honey? Jake Carpenter, I am not 'honey' to you! I am your business partner and that is all. Got it?"

He nodded, but I thought I saw the sides of his mouth twitching with a suppressed grin.

"What was so important we had to walk all the way out here to talk about it?" I demanded.

"I got a call from one of my contacts at the P.D. before we left," he said. "The guys that chased us out of Joey Smack's didn't make it."

I thought back to the vision I'd had in my rearview mirror of the car exploding into a fireball as it hit a tree, and shuddered.

"That's not all," Jake added. "I read over the report Mia's private investigator sent her and…" His voice drifted off, his attention caught by something behind me.

"And?"

Jake wasn't listening. His rod suddenly jumped, flying out of its sand pocket and skittering across the beach. Jake ran after it, dived and came up with it in his hands, pulling hard as something on the other end fought him.

"Damn, Stella, look at that!"

I followed him to the edge of the water, peering out where he pointed and saw an explosion of white surf and black bodies.

"What is it?"

Jake was struggling to hold his line, a fine sheen of sweat breaking out across his forehead as he wrestled.

"A blitz! It's a fucking blitz!" His words came out between gasps of exertion and he moved slowly closer to the water.

"Jake, let it go!" I yelled. "Whatever that is, it's pulling you in!"

I followed him, about to reach out and grasp his arm. The surf was filled with fish, thousands, all roiling around in some sort of frenzy.

"Jake, don't!" I cried.

He ignored me, wading a few steps into the water as he slowly reeled the line in on the rod that was now bent almost double.

"This is outstanding!" he cried. "We're going to catch the hell out of fish now! Do you understand how rare this is?"

Jake wasn't expecting an answer.

"A blitz hardly ever happens, and never in winter!"

With a mighty heave, Jake stepped back, jerking the rod as he did so, moving with the momentum of the incoming wave to land his catch.

A black shape, writhing and flipping with the effort to escape, flew past us, landing with a loud thud on the sand.

I looked and saw the other men having similar luck, reeling in fish after fish. The water was filled with them and the moonlight reflected off their scales, creating a shimmering cauldron of shape and motion.

The man standing closest to us cried out, wrestling with something that tugged and fought, bending his rod nearly double.

Jake threw his catch farther up onto the sand and moved toward the other man, his attention completely riveted to the man's struggle. The others did the same, all converging on the man with the big catch, shouting out advice and moving to assist him.

With a sigh, I followed, drawing closer just as the fight came to its conclusion.

A huge, dark lump came rolling in with the surf, swirling to a stop on the firm, frigid sand. The man bent over his catch, reaching to pull it up farther onto the beach, assisted by the others.

One of them cried out, recoiling and running several yards away where he bent over and vomited.

I ran the remaining few yards, stopping a few feet away from Jake. For a brief moment my view was blocked by his back, but then he moved, giving me a clear view.

A woman lay dead on the sand, her long, dark hair fanned out around her body in swirls that ebbed and flowed with the incoming tide.

"Shit!"

Jake and another man tugged at the body, attempting to pull her farther away from the water and up onto dry land.

I took in the scene, reverting to my professional training and detaching from the normal emotional response of a civilian. It was obvious that she was far beyond our help. Her face and torso were bloated. The body, or what was left of it, wore jeans and a sodden, navy pea coat. The blitz of fish had done its damage, ravaging her face and hands and making an easy identification impossible.

Jake and I stood there, studying her for almost a minute before either of us spoke. We had both gone into our past professional modes, the soldier and the cop studying the effects of human rage. There was no doubt in my mind that this woman was the victim of a crime and not an accident. Her hands were firmly tied behind her back and her ankles were bound together by duct tape.

"Got your cell phone?"

I nodded, pulled it out of my pocket and looked toward the boardwalk. "I'm not sure where we are exactly."

Jake nodded back toward the street. "Tell them we're at the bottom of Forty-sixth Street, on the beach. They'll find us."

I made the call, listened to the bored communicator take down the details, and then hung up. I figured that a beach town in winter might have one cop on duty, if that, and prepared for a long wait in the frigid night air. It surprised me when I heard the wail of sirens almost immediately.

"What do you think happened to her?"

Jake had been silently inspecting the body, reaching into her pockets for identification while the others watched, checking the labels in her clothing and carefully searching for additional clues to her cause of death.

"I can't really tell," he said.

I stepped closer and knelt by the victim's side. I'd been a cop in a beach town. Drownings weren't new to me, but our victims were usually recovered quickly. The woman lying on the ground was too swollen and disfigured to make cause of death discernible. It would take a medical examiner to tell us any more, but then, as bystanders we'd only read about it in the paper.

"Don't let the cops catch you touching the body," I whispered to Jake. "It's a crime scene now. They won't want it contaminated."

"Jesus!" One of the men standing clustered behind us swore and fell back, the others following. A huge dog, maybe not even a dog but a wolf, appeared, teeth barred, and stood maybe five feet away from us.

The dog's attention seemed focused on the body.

I straightened very slowly and stepped between the dog and the victim. Jake did the same.

"Git!" one of the men cried. "Go on, git!" He lunged, holding his long-handled net out in front of him, poking it like a weapon in the animal's direction.

The wolf-dog stood its ground, fangs bared.

"Don't move," Jake said.

The dog whined, wanting to move closer, but was leery of humans. The sirens in the distance grew louder as the emergency vehicles drew closer. The huge dog threw his head back suddenly and emitted a long wail of unmistakable grief.

Lloyd had held back until this point, tail down, ears back, watching. Now he started toward the wolf-dog, as if drawn by the plaintive wail.

"Lloyd, stay!"

He ignored me, slowly advancing toward the other dog. I moved and Jake grabbed my arm, stopping me.

"Don't!"

"That dog will kill Lloyd!"

I tried to shake off his grip, but it was too late. Lloyd kept on going, closing the gap, tail wagging softly. A strobe of headlights and blue lights flashed, bouncing as the vehicles left the street and hit sand. A fire truck, a police car, an ambulance and several Jeeps converged, heading directly for the spot where we waited with the body.

The large dog's attention was drawn away from Lloyd momentarily. As the convoy drew closer, the dog turned, gave one look at the body and ran with Lloyd following.

"Lloyd!" It was no use. Lloyd ran behind the other dog, becoming a shadowy form as the moon ducked behind a cloud and left the shoreline in darkness.

The emergency vehicles reached us, halting a few feet from where we stood. Doors flew open and within an instant we were surrounded.

A familiar figure, curly-haired and tall, with an open, easy smile, stepped to the front of the crowd and seemed to take charge.

"All right," he said to the others, "everybody wait right there until I get an idea of what's going on."

He walked toward us, taking in the details of the scene before him. When he reached me he said, "You again. You're getting quite an introduction to Surfside Isle."

I nodded, feeling the chili he'd recommended churn in my stomach.

"I'm not liking this part of town as well as I did Marti's Café," I said. "So you're a cop?"

How had I overlooked this? I thought I was good, especially at picking out a fellow officer, but he'd gotten by me.

Tom chuckled. "Yep, they made me an offer I couldn't refuse. I was working in Virginia, came home on vacation and well, you see the result." He shrugged and turned to Jake.

"So she found you. That was quick."

"Oh, no, this isn't the guy."

Tom shot me a puzzled look and I realized he had to be wondering why I'd come to town looking for a man I'd met in New York when I had Jake here, as well.

"He's my cousin," I interjected.

Jake looked completely confused, but recovered, introducing himself and shaking hands.

"I thought I'd try out the rod, and well, there was a blitz and then this." Jake indicated the victim's body.

Tom squatted in the sand beside the victim and inspected her carefully.

"Are you the one who hooked her?" he asked Jake.

"No, I was." The other fisherman, a small, squat, middle-aged man shuffled forward and Tom turned his attention to him.

"All right. Hang on." He signaled to an older gentleman. "Let's see what Doc can tell us."

Tom looked up at the others. "I'll need statements, names

and addresses," he said. "Why don't you folks wait over there by the police car and I'll get to you as quick as I can."

The process was beginning. Flashes exploded as the scene was preserved on film and the evidence gathering began. Tom gave orders in a calm, understated tone, watching as the others moved to carry them out.

"Here." Tom shoved his notepad in our direction. "Would you mind writing down your full names and where you're staying? I guess we might as well get your home addresses while we're at it. I doubt I'll need too much more from you tonight, but I'd like to get a formal statement tomorrow."

Jake took the pad and began writing. I inched closer to the medical examiner, hoping to hear more.

"Not over twelve hours," he muttered. "Doesn't look like she was conscious when they dumped her."

Tom nodded, caught me eavesdropping and said, "You got your contact numbers on there, too?"

"Does this sort of thing happen a lot around here?" I asked.

He smiled. "What, you think 'cause this is Jersey the Mafia uses the beach for a dumping ground?"

I shrugged. "Well, you gotta admit it's a bit weird, a woman duct-taped and dumped. I'd expect it more here than in, say, Florida."

Tom shook his head. "No, we don't find bodies washing up onshore any more than you would anywhere else. Surfside Isle hasn't had a homicide in—"

Before he could answer, the M.E. interrupted. "Well, you got one now," he said. "No way around it."

Another flash went off, startling us. A middle-aged woman holding a huge camera stood just a few feet away, snapping pictures while simultaneously trying to keep her long red hair from flying across her face and into the camera lens.

"Hey, Megan, knock it off! You're corrupting a crime scene."

Two volunteer firefighters moved toward the woman, but she stood firm. "It's news, honey," she said. "I got rights the same as you. The public has a right to know about news in their community."

"For God's sake, Megan," Tom said. "We don't even know the victim's name. How'd her family like it, finding out by seeing pictures of her body splashed all over the front page?"

Megan gave Tom a look. "I'm doin' my job, sport," she said.

The M.E. hastily covered the victim's body with a sheet provided by the EMTs. Tom moved toward the reporter, his hand extended.

"Give me the film, Megan. I'm confiscating it."

Megan shook her head and took a step backward.

"Megan, don't make me arrest you."

She stood there, uncertain, for a long moment, and Tom waited.

"Ah, shit!" she swore. "Here!"

She pulled the length of film from her camera, tossed it onto the sand in front of Tom, and just as quickly popped in a new roll.

"No pictures of the body, but I get everything else," she said, and started snapping.

Jake grabbed my arm, spun me around and started walking me away from the others, down the beach in the opposite direction of our beach house.

"Move it, we don't need to have our faces plastered across the local paper," he whispered.

I let him lead me across the firm sand, but looked back when I heard someone cry out, "Hey!"

The flash went off again and Megan lowered the camera. "I wanna talk to you two," she called.

"Take a number," I muttered.

We put on speed, not exactly running, but in no way lingering to acknowledge the reporter's request. That would be all we needed, an article in the local paper mentioning that two private detectives were in town. If Mia Lange wanted a private reunion with her brother, a newspaper article that so much as mentioned our case would ruin her chances. Worse, if Joey Smack had contacts in New Jersey, and what mobster didn't, he'd find us before we could devise a plan to thwart his efforts.

"We'll go down here and then cut back up toward the house," Jake said.

I scanned the shoreline ahead of us, searching for a sign of Lloyd. Where had that dog disappeared to, and had the other dog hurt him?

As if hearing my thoughts, two blurs appeared in the distance ahead of us, running across the sand, then up toward the houses that lined the beach.

"Look! There he is!"

I started off in Lloyd's direction, aware that Jake lagged behind. When I turned to hurry him up, I stopped, surprised to see the grimace of pain that momentarily contorted Jake's features.

"Hey, you all right?"

The grimace was replaced by a quick smile that I knew took effort. "Never better."

"You're hurting. You want me to go get the car for you?"

Jake shook his head emphatically. "Isn't that Lloyd?" He nodded toward a large house that sat oceanfront. As we drew closer I could see Lloyd standing at the foot of a large Victorian. The big dog stood watching Lloyd from the shadows of the home's wraparound porch, his eyes glowing like marbles in the darkness.

"Lloyd! Come here!"

I kept my eye on the big dog and closed the gap between myself and Lloyd, fumbling in my pocket for his leash and cursing myself for not putting him on it in the first place.

Lloyd's tail was wagging, his attention completely taken by the other animal. He barked a friendly Lloyd bark and the other dog whined in return.

I looked at Jake. "You don't think they like each other, do you?"

Jake smiled. "What's not to like? Lloyd's a pleasant enough fella."

I scowled. "Not like that! I mean, that wolf-looking thing isn't going to attack Lloyd, is he?"

Jake stared up at the porch and smiled. "I knew what you meant. All I'm saying is love has made stranger pairings than these two."

I must've looked confused because he added. "That isn't a he-dog, it's a she."

Lloyd's tongue hung out of his mouth and he was panting when I reached down to snap the lead to his collar.

I looked up at the big dog and sighed. "Lloyd, she's way out of your league. For one thing, you'd need a ladder to—"

The words died in my throat. What was I doing, explaining basic doggie sex education to a dog? Like he could understand me? I shook my head. The cold had obviously gotten the better of my brain.

"Come on, it's late. Let's get you home." I glanced at Jake. "You sure you can make it? It wouldn't take five minutes to get the car."

Jake wouldn't have it. He insisted on walking the five or six blocks back to the cottage but his face was pale by the time he climbed the steps to the front door. His pace had slowed even more after reaching the sidewalk and he hadn't spoken since leaving the crime scene. As I stood beneath the front porch light, fumbling to put the key in the lock, I could see beads of sweat standing out on his forehead. His skin looked almost gray and it was obvious from the way he favored his left side that he was in pain.

"We'd better get you to bed," I said, swinging open the door and holding it wide for him.

"I'm fine," he said, but his voice barely rose above a whisper.

The cottage was quiet and the only light still burning came from the hood over the stove. Lloyd padded out into the living room and licked my hand.

"They all go to bed?" I asked.

Lloyd gave me another quick slurp, then retreated down the hallway toward Aunt Lucy's bedroom.

"Guess that's a yes," I muttered.

Jake leaned with his back against the front door and closed his eyes.

"Think you can make it upstairs?" I asked.

He nodded but didn't make an attempt to move. I reached out and took his arm, pulling him gently toward the steps. I saw him wince, then bite down on his lower lip.

"Pain meds wore off, huh?"

He nodded.

"All right, well, let me get you into bed and I'll go bring you water and another pill."

A faint smile crossed Jake's lips. "About time," he whispered.

"About time?" I echoed.

"Yeah. About time you dragged me off to bed. I knew you couldn't resist me, ever since this afternoon. You can't get me out of your head, huh?"

"In your dreams, Carpenter!" I answered.

"Mmm," he sighed. "Yeah, that, too, dreams."

We reached the top of the steps and I looked down the hallway. Nina and Spike had taken the room with the queen-size bed, leaving the room with the two doubles for me and Jake. Thank God.

Jake was making the trip under his own power, but it was clear to me he wouldn't last much longer. I rounded the corner into the bedroom and slowly guided him down onto the bed.

"I'll go get you a glass of water," I said.

"I'll be waiting." He closed his eyes and lay back on the bed, an expectant smile plastered across his face.

I fled downstairs to the kitchen where I poured a short tumbler full of Aunt Lucy's Chianti and filled another tumbler with water. I grabbed Jake's bag, a green army duffel, and half ran back upstairs.

"I didn't want to go through your things—" I stopped mid-sentence. A pair of boots, faded jeans and a T-shirt lay in a clump on the floor beside the bed. Jake, bare-chested and probably naked, lay under a thin blanket in the bed where I'd left him. He was sleeping.

I stood there, the wine in one hand, the water and his bag in the other, and wondered if I should wake him just to give him a pain pill so he could sleep. Probably not. I took a swig of Chianti and leaned against the doorjamb, studying the curve of Jake's mouth, the hard angles and planes of his face and the way the lines of his neck blended into the strong muscles of his shoulders.

I closed my eyes for a moment and remembered the feel of his work-roughened fingers on my breasts. A thrill of pleasure and excitement surged through my body and I quickly opened my eyes to shut out the feelings that accompanied the memory. No. No Jake. No passion. No romance. Work. We were here to work, not play, and definitely not to open a new can of whoop-ass relationship.

I walked out of the room and left him sleeping. I wandered downstairs into the darkened living room, and stood by the bay window in the kitchen, staring out at the deserted sidewalk and beyond that to the water. From my vantage point, it all looked so peaceful, but I knew, barely out of my line of sight, a forensics team still scoured the beach, trying to piece together the story of the dead woman's identity.

By nearly 3:00 a.m. I still wasn't at all sleepy. I poured a second glass of Chianti and returned to my watch by the window. At some point, Lloyd joined me. For a little while the two of us stood there, studying the blank square of concrete beneath the streetlight. When he'd had enough, Lloyd padded to the door and scratched to go out. When I didn't respond, he whined.

"No, way, dog. You've had enough action for one night."

Lloyd moaned his disagreement. "It'll never work. For one thing, she's too tall for you. For another, she's vicious, like the black widow spider of dogs. If you were lucky enough to gain access, she'd probably suck your blood dry afterward."

Lloyd moaned again and stared up at me. He was grinning.

"Just like a man," I muttered.

Lloyd didn't want to hear it. He flopped down on the cold, vinyl floor, his chin propped up on the bay-window frame, and stared after his beloved.

"Okay, be that way," I said, "but I'm going to bed."

I left him there and headed upstairs. Jake was snoring softly when I tiptoed back into the bedroom. I stood there, watching him sleep for a moment and then realized I was the only one who'd come to the Shore totally unprepared. The others had grabbed toothbrushes and a few quick changes of clothing, but I'd been in too much of a hurry to even stop on the way and buy anything.

"Damn!"

I walked into the upstairs bathroom, borrowed Nina's toothpaste and brushed my teeth with my index finger, but this still left me without pajamas. I walked back into the bedroom and studied him again for a moment. He was definitely sound asleep and with as much activity as he'd had in one day, I very seriously doubted he'd be a threat to me anytime soon. Surely I could sleep in the vacant bed for just one night. Tomorrow night I'd take the downstairs couch, but tonight the bed just looked so inviting.

I stripped down to my shirt and panties, hopped under the covers and closed my eyes. Tomorrow, I sleepily promised myself, it would all come together tomorrow.

I fell asleep to the distant pounding of the waves against the beach and dreamed that night of Lloyd and Fang the wolf-dog, happily frolicking on the beach as body after body washed up onto the sand behind them.

Chapter 6

I awoke to the smell of bacon and coffee. Bright sunlight flooded the bedroom and for a moment I lay in bed, disoriented. The bed beside me was empty, the covers neatly pulled up and tucked securely into the mattress. Jake was gone. A shock wave of memory flashed through my head as still photographs from the day before flooded into my head.

What time was it? Where was everyone? I jerked the covers back, reached for my jeans and hastily pulled them on. The sound of voices drifted up from downstairs and I stumbled to the bathroom in a sleep-deprived fog. I brushed my teeth with my index finger and borrowed toothpaste, planning the day as I splashed water on my face and tried to tame my hair into something presentable.

Spike looked up as I walked into the kitchen and smiled. She was sitting at the table, the newspaper neatly folded in half before her, reading and sipping coffee from a large brown mug.

"Sounds like you and Jake had an eventful evening."

Aunt Lucy stood by the stove, frying bacon. When she saw me, she gestured to the coffeemaker to her left.

"Always with the late nights," she murmured.

Jake and Nina were nowhere to be seen. I crossed to the coffeepot and pulled a mug from a cup hook above the counter.

"Jake tell you about our adventure?"

Spike chuckled. "Yeah, but only after I showed him this." She gestured to the front page of the paper, sliding it toward me as I approached the table.

There, splashed above the fold, was a huge color photograph of Surfside Isle's finest, Jake and me, all huddled around a lump on the beach: Body Washes Ashore. Foul Play Suspected.

"Oh, that's great! Just what we need, publicity."

Spike waited in silence while I read the article. The red-headed reporter had done a thorough job reporting the grisly details. She referred to us as vacationing tourists and I mentally thanked Tom for not giving out our names.

Nina blew through the front door just as I finished, weighted down with blue plastic bags and grinning triumphantly.

"Oh, we are so prepared!" she said.

"Is that it, honey, or do you need help unloading?" Spike met Nina at the kitchen entrance and took the bags from her, setting them down in a cluster on the counter.

"That's it. I got sweatshirts and pants for all of us, in black, of course, and a board with erasable markers. I even found tofu—we can put some in our omelettes!" She saw me and smiled. "I got you a couple of pairs of jeans and some other stuff. I figured you didn't get a chance to grab anything when you left town, huh?"

"Thanks!"

Nina winked. "Don't thank me! I took the money out of the petty-cash box before we left. We're loaded!"

"Tofu? What's tofu?" Aunt Lucy had wandered over to inspect Nina's purchases.

"Bean curd," Nina answered. "It's an awesome source of vegetarian protein."

Aunt Lucy pulled a small white square out of a bag and stared at it. "Looks like a hunk of lard in dirty water," she pronounced. "I'm not eating that!"

Nina sniffed. "It's very good for you. Totally fat free."

"Tasteless, you mean." Aunt Lucy walked back over to the stove and began turning the bacon.

"Where's Jake?"

I was only half trying to avert a skirmish between Aunt Lucy and Nina. If Jake was missing, it could only mean he was on the track of something way more interesting than the Tofu Wars. I was beginning to realize that I had Jake-dar. I had the ability to instinctively "know" Jake was on the track of something pertaining to our investigation, and there was no way I would let him get the upper hand.

"He's fishing, I think," Nina answered. "I saw him leave early with his new rod and a bucket."

So much for instinct. Fishing. I sat at the table drinking coffee and fuming. We had work to do. The man had an injury and only so much energy; how could he waste it throwing fake minnows into the surf?

On the second cup of coffee, I realized that Jake's car was no longer in the driveway. Shit! Why didn't I ever trust my instincts?

I ran upstairs, grabbed my purse and the keys to Aunt Lucy's Buick, and then double-timed it back downstairs.

"I'll be back," I called.

Nina ran after me. "Wait! Aren't we going to make a plan for the day?"

This stopped me momentarily. "Plan?"

Nina's foot tapped impatiently. "You know, we *are* on a

case here. Don't you want to meet as a team and decide who's going to do what? See? Lack of planning!"

Nina's eyes darkened dangerously and I found myself scrambling for an out.

"I'm all about the team effort, honey, that's why I'm going to find Jake. He's a part of this thing and I just can't believe he'd run off and forget about it. That is *so* irresponsible!"

Nina wasn't having it. She shook her head. "No, I told him about the meeting and he said he was going to go clear his head so he could be focused on our work. He'll be back by ten, he promised."

I looked at the clock on the wall behind her. He had eighteen minutes to reappear; only, I knew he'd blow Nina off entirely if a lead developed. Damn him! How could he run off without me?

"Okay, well, um, I need to clear something up with him before we start. It's about last night. I, uh, couldn't begin to think about a mission statement when there's negative energy between us."

I tried to look sincere. Nina was searching my face, trying to decide whether I was making up a story or being honest with her.

"Ten o'clock," she repeated ominously. "If you two aren't here by ten..."

"Nina, nothing means more to me than moving this agency forward. I'll find him and get back here as fast as I can."

Nina nodded, but she wasn't happy. I left her standing in the doorway staring after me as I unlocked Aunt Lucy's car and slid behind the driver's seat. I pulled out of the driveway and turned the car toward the beach. I knew Jake wasn't there, but Nina didn't.

I drove to the end of the street anyway, scanned the almost empty parking lot and drove on toward the pier. When Jake's car wasn't there, either, I turned and headed for the main part of town. I found Jake's car in the parking lot of Marti's Café.

I found Jake sitting at the counter next to Tom, kidding Marti and acting for all the world like a local.

"There she is!" Marti called as I walked through the door. "Jake, here, said you'd be along shortly."

I shot Jake a curl-up-and-die glare, which Marti mistook for caffeine addiction. She slid a thick mug of coffee across the counter in my direction and smiled sympathetically.

"Heard it was a long night for you guys. Want breakfast?"

"No, thanks. We're in kind of a rush."

Jake grinned and patted the stool next to him. "Aw, now, cuz, there's nothin' that won't go better after a good, hearty breakfast."

If I could've squashed him like a bug, I would've done it and enjoyed myself. There he sat, serene, well-rested and obviously in the catbird seat. What was I supposed to do? What could I do? I slid onto the stool, looked at Marti and said, "I'll have two eggs over easy, a side of crisp bacon, raisin toast and hash browns."

Marti leaned over to refill Tom's mug and whispered something in his ear before moving off toward the kitchen. Tom grinned after her, looked at the two of us for a second and called to Marti.

"You're on!"

"Well, I guess you know how to have a hearty breakfast," Jake said.

I shrugged. "Well, it's your funeral. Nina's expecting you in five minutes, and you know how she hates to be kept waiting. I told her I'd come after you and try to make sure you showed up on time, but if you're late, it's you she'll be looking for, not me."

Tom sat drinking his coffee, watching Marti through the kitchen pass-through and acting as if he wasn't listening to our every word. By now I knew better than to dismiss him as a regular guy. Tom was a cop and cops are sneaky at best— trust me, I was one once.

Jake was staring at me, still smiling, but his eyes were

working on another message, a message I couldn't quite read. He inclined his head ever so slightly toward Tom and I let the matter of Nina and our corporate mission statement drop. Jake was working, and even though we were going to have a long talk about running off like the Lone Ranger and leaving me in the dust, I had to back him up.

Tom's pager went off and he pulled it out, staring at the screen and frowning.

"Duty calling?" Jake asked.

Tom shook his head and popped the pager back into its holster. Dark circles rimmed his eyes and he looked tired. At some point he'd changed into dress pants, a sports coat, and a shirt and tie, but nothing about his outward appearance said police. Nothing, that is, until he lifted his arm and leaned forward to reach for the coffeepot. The black butt of a gun stuck out of its shoulder holster.

He caught me staring at the gun and smiled. "Jake tells me you were on the job. Ever miss it?"

My heart skipped a beat and I started wondering what else Jake had told Tom. It wasn't as if we'd exactly discussed my earlier meeting with Tom, or planned our strategy. No, that would be entirely too efficient. That was why people like Nina organized meetings.

"A little," I answered.

Tom smiled, but he was watching me like a cop. Jake intervened, laying one strong hand on mine and sending a shiver of sensation up my spine even though I was trying to stay completely focused on the game at hand.

"I told Tom about the family business."

"Ah, so you did that, huh."

Okay, somebody was gonna die, and I was thinking Jake looked like a pretty good victim.

"Yeah, you know, I thought it best to let him know, common courtesy and all. I'd want to know if I were him."

What in the hell had Jake told him? I gave myself a mental shake, just to clear my head, and kept on nodding like an idiot.

Tom smiled. "Well, since you didn't know who I was, I can see how you wouldn't want to talk about it to a stranger."

I smiled. "Well, I would've come to see you as soon as possible, common courtesy being what it is."

Jake was enjoying himself. He was actually smirking.

Marti was bearing down on me with a loaded plate and I seized the opportunity to change the subject.

"Looks great! I'm starved!"

Jake leaned dangerously close, inspecting my order and snagging a bacon strip. His shoulder touched my arm, his thigh brushed against mine, and I caught a whiff of spice and something undeniably male before he drew back.

I stared at my plate, felt the color rise in my cheeks and knew Tom or Marti would see it and wonder. After all, Jake was my cousin, wasn't he? I gave myself an imaginary bitch slap for that one. Couldn't I have concocted a better story than that?

"So have you found out any more about your victim?" I was trying to sound interested, and while I was curious, I was way more interested in moving the topic away from my life and onto something neutral.

Tom chuckled. "Well, I doubt it has anything to do with you being here," he said.

"Well, of course not! Why would—"

Jake rescued me. "Now, Stella," he began. "I know you're scared, but—"

"Scared? I'm not scared!"

Jake actually reached over to pat my knee as though I was some frail flower of a woman. He gave Tom one of those man-to-man smiles. And had he not also reached to take my hand, I believe I would've smacked him. His grip on my fingers prevented me from doing anything but nonverbally promising him retribution.

"I told Tom about your little problem with Joey Smack. Don't worry, nothing's going to happen to you now."

Tom nodded. "I'm just glad you gave me a heads-up, Jake. I imagine riling up a mobster like Smack is about the same as spraying gasoline on a hornet's nest."

The two men chuckled like conspirators in a locker room.

"I bet Stella can handle herself."

The unexpected comment coming from Marti brought Tom's manly act to a grinding halt. He knew with one quick glance at his redhead that he'd stepped in it and stepped deep.

"Oh, now, ladies," he said, his hands held palms up, traffic-cop style, "I didn't mean to imply…"

"Really?" Marti's hands were on her hips, her head cocked to one side, and a dangerous glint twinkled in her eyes.

"Well, if I did, I…"

"Uh-huh," Marti said. "Well, maybe you did and maybe you didn't. All's I'm saying is, maybe you'd better not go around underestimating folks, 'cause maybe there's a lot of us stronger than you think."

A customer slid his mug forward halfway down the counter and Marti began to move off toward him, coffeepot in hand.

"Oh, shit," Tom murmured.

I grinned. I had a new friend.

"Stella," Tom said, "I didn't mean to imply you couldn't take care of yourself. I just meant that I'm here if you two need me, that's all. I'll keep my eye out for him."

I tried to smile, but I had a mouth full of raisin toast.

"Yeah, the repo business ain't always pretty," Jake said, "but it's a livin'!"

He reached for the check and stood, pulled a few bills from his wallet and tossed them onto the counter between us.

"That should cover yours, too, cuz. Now don't dally too long. Remember, we're meeting Nina and—" he paused, inspecting his wristwatch "—well, we're already late."

Before I could swallow the toast, Jake was gone, out the door, into his car and out onto the road. I was fuming. If this was his idea of fun, well, I had a few things to teach him.

"Looking for a man and his dog, eh?" Tom chuckled. "What a story!"

"What?"

"He's not your cousin, either, I suppose?"

I met Tom's eyes. Shit. "No, he's not my cousin. He's my partner in the repo business."

Tom was shaking his head. He looked down the counter at Marti. "Well, this'll please her."

"What're you talking about?"

"Hey, Marti, come here!" He pulled out a five-dollar bill, and when she approached, he stuck it in her open palm. "You were right."

Marti looked at me and grinned. Without another word, she pocketed the money and rushed off to refill more coffee cups.

"What was that all about?"

Tom nodded to Marti, open admiration in his eyes. "When you came in, Marti said you two certainly didn't look like cousins. I couldn't understand what would make her say that, so I said you were and she said she'd bet five dollars you weren't."

I could feel my cheeks turning scarlet and the diner suddenly felt like a sweltering summer day without air. Somehow I felt certain none of this would be happening if we'd only followed Nina's advice sooner. We needed a corporate mission statement, something clean and clear, something that said we will not go off half-cocked, making up stories that were as transparent as my embarrassment was now.

I don't even think I said goodbye to Tom or Marti. I drove the few short blocks back to the beach cottage in a red haze of humiliation and fury. Jake Carpenter had gotten the best of me for the very last time.

I pulled up in front of the cottage, narrowly missing a departing white panel van and made a beeline for the front door. Nina was standing there, watching me, waving me in like a third-grade teacher ending recess.

I suppose that's why I didn't see the immense pile of dog crap; the thick, brown mountain of doo-doo that could only have been produced by... I looked up at the house next door, saw the blind slats twitch and raised my fist irritably. I didn't care if he was a senior citizen, some things you just don't do. Scoop your poop!

"Hurry up!" Nina yelled, but when I came within ten feet of her, she wrinkled her nose. "Ew! What is that smell?"

I stopped at the bottom step, scraping my foot against the edge of the walkway and gave her the evil eye.

"What do you think it is?"

She looked over her shoulder, then back at me. "Lloyd?"

Lloyd appeared in the doorway behind her. I climbed the steps, gingerly removed the offending shoes and started into the house. Lloyd blocked my progress, sniffing vigorously, tail wagging in a doggie orgy of unrequited lust. It was the scent of his beloved.

"Lloyd, back it up. I'm late."

I fully expected a lecture, but nothing could've prepared me for the scene inside. They were all wearing black sweat suits, all of them. Even Lloyd wore a toddler-size black sweatshirt. The furniture had been pushed back against the walls. New Age music played softly in the background, and the smoky scent of patchouli incense had obliterated the breakfast smell of frying bacon.

But it was the floral arrangement that had me. They were all standing around the kitchen counter, studying a monstrous arrangement of deep red roses, lilies, carnations, greenery, birds of paradise and tall spires of purple statice. It was easily four feet tall, including the giant urn, and must've taken two men to deliver.

"Nina, did we really need flowers? Isn't this a little bit much?"

Nina's eyes widened. "I didn't do this."

I met Jake's eyes, saw the grim set to his jaw, and knew somehow we'd been made.

"They've got your aunt's name on the card," he said, and handed me the small white square of card stock. "Doesn't say what florist delivered them, either."

I took the card and studied it. There was no message inside, only Aunt Lucy's name and address. I looked up and saw the worried expression on my aunt's face.

"Did you tell anyone where you were going?" I asked.

She started to shake her head and stopped. "Well, I told Maria McCarthy, but I had to, this is her house. But I didn't tell anyone else."

"Would she?"

Aunt Lucy's eyes slowly closed. She pulled her lips together in a tight line and shook her head. "I didn't tell her not to," she said at last. "I figured if I made it a secret, then she'd be more tempted to blab. If it was just a vacation, well—" she shrugged "—what's the big deal?" Aunt Lucy began to panic. "But she doesn't know… I mean, I don't even know this man. Who is this man?"

I slipped my arm around her waist and stood looking at the flowers. "Honey, you've got an admirer. First a parade float, now the flowers. Somebody saw you on TV and now he's smitten. Mrs. McCarthy probably knows him. Maybe she told someone else and they know him."

I locked eyes with Jake again. "It's no big deal. I'm sure he's harmless, but why don't you give her a call and just see? It'll make you feel better to know who it is. Then you can maybe send the guy a nice thanks-but-no-thanks note and call it a day. Okay?"

The spark came back to my aunt's eyes. Aunt Lucy was feisty most of the time; determined, strong-willed and very much in charge of her life, but I'd noted recently that it was the little things that threw her. I figured my uncle's murder had done this to her. She'd lost her footing in the world. Uncle Benny had always taken care of the details. Now, Aunt Lucy had to be overwhelmed.

Aunt Lucy stepped away from us and reached for the phone that hung on the kitchen wall. No one said a word as she dialed. Behind us Nina's woo-wah music changed to the sounds of a tropical rain forest. A macaw screeched and we all jumped.

"Maria, it's me, Lucy. Listen, I gotta ask you something."

Two minutes later we all knew the score. No, Maria hadn't told a soul and now she'd make double sure she didn't, although she was delighted to hear that my aunt had a secret admirer. Maria had also wasted no time in giving Aunt Lucy a bit of town gossip and opinion, as well.

"She said she'd heard about someone stealing Joey Smack's sleigh, and said there's talk it was you, Stella, who was responsible. She said, 'Your niece wouldn't do a terrible thing like that to that nice man, would she?'"

"Aunt Lucy, he didn't pay for the sleigh. It's not my fault it got repo'ed."

My aunt threw up her hand. "Don't tell me! Joey Smack's a lying dope dealer, that's what he is, but you can't convince some people."

Some people indeed! I shook my head.

Nina had wandered closer to the flowers and was now pulling back stalks and peering intently into the center of the arrangement.

"What're you doing, baby?" Spike asked.

Nina's muffled voice came back to us through the greenery. "I'm just checking to make sure it's not booby-trapped or anything. One time I watched this movie and..."

I gave Nina a nudge with my hip, just a little "shut up you'll scare Aunt Lucy" nudge, but it was stronger than I intended. She went flying forward, into and through the flowers, arcing into an accidental somersault that brought the faux-Greek urn tumbling along behind her.

Flowers went everywhere. Water spewed. Nina shrieked and Lloyd came dashing to her rescue, making an already chaotic situation worse.

"Get off me, dog!" Nina cried.

The macaw on the tape screamed bloody murder. Lloyd scampered to escape Nina, and somehow, in all the turmoil, the urn broke into large chunks.

I found the tiny black button among the pottery shards. I picked it up, folded it over into my palm and stuffed it into my jeans pocket. I had worked Vice Narcotics long enough to recognize a listening device when I saw one.

Jake didn't miss it, either. I looked up, saw him watching me, and mouthed "bug." He nodded toward the stairs, turned and slipped off before the others noticed. Within moments I followed.

When I reached the bedroom I found Jake staring out a window at the street below. I crossed the room and stood beside him, inspecting the empty street and the beach beyond that.

"See anything?" I asked.

Jake shrugged. "I'm not sure. I just figured they'd have a listening post nearby. But I don't see a thing."

I scanned the street again. It was completely empty.

"Two possibilities come to mind," I said. "Aunt Lucy could have a stalker on her tail, or Joey Spagnazi's found us. I think we should check the local florists and see if the flowers came from a local shop. It's a long shot, but it's possible."

Jake nodded. "All right, you do that and I'll—"

"Whoa, Jake, we need to get something straight here. I am not your employee. This is my agency."

"Actually, I believe it's our agency. I went in on this fifty-fifty. I put the deposit down on the phone system."

"And I put the security deposit down on the office and paid the first month's rent. I believe I was the one who came up with the idea for this business anyway. I invited you, not the other way around."

Jake nodded, as if he finally understood. "Oh, I see. You asked me, so that makes it your business and I work for you, right?"

"Right."

"Wrong, Valocchi. You might've come up with the idea, but I'm the one who scored the repo contract for Lifetime Novelty. This is a partnership, Stella, even up, equally divided."

I couldn't believe we were arguing about this when my aunt was being stalked and we had yet to begin our first real job.

"Jake, we don't have time for this. We can talk about it later. Right now we have to—"

Jake folded his arms across his chest. "No, we clear it up right now. I'm nobody's employee. Either this is a partnership or it isn't."

It was a standoff. Neither one of us spoke for what seemed like an eternity. I was feeling more and more desperate by the moment. I needed to know what was going on with Aunt Lucy's secret admirer. I needed to know if Joey Smack had sent the flowers hoping to scare me because I'd realize he knew where we were, and that if flowers got through to my aunt, so could he.

"You need me, Stella." Jake spoke softly, almost whispering.

"No, I don't."

He stared at me and for an instant I saw hurt and knew I'd wounded him somehow.

"Yes, you do. You can't work Mia's case and look out for your aunt all by yourself. Besides, I have Mia's manila envelope. Without that, you can't reach her. You can't read what the last investigator found."

For some reason, I didn't want to give in. I didn't want to give him that much power or space in my life, even if it was purely business. But then, what choice did I have? I referred to him as my partner, but I hadn't really thought of him as my equal partner; somehow the word *equal* just stuck in my throat like a lump of wood.

"All right," I said. "We're partners." When I saw that he was still waiting, I added, "Equal partners. But you can't keep issuing orders."

"You, either."

I nodded. "Fair enough. We discuss it, then we do it. No running off to investigate on our own without telling the other one. It's dangerous, anyway."

"I agree. We discuss it." Jake walked to the chest that stood between our two beds, opened a drawer and pulled out the manila envelope.

"Here you go," he said. "There isn't a report from another investigator in here. Looks like Mia wrote down what he told her, but there's nothing formal."

"Did she write down his name? Maybe we could talk to him and—"

Jake shook his head. "All she has down here is that her brother was born here and adopted by a local family. She doesn't have his name. She thinks he was born in 1962, but she's not sure."

"Damn. That doesn't give us anything. I'll have to go through newspapers, birth records and whatever else I can find to figure out who was born and raised here and who was also adopted. This could take forever."

"It'll give Spike and Nina something to do," Jake offered. "That would free us up to go find out what we can on the flowers and the bug."

I nodded, my thoughts racing. There should be mention of Mia's parents' deaths in the paper and certainly in the county records. We could track him that way.

"I've got a few friends who might be able to tell us more about the bug," Jake said. "It might help to know where it came from and how easy it is to buy them."

"Are you two having sex, or what?" Nina yelled from downstairs. "I thought we were going to meditate."

Nina's tone was ominous.

"Great! Now Nina's going to be pissed off. We really don't have time for this."

"Family business," Jake said. "Sounds great in theory, but in practice…"

I ignored this and started past him toward the stairs. He grabbed my arm, stopping me.

"What?"

"It's not so bad, is it?" he said.

"What?"

"Being equal partners."

I frowned and attempted to slip out of his grasp, but his hold tightened. He reached out with his other hand and tilted my chin up, forcing my eyes to meet his.

"Is this so bad, Stella?"

I felt the pilot light in my stomach catch and ignite slowly into a steady flame of awareness. I wanted to move, ordered myself to go, to run away, but found my body wouldn't act. I saw him bending closer, felt the taste of his lips on mine even before he kissed me, and realized that my eyes were slowly closing in delighted anticipation.

What was happening to me? One moment we had been fighting over an equal partnership, the next we were doing this.

As Jake's lips found mine, I let my arms reach up, circling his neck and drawing him closer until I felt my body move against his.

"You two are having sex, aren't you?" Nina called again. "This is so like totally not the way to run a business."

Jake nibbled my ear. "If you take them to the library and

courthouse, I'll check the florists." I felt his hand trace the top button of my shirt, caught my breath as he slowly unbuttoned it and moved to the next button and then the next. As the last button gave way, I felt the warm, rough touch of his hand sliding across my skin.

I closed my eyes and gave myself over to the sensations as every nerve ending in my body cried out "More!" His hands answered, sliding up beneath my bra slowly exploring and exciting.

His fingers searched for and found the tender tips of my breasts, squeezing them gently, rubbing his work-roughened skin across the sensitive nipples. "Does that work for you?" he murmured.

I sighed, my head tilting back against the wall as he slowly, very slowly, teased and excited my neck with his tongue. I tugged his T-shirt free from his waistband and ran my fingers across his smooth chest.

"It works," I whispered. "It works just fine."

"Stella!"

At the sound of Aunt Lucy's voice, I jumped away from Jake, hastily buttoning my shirt as I ran for the steps.

"I'm coming," I yelled. "We were just discussing the case."

I appeared at the top of the landing, breathless, and saw Spike conceal a giggle. I ran the rest of the way down the steps.

"I hate to do this to you, Nina," I said. "But we've got to get moving on our missing person's case and I really could use some help from you and Spike."

Nina's demeanor went from pissed off to excited in one second flat. "Will it be dangerous? I really like it dangerous."

Spike walked up beside Nina and bent to whisper in my ear, "Your shirt's buttoned wrong."

I looked down, saw the cock-eyed buttons and winced.

"Uh-huh," Aunt Lucy snorted. "Working, eh?"

"Really, we were. And we've got a plan."

I outlined the afternoon's research project, giving Spike the courthouse-record detail and Nina the library and newspaper archives.

"Jake and I are going to check out the local florists."

With a start I remembered we hadn't thought to cover Aunt Lucy. "And you can come with us," I added.

Jake joined us just in time to hear my aunt say, "Absolutely not! I've got work to do. I'll stay right here."

I started to argue with her, but she cut me off. "Your uncle will be here with me. He won't let anything happen. Besides, if anything does happen, I can always call your cell phone."

Jake didn't seem to be any more pleased than I was. "Take the girls and go on. I'll call all the florists in the phone book while you're gone. When you get back, we should have something to go on."

When I didn't move, he said, "Stella, that's not an order, it's my idea. If you want to do it differently…"

"Actually," I said, "I was waiting for you to move. You're standing in front of the coat closet."

I smiled sweetly up at him, ignoring the way he double-checked my facial expression, trying to figure out if I was playing him. I couldn't look at him for long without my knees going weak, but I couldn't seem to stop staring, either.

"You were so having sex up there!" Nina hissed in my ear.

"So not!"

She rolled her eyes and shrugged into her coat and multi-colored knit stocking cap. With a flounce she was out the door and down the steps to the car, Spike right behind her.

"I'll be back as soon as I drop them off."

Jake nodded. "Don't worry. I've got calls to make." His eyes lingered just a bit too long on my lips. My stomach fluttered and I couldn't take another second of attention. I half ran out the door, heard him call my name and turned to see him standing with my coat in his hand.

"Need this?"

I snatched it and ran, knowing Aunt Lucy had witnessed everything and was making her own judgments about the two of us.

"Nothing." I scolded myself under my breath. "He's nothing to you, do you hear? Business and nothing more! You are such a weak-willed person!"

I opened the car door and Nina immediately pounced. "Okay, what's going on with you two?"

"Nothing!"

"Stella, he's got you walking around talking to yourself. You think we didn't see you just then? Now, give. Every detail!"

Spike leaned forward from the back seat. "You don't look like it's nothing," she said. "You really have been acting a little funny."

I gave myself a huge mental bitch slap and reminded myself that this was exactly why you shouldn't work with family members. They'd known you since childhood. Pulling the wool over their eyes was impossible. Of course, Spike wasn't family exactly, but her connection to Nina made it just as bad.

"All right, I'll just tell you," I said, backing the car out into the street. "I don't know what's going on. All I know is that it isn't safe for me to be in a room alone with Jake. It's like we have this chemistry…"

"Ohh, I love chemistry," Nina breathed.

"Yeah, well, I don't. Jake Carpenter and I do not have a future. We tried it before and it ended in disaster. And look how things ended with Pete. He ran off with my partner and I wound up quitting the force because of it."

Spike clucked her tongue softly. "But weren't you and Jake together back in high school? Of course your relationship wouldn't work out back then—you were too young. Nobody knows what they want when they're young. You've both grown up since then."

Nina sighed and reached back across the seat to touch

Spike's arm. "I certainly wouldn't have known what to do about you back then," she said softly. "And I was a Girl Scout, too."

Spike and I exchanged puzzled glances in the rearview mirror.

"Why would that matter, Nina?" I asked.

"Well, silly, I mean our motto was 'Always Be Prepared.' I wasn't prepared for *this*. I mean, in case you hadn't noticed, Spike's a girl. I liked boys back then. How can you prepare to like a girl when you like boys? Liking someone you're not supposed to like is scary. Me and Spike are just like you and Jake. I wasn't supposed to like a girl, and you're not supposed to like Jake because he hurt you, remember?"

I wanted to say, "How could I not remember that? He was my first love and he broke my heart." Instead, I kept my mouth shut and drove.

When I spotted the library I said a silent thank-you to the great Girl Scout leader in the sky and drove a little faster. I pulled up in front of the small, serpentine building and promised I'd be back to collect Nina by four o'clock.

"There's a nice diner about two blocks down," I told her. "But I doubt they have tofu."

Nina rolled her eyes and looked back at Spike. "Meet me there at one?"

Spike nodded and pointed to a brick building in the next block. "That's the courthouse," she said. "If I finish before one, I'll come up here and help you."

Nina squinted into the late-morning sunlight, peering off in the direction of the courthouse.

"That's the courthouse, really? I thought you hadn't been here before."

Spike smiled. "I haven't."

"Then how do you know that's it?"

I looked at her and pointed. "I think the sign over there was a clue. It says Ocean County Courthouse."

Nina bristled. "Well, just totally excuse me." she said, sniffing. "I can't help it if I have allergies."

I didn't even ask.

I let Nina and Spike out, waved goodbye and waited until I'd rounded the corner to pick up the cell phone and dial. Pete answered on the third ring, his voice thick with sleep.

"It's me," I said, suddenly at a loss.

After all, what did you say to the old boyfriend you'd caught boinking your partner? True, it had been almost three months since I'd walked in on the two of them, and yes, a lot had happened in that time. We'd done some work to bury the hatchet, but the awkwardness would always be there between the two of us. He wanted me back, I knew that, but I wasn't going to return and he knew that. It was just weird, and had I not needed a favor, I probably wouldn't have called, we both knew that.

"Stella, baby. How are you?"

I swallowed as the mental image of him and Lou Ann having sex suddenly popped into my head. I shuddered and asked him anyway.

"I need a favor," I said.

"Sure, baby, anything!"

"I need you to run a check on someone."

"I knew that guy was no good, Stella."

I turned Aunt Lucy's Buick onto a side street, drove to the end and pulled into a slot in the public parking area.

"Who—Jake?"

Pete had run into Jake on his failed mission to bring me back home to Florida. Pete was a dog with women, but he had impeccable cop instincts. He smelled danger on Jake and I knew it.

"Is that his name?"

I rolled my eyes. Pete knew Jake's name as well as he knew mine.

"It's not him. I took on a missing person's case. I want you to run my client."

"So your new boyfriend doesn't have connections? He can't get you what you need?" Pete sounded smug, as if he thought I was crawling back to him.

"He worked for the feds, Pete. He's not a cop."

There was no way I was going to tell Pete I didn't want to ask Jake because I wanted to be one up on my new partner.

There was a momentary silence. In the background I thought I heard the faintest murmur of a female voice. Lou Ann. Pete was still boffing my old squad partner.

"All right," he said. "Let me get something to write with. I'll run her when I go in tonight."

"You still seeing Lou Ann?" I asked.

Pete choked. "No, baby. Whatever gave you that idea? Now, what's that name?"

I gave him Mia's name, spelled it out for him and then said, "That's all I have on her for now. I don't have a social, birth date or tag."

"I'll do what I can, honey."

I heard the woman's voice again and Pete quickly muffled the phone.

"Just call my cell when you know something," I said, and pressed my lips together hard in order not to say something. Pete was the only cop contact I could rely on to look up something without a lengthy explanation. He was too busy digging himself out of the doghouse to ask questions.

"Oh, and tell Lou Ann I said hey."

I broke the connection before he could say anything and sat for a moment with my head resting against the steering wheel. My head was spinning with random thoughts. I didn't want Jake to know I was checking Mia out. Something about that woman didn't ring right and I couldn't explain it to Jake as anything other than a feeling, an instinct.

Jake would probably think I was jealous because she was attractive and obviously attracted to him. I also didn't want Jake to know I'd called Pete, and I didn't know why. I found myself thinking about Joey Smack and wondered why he couldn't accept that we'd only been doing our jobs.

I raised my head and stared at the steps leading up to the boardwalk and then down onto the beach. Maybe a walk would clear my head. I climbed out of the car, locked it and pocketed the keys. A walk was just what I needed. What better way to generate a plan?

I walked to the edge of the water and stood staring out to sea, lost in thought again. This time I slipped far away from today's problems, choosing instead to think about the long-ago past. I could never spend time by the ocean without missing my mom and dad. When I was thirteen, my parents had taken a second honeymoon. They'd boarded a huge jumbo jet and left for Ireland, never to return. On the return trip, their plane developed some kind of sudden problem and was lost over the Atlantic Ocean.

For years I blamed myself, thinking I'd driven them away with my teenage rebelliousness. My uncle Benny was the one to see through that. Ever so gently he picked away at the layers of guilt and remorse, until at last he found my secret core.

We were fishing, the way we did almost every afternoon the summer after I lost my parents. Uncle Benny was baiting his hook with a plastic worm, smiling to himself as if he had some secret knowledge.

"Stella Luna," he said at last, "did I ever tell you about the time your aunt Lucy, your mother and I got arrested?"

I had been reading *A Tale of Two Cities,* part of my do-good-be-good penance program. I remember lowering the book to my lap and staring at him, silently waiting for the story and too proud to urge him on.

"Yes, your mother and your aunt snuck out one night, right around Halloween it was."

My mother? My mother had been a saint. She'd never done anything wrong in her life.

Uncle Benny nodded. "Yep, the two of them McClannahan girls were wild as coot owls, always into the trouble, they were. Preachers' daughters, you know. Anyway, that particular night we were mad at the mayor. Now, they were always mad at the powers that be for one reason or another. Your mother, you know, was quite the rebel."

I couldn't help myself. "She was?"

Uncle Benny smiled at me, eyes twinkling. "Ah, so she didn't tell you, eh? Well, I think she saw so much of herself in you it scared her. I think she realized that some of her little stunts were dangerous and she didn't want her precious daughter getting hurt."

"How did she get arrested?"

"Well, there was a slight miscalculation when we released the brakes on the mayor's car. Instead of it rolling harmlessly into a field, it landed in the millpond and we were in it at the time."

I frowned. "Why didn't you run away?"

Uncle Benny smiled. "Well, we were going to, but it didn't seem anybody noticed, so we, um, decided to go for a little swim first. That's how the police found us."

"You didn't see them coming?"

Uncle Benny blushed furiously. "Your aunt'll have my ass if I tell you," he said.

"Please, Uncle Benny, tell me what happened."

"Well, we'd sort of written our policy position on whatever it was, segregation I suppose, across his front door in red paint, and were celebrating with, um, well…"

"You were drinking?"

"Oh, yes, I'm afraid we were. Slowed us down quite a bit,

that and your mother and her sister couldn't quite find all of their clothes."

"Uncle Benny!"

He laughed. "Ah, kids. They all do something crazy and rebellious now and then. Your mother and her sister were just feeling their oats."

"I don't believe it!"

Uncle Benny crossed his heart and looked suddenly serious. "All kids have to rebel, otherwise how can they grow up and be their own person? Your mother told me she saw herself in you. She said it was the most amazing thing, to be on the other side looking back at herself. You know, I think it made her proud."

"No, it didn't." I felt tears welling up and spilling over to run down my cheeks. "I was awful."

"Stella Luna, the week before your mother left she was over at the house, sitting at the kitchen table telling us how you sassed her and she was laughing. 'I'll never worry about that one falling in with a bad lot,' she said. 'She's too strong-willed to let herself be led around by the nose.'"

Uncle Benny leaned over to hand me the bandanna he always kept handy in his back pocket.

"They were so proud of you, Stella. They died knowing you'd be fine. Don't let them down by punishing yourself for the very thing they loved in you."

I looked out at the ocean and felt my chest tightening. Sometimes, despite my aunt and uncle's love, I felt so alone without my parents. Now Uncle Benny was gone. A wave of grief swamped me when I thought about him and for a moment I couldn't breathe. Sometimes life was just so unfair.

I turned away from the ocean and started back toward the boardwalk. Enough self-pity, I told myself. I stiffened my shoulders and raised my head. That's when I saw the two men walking toward me.

Chapter 7

At the same moment my cell phone rang. I reached into my
pocket, watching as the men continued to approach, praying
Jake was on the other end of the line and could reach me if I
needed him. I tried to convince myself that they were harmless, guys heading toward the surf to fish. I took in the black
business shoes and sighed. Nope. They didn't even carry rods
or tackle boxes.

Maybe they were tourists, or in town on business and hoping to take in a quick walk along the shoreline. I studied the
cauliflower ear on the big guy to the left and ruled nature lover
out of the program. The gun prominently displayed in the
waistband of the guy on the right seemed to rule out tourist.
The way both of them zeroed in on me left no doubt in my mind
that this was a business call and I was the intended victim.

I fished harder for the cell phone, digging deep into my
jacket pocket, and finally succeeded in pulling it out.

"Hello?"

Someone gave a short impatient sigh on the other end of the line. "Is Jake there?" Mia asked. "I really need to talk to him."

Please, I thought looking at my two visitors, you only think you need to talk to Jake.

"This isn't a good time, Mia," I said. "And he's not here anyway."

The two men stopped momentarily, conferring. Maybe they thought I was calling the police. Right now, calling the police sounded like a good idea, only what would I say? Two men are staring at me and one has a gun? Most of the male population in Jersey carried guns. They carried guns like women carried purses. What if I was wrong about them? What if they were police working the case from the night before? Maybe I should keep Mia on the line and just pretend she was the police.

"Can I do something for you?" I asked.

"Well, I was really hoping…"

"I know, I know. You were hoping to talk to Jake, but that's impossible, so what is it?"

"I was talking to my sister and she remembered a few more things about my brother," she said.

I had stopped and was watching the two men in front of me. They stood blocking the steps leading up onto the boardwalk and while they weren't openly menacing, they didn't look friendly. This required a plan.

I veered off to the left, trying to act as if I was studying the houses that lined the beach. I kept the cell phone out where the two men could see it and hoped I'd been imagining things.

"What did your sister remember, Mia?"

Damn. The two men hesitated, and then started following me, keeping their distance, but still bird-dogging me.

"Well, it's not so much what she remembered as what she found."

Mia seemed to enjoy doling out the information slowly, and

I wasn't about to indulge her by asking, so I waited. After a long moment, she continued.

"Both of us have tried to find our brother. We've hired private investigators, tried to find adoption records, all that, but we never could get beyond the basics. We believe he was adopted by a family in Surfside Isle and that he grew up there."

Mia wasn't telling me one new thing and I began to wonder if she'd only called to flirt with Jake. In the meantime, the two men had moved in closer. I looked ahead, trying to figure out my next move, and realized why they felt safe in closing the gap. A stone jetty poked out into the water a block away. The channel leading from the sound side of the island to the ocean lay just before me. I was running out of beach and would have no other option but to turn back.

"I thought you said your sister remembered something new," I said.

Mia sighed. "A year or two earlier she received an anonymous letter. Inside was an old picture of a family standing in front of a beach house. Someone had written, Summer, 1967 on the back of it."

I held the phone away from my head and scowled at it. "And she just now told you this?" I asked.

"Well, it's not exactly like we were close or anything. After all, she didn't find me until last month. I'd only talked to her on the phone. We didn't even meet face-to-face until a week ago. Besides, she's really sick. She doesn't remember things well. I mean, she's on dialysis, for God's sake!" Mia sounded exasperated. "Do you want the picture or not?"

"What if someone was playing a joke on her?"

"At least you'll have something to go on," she said. "Show it around. Maybe someone will recognize one of the people in the picture. I'll fax it to you. Where are you staying?"

I gave Mia the address. "Overnight it," I said. "It's a little beach house. It doesn't have a fax."

I was studying the boardwalk, praying for signs of life, witnesses, open businesses, but Surfside Isle was deserted. When I glanced over my shoulder I saw the two men had stopped and were staring up at a house, pointing and gesturing to something I couldn't make out. I breathed a sigh of relief.

"I can't believe you don't have a fax," Mia said.

"I don't even know where there is one around here," I said. "Everything's closed up for the winter. I can't imagine we'd need the picture before tomorrow anyway. If you think we do, you can either drive it or have it sent by courier, but that'll cost you."

Mia paused, considering her options. I half thought she'd elect to drive, just so she'd see Jake, and was surprised when she said, "No, I'll overnight it."

She hung up before I could say another word. I turned to walk back toward the boardwalk, scanned the beach and saw no sign of the two men.

My attention strayed back to Mia's call. Why would someone send an anonymous picture to Mia's sister? Who knew she was looking for her family? Who would've known how to contact Mia's sister anyway? Did she run an ad in the paper? Did she leave her name and address with someone? I just couldn't get over the feeling that Mia wasn't telling us the whole truth about her situation. I made a mental list of questions for Mia to answer for when we next spoke.

I flipped open the phone and started to call Pete, then realized he hadn't even gone into work yet. He wouldn't be able to give me anything on Mia until well after midnight.

I was walking faster now, intent on returning to the beach house and still checking for the two men who'd seemed to be following me. I almost missed the Victorian house that sat just a bit apart from the other oceanfront homes. I saw it and stopped, recognizing it as the house where Lloyd's new friend might live.

It appeared to have been abandoned. Sheets of plywood covered the doors and windows, making the house far more secure than if it had been closed for a seasonal shutdown. A metal For Sale sign was stuck into the sand by the front entrance, dangling loosely by one remaining screw. The place looked as if no one had lived there for quite a while. I thought I spotted movement beneath the porch, and squinted and studied a piece of loose latticework. Had I seen a flash of gray fur? The glint of wild wolf eyes?

I kept my eyes trained on that one spot as I passed, wondering if the big dog was a stray who'd found shelter in the abandoned house. I couldn't believe the house had been allowed to fall into such a state of disrepair. With fresh paint and a few repairs, it could've been a showplace. Beachfront property usually moved no matter what condition it was in, so why was this still on the market?

As I started up the stairs, I looked back out at the ocean. Clouds had begun to move in, obscuring the sun and adding to the chill in the air. I shivered, pulling my coat tighter around my body, and turned away. I smelled snow and salt, not unpleasant but definitely unfamiliar.

I started down the steps and stopped, frozen by the scene before me. Every tire on Aunt Lucy's prize Buick had been flattened and red paint covered the windshield.

"Shit!"

I dug in my pocket for the cell phone as I moved down the stairs. Something caught my ankle and I felt myself pitch forward. I reached out to grab the railing and break my fall, missed, and hit every single sharp angle on my way down. But the pain from the fall was the least of my worries.

Cauliflower Ear was waiting for me by the bottom step, and when I landed he reached down, snatched me up by the coat collar and dragged me effortlessly behind the steps, under the boardwalk.

I opened my mouth to scream and Cauliflower slapped me hard across the mouth. I tasted blood and looked up at my two assailants. Hitting me had been the very best thing Cauliflower could've done. It made me mad, and anger was a very productive emotion.

"Where is it?" Cauliflower's partner asked me.

"Up your ass, I suppose."

Cauliflower held me from behind and this time his partner hit me. The heavy nugget ring on his right finger connected with my cheekbone and I felt the skin split beneath my eye.

I heard the sharp cry of pain escape my lips and tried to detach from it. I had an armed man standing in front of me and a hulk of muscle and steroids restraining me from behind. I had to welcome the pain if I wanted to live, not give in to it.

I leaned forward as far as Cauliflower would allow and spit blood onto the gray sand at my feet. "What do you want?" I asked.

"Don't play games with us," the short guy said. "You got something and Joey wants it back."

I straightened up, figuring that if he were to come one foot closer I could kick him in the groin.

"Tell Mr. Spagnazi he's barking up the wrong tree. We repossessed his sleigh and turned it over to Lifetime Novelty. Take it up with them."

For some reason this didn't please my captors. The short guy looked at Cauliflower, took a cigarette out of his coat pocket and lit it.

"Pin her," he said.

Cauliflower swung me around, pushed me up against a piling and held me there. The short guy approached, took a long, deep drag of his cigarette, and nodded to Cauliflower.

I felt cold air hit the side of my neck as he ripped the coat away, exposing bare skin. When he pulled my shirt away, fabric tore, buttons popped, and I struggled to get away from the two madmen.

"Last chance," the short guy whispered. "Where is it?"

Tobacco smoke stung my eyes, making tears stream down my face. When the red ember bit into the soft skin at the base of my neck I screamed again, unable to stop the terror from overtaking me.

I heard something behind us, screamed again and this time heard the short man scream. Cauliflower dropped me and I sagged against the tar-stained post. The short man was screaming, terrified and in pain.

I pushed myself away from the pole, turned and saw the wolf-dog sinking her fangs into my attacker. Cauliflower had vanished, his footsteps echoing across the parking lot as he fled. The dog held the smaller man down, gripping his forearm in her massive jaws, snarling and jerking the arm back and forth.

"Help!" the man screamed. "Help me!"

The cigarette lay on the ground a few feet away from my attacker; his gun had also fallen inches from his writhing body. He spotted it and was trying desperately to reach it.

I leaned down, picked up the gun and stepped back.

"Is this what you wanted?" I asked.

"Help me, please."

My new friend, Fang, stood still, her eyes on me, the man's arm still firmly clenched between her jaws.

"I don't know," I said. "I don't think you've been a good boy. Maybe you need to be taught a lesson. Maybe the dog's hungry."

The pain from the burn on my neck was almost unbearable. It joined in with my other cuts and bruises in an overwhelming abundance of painful sensation. The brief temptation to shoot the guy hit me and I gripped the butt of the gun hard to keep from squeezing the trigger.

I looked at the dog, saw her watching me, and tried to smile. "Good puppy," I said softly. "Good, good puppy."

Her prisoner moaned. Blood was soaking the ground beneath his arm and I realized that calling the police might not be my best option. The cops would ask questions I didn't want to answer. Besides, what would they do with Fang? What if she hadn't had her shots? What if they put her down? They could do that, even though Fang had been defending me.

I looked down at Fang and her prisoner and had another thought. This man could tell Joey Smack that I didn't have whatever he wanted. He could be my messenger. Maybe Joey would get off my back. I very slowly knelt to Fang's level. "Fang, release him." I held my breath, hoping Fang might recognize the command. Her eyes met mine, soft, liquid and pleading. She whined.

"Fang, release him."

The dog's jaws dropped open; my attacker jerked his bleeding arm away, and scrambled up into a half-crouching position.

"Tell Joey Smack I don't have anything of his. I have no idea what he's after. Tell him he tries a stupid stunt like this again and we'll deal with him on a very personal and up-front manner," I said.

The man took off running without another word. Fang watched him leave, snarling and barking viciously at his retreating figure.

I sank onto the sand, suddenly weak, and felt my body begin to shake. Fang's attention turned to me and the giant dog took a few hesitant steps in my direction, sniffing the air around my body cautiously.

"It's all right," I murmured. "I'm Lloyd's mother. I won't hurt you, baby."

I slowly stretched out my hand, offering Fang the opportunity to check me out for herself. When she did, I very carefully stroked the fur beneath her bloodstained muzzle.

"I don't know who you are," I whispered, "but I'm mighty glad you decided to come along."

The dog licked my finger and whined softly.

"I called you Fang," I said softly, "because I don't know your name, not because you're, well… What I'm trying to say is, I hope you don't mind."

I felt my energy dropping off into exhaustion and knew I needed to get someplace warm and safe before I passed out and succumbed to hypothermia. Jake was wrong about the weather, I thought idly. The temperature wouldn't come anywhere near fifty degrees. I peered out at the lowering skyline. It looked like snow.

I switched the gun to my left hand and dug deep into my coat pocket for the cell phone. I punched in Jake's cell number and rested my head against Fang's soft furry shoulder.

"Wanna come home to my house?" I asked her. "I bet it beats living underneath a porch."

She whined and licked the side of my face.

"You're just a sweetheart," I said.

"Thank you," Jake's voice said in my ear. "All this time I thought you were sort of ambivalent."

"Not you. Fang."

"Who's Fang?" he asked. "Even better, where are you? I thought you were going to drop the girls off and come right back. Didn't we just talk about…"

I buried my head back against Fang's soft fur. "Jake, I need you to come get me."

My tone must've alarmed him.

"What happened? Where are you?"

"Don't tell Aunt Lucy," I said. "The car is in a parking lot at the end of Forty-first Street or somewhere close to that. I wasn't paying much attention at the time."

"Where are you?" His voice was slow and deliberate.

"Under the boardwalk. I don't think I want to try walking out just yet."

"On my way," he said, and broke the connection.

He made it to me in less than three minutes. Fang bristled when she heard the car door slam, the hackles rising on her neck as Jake ran toward us.

"Fang," I said, "it's all right."

Jake appeared, saw the dog and stopped, assessing the situation. A muscle in his jaw twitched and his hand slowly crept to his jacket pocket.

"Don't," I said. "She's the one who saved me."

Jake relaxed, took his hand from his pocket and stepped slowly forward. "It's all right, girl," he murmured. "I'm one of the good guys."

Fang growled low in her throat and backed away from me.

"Come here, puppy. It's okay."

Fang looked from me to Jake and back again, deciding for herself. A moment later she turned and trotted off, leaving the underbelly of the boardwalk and loping away in the direction of the beach house.

Jake knelt by my side and gently stretched out a finger to touch the swelling skin on the right side of my face.

"Hate to see the other guy," he said softly.

He was smiling, giving it the nonchalant, no-big-deal treatment, but his eyes were another story. Jake Carpenter's eyes were dark with unexpressed anger.

"Help me up, would you?"

I struggled to stand, unable to hide the effort and the pain it took to move. When Jake slid his arm around my waist to support me, he noticed the burn.

"What happened, Stella?"

I bit down on my lip. I wanted to cry but wasn't about to let him see me weaker than I already felt.

"Oh, you know, I was tired of you getting all the attention with that gunshot wound, so I ran across a couple of guys who said they'd kick my ass for free, so I let them."

We were up and moving now, emerging into the parking lot where Aunt Lucy's car sat resting on its rims.

"Stella!"

So I told him while we waited for the wrecker to come for the Buick. I tried to gloss over the details, like how scared I'd been, or how badly the two men had hurt me, but it was no use. Jake had a way of looking at me and reading every unspoken nuance.

We sat in his car, engine running, heat on high, and talked, or rather I talked and he asked question after question.

When the tow truck arrived and carried Aunt Lucy's car to the nearest auto-body shop, Jake drove me back to the beach house. He pulled up into the gravel driveway, cut the engine and was preparing to open the door when I stopped him.

"Jake."

"Yeah?"

"I think we should be straight up with Aunt Lucy and the others about what happened. I mean, they need to be careful, especially if Joey Smack's looking to make trouble. But I don't want my aunt knowing how rough it got out there, okay? She'd worry."

Jake raised an eyebrow. "You don't think she'll take one look at you and know something happened?"

I tried to shrug but stopped as a searing pain ran up my arm and radiated out across my shoulders.

"Sure, she'll know they tripped me and I fell, but she doesn't need to know about the thing with the cigarette, or any of the gory details, okay?" I reached into my pocket, pulled out the short guy's gun and handed it to Jake. "Put this somewhere, okay?"

He nodded and stuck the gun in a jacket pocket. We locked

the truck and started inside to face Aunt Lucy. My aunt was a sharp cookie and I knew it wasn't going to be easy to tell her a story and have her not read between the lines.

The evidence of this lay on the kitchen counter beside her when we entered the house. A Colt 45–caliber revolver rested next to a pan of lasagna. Aunt Lucy didn't often rely on others to take care of her. She didn't have to.

She looked up from her Bunsen burner, saw me, and immediately went into the role of nurse and surrogate mother.

"What happened to you, car accident?"

She asked this as she pulled the ice bin from the freezer and began loading small plastic bags with ice.

"Among other things," I answered.

"Sit down at the table," she instructed. "Let's get you cleaned up."

She reached into a paper grocery sack, pulled out an unmarked silver tube and headed toward me.

"Joey Spagnazi do this?" she asked.

Jake and I nodded.

"Son of a bitch."

"My sentiments exactly," I said.

Aunt Lucy unscrewed the cap on her silver tube, squeezed a dab of clear cream onto her finger and began gently applying it to my cheek.

"This should bring the swelling down," she murmured. "He did this to you?"

"Indirectly. One of his goons tripped me as I was coming down the boardwalk steps. I hit my cheek on the steps."

Aunt Lucy inspected the cut carefully. "Hmm. Those steps burn your neck, too?"

I reached up and realized my collar hadn't quite covered the mark on my neck. Damn.

"It probably looks worse than it is."

Aunt Lucy didn't say a word. She turned and walked back

to her grocery sack, pulled out another silver tube and returned to the table. I saw her exchange a look with Jake before she reached out and gently eased my shirt collar away
from my neck.

"This should make it so there won't be a scar later," she
said. "What did the police say?"

I looked at Jake. No help there.

"Did anything happen while I was gone?"

"No," Aunt Lucy answered. "What did the police say?"

This time my cell phone saved me.

"Hey," Nina said. "Are you guys coming up here to lunch?
I think we found some information. I'm not sure it's what you
want, because I don't really know what we're looking for."

Aunt Lucy was poised over me, two silver tubes in hand
and a determined look on her face.

"Absolutely," I said. "I'll be right there. Don't worry."

"I'm not worried. I just thought—"

I flipped the phone shut, stood up and felt the room swim
around me for a moment.

"Gotta go," I said. "Nina doesn't know what she's doing."

"Like that's new," Jake muttered.

I gave him the evil eye and stuck out my hand. "Keys, please."

He raised an eyebrow. "Are you forgetting the new policy?"

"No. I didn't think library work was your forte, that's all.
I figured you were on bodyguard duty here."

Aunt Lucy glared at the two of us. "Do I look like I need
a bodyguard?" she demanded. She inclined her head toward
the big gun on the counter. "I've got your bodyguard right over
there. If Jake leaves his cell phone I can call for help if I need
it. But you," she said, directing her attention to me, "don't look
like you'd be a help to anybody. Anybody stupid enough to
think I'm gonna believe they fell down a flight of steps and
accidentally landed on a cigarette doesn't need to be rushing
off to help anybody else. You should lie down."

The air in the beach house suddenly felt too thick to breathe. The dark-paneled walls were closing in on me and no amount of natural or artificial light was enough to brighten the house's atmosphere.

"I'm fine, really. I've got a couple of bruises and…"

"And a lot you're not telling me," my aunt finished.

She frowned at Jake. "Looks like Stella needs more caretaking than I do. You gonna be the one responsible for her?"

Lloyd padded out into the kitchen, took one whiff of my jeans and went into a sudden doggie-lust frenzy. He jumped up and pawed at my pants, his pink tongue lolling out of his mouth as he drooled all over me.

"Lloyd, get down." I grabbed Jake's keys off the kitchen counter. "Aunt Lucy, Jake doesn't need to take care of me. I'm responsible for me. I don't need a keeper."

"Well, I don't, either," she snapped. "I may be old, but I'm not half beat to death, and I've got a gun. Where was yours?"

She had me there. I'd never walk on the beach again without it.

"Do I get a say in this?" Jake interrupted.

"No!"

It was the only thing Aunt Lucy and I agreed on at the time. Neither one of us felt much like having a baby-sitter or taking it easy. I was too mad to slow down and be careful. I wanted to wipe Joey Smack off the face of the planet. I wanted to take action, not read about it later. Apparently, Aunt Lucy felt the same way.

"I've got work to do," she said. "If you don't want to take care of yourself, then you're certainly old enough to suffer the consequences."

I looked at the mess of bowls and pans she'd scattered across the kitchen counters and realized Aunt Lucy had created a make-do laboratory.

Jake peered into a stainless-steel bowl and inhaled deeply.

"Mmm, this smells good. What is it?"

He dipped a finger into the bowl, swiped a sample and was about to taste it when Aunt Lucy slapped his hand away.

"Get out of there! It's stain remover. Eat that and you'll be blowin' bubbles outta both ends for days."

I slipped toward the door and was almost gone before they noticed. Jake wiped his finger on his jeans.

"Lock the door after us. We'll be back as quickly as possible," he said, and was right behind me as I started down the steps.

He grabbed the keys from my hand, pressed the remote to unlock the doors and waited until I'd climbed up into the truck before he lost his temper.

"Stella, what is it with you? Do you think you're the only person on the planet with a stake in the outcome? Do you treat your friends like they're idiots, too, or just your aunt and me?"

He started the car and backed out of the driveway. The tiny muscle in his jaw twitched and he wouldn't look at me.

"I just felt like moving so I wouldn't stiffen up. I didn't mean to—"

"Don't start, Stella, all right? Just don't start. What do you take me for, huh? You think I'm just some dumb car mechanic or the boy you left behind ten years ago?"

"Eleven," I corrected. "And you left me first."

Jake veered into the driveway of a vacant beach house, slammed the car into Park and stared at me.

"You see? You're doing it right there. Stella, let's get a few things straight, all right? Number one, we were seventeen when I asked you to elope with me. We were too young to get married and we were just lucky your uncle stopped us. It would've been a terrible mistake and you know it, don't you?"

I opened my mouth to agree with him, but he wasn't looking for an answer.

"Okay, so I'm guilty of avoiding you after that. What can

I say, Stella? Your uncle was the closest thing I had to a father back then. I let him down. I let you down. I was embarrassed. No, I didn't handle it well, but did you? You've carried your grudge against me ever since then and you want to talk about mature?"

"Now, just wait a minute," I said, but Jake was too intent upon emptying his cup to even hear me.

"Number two. If you hate me so much, what are you doing in business with me?"

He looked at me then, and I felt he could see things inside me that even I couldn't see. If I'd felt claustrophobic in the beach house with Aunt Lucy, I now felt absolute panic. I wanted to run away, fast and forever. What was I doing in business with him?

"You're so busy trying to run me off, but your body tells me you want me, Stella."

I came at him like a trapped animal.

"Stop it, Jake."

"You want me, Stella, and you're afraid. What's so bad about that?"

"You're wrong. I don't want you. I'm in business with you because you have a lot of skills that would make us a good team, and because you were good to my aunt and uncle. It makes good business sense," I finished.

"Good business sense?" he echoed. "Was it good business sense when we were up in your bedroom yesterday?"

Now I couldn't look at him. I smiled coolly and focused on a spot just below his right earlobe.

"That was just…instinct," I said. "Probably a reaction to all the stress of the night before. It was an unconscious way to remind myself that I was still alive, that's what Freud would say. Lust should not be mistaken for a relationship."

His response threw me.

"Who said anything about a relationship?" he said. "Stella,

I'm not looking for a serious relationship. I just got out of a bad marriage, why would I want to get bogged down again?"

"Bogged down?" I threw up my hands. "See, you haven't changed one bit. You were afraid of commitment when you were a kid and you're afraid of it now."

"Oh, I get it," Jake said, nodding. "You haven't changed either, no pleasure without pain. No sex without marriage."

"I didn't say that."

"Well, isn't that how it is? Isn't that why you come on to me one minute and run away the next?"

I glared at him. What kind of person did he think I was? I wasn't like that, was I?

"I'll have you know, Jake Carpenter, that I've had plenty of sex without feeling the need to get married."

"So it's just me, then. You don't want to sleep with me unless I marry you. Why, Stella, I'm flattered."

Damn, how had we gotten here?

"No, I don't want to sleep with you because I'm not attracted to you."

"So you were faking it yesterday?"

Hell and double damn!

"No… I mean…"

"So you did want me."

He grinned and relaxed back against the driver's-side window.

"I have my own theory," he said. "I think you're afraid that if you let down your hair, you might enjoy yourself and that scares the hell out of you because you wouldn't be in control. Marriage isn't a guarantee, Stella. I learned that the hard way."

He tapped one finger against the steering wheel and seemed to be considering something.

"You know," he said at last, "you haven't really changed. You were an uptight, Goody Two-shoes when I first met you. The only difference between then and now is you're a woman and not a little girl. Women have a harder time with temptation."

I struggled to stay calm. He didn't know me, not really. All Jake had known was the grieving girl who had tried to be good enough to make up for causing her parents' deaths.

"You don't tempt me, Jake," I said.

"Don't I?"

He leaned toward me, grabbed my arm and pulled me toward him.

"Prove it."

I started to melt into him and hesitated. I was pretty much damned if I did and damned if I didn't. If I gave in, he'd be right and if I didn't, well, he'd be right again.

He reached up and gently stroked the side of my face, ran his fingers through my hair and settled his hand at the base of my neck.

"One minute at a time, Stella," he whispered. "Just one minute at a time."

I felt his lips meet mine and relaxed into the waves of warmth that welled up inside my body. One kiss, one moment. Was there really anything wrong with that?

I brought my hand up and touched the side of his face, felt the sandpaper stubble along his chin and memorized the angle of his neck with my fingertips. I met his tongue with my own, explored all that was to be discovered in that one kiss, before slowly pulling away.

"We'd better go," I said. "It's one. They'll be waiting at the diner."

"Scared you, huh?" Jake said.

"Nope."

But I was lying. Jake Carpenter terrified me. He was like free-falling out of an airplane and trusting my parachute to open.

Chapter 8

No one even bothered to look up as we entered the diner; they were all watching Nina. She sat front and center at the lunch counter, Spike by her side, regaling her fellow diners with some apparently fascinating tale.

Marti stood across from Nina, eyes sparkling, mouth open in a wide grin of amazement.

"No way," she said.

"Way," Nina answered. "So I said, oh my God, I was in love with him, like passionately all through middle school. I mean—" she turned and patted Spike's knee "—before I knew I was, well, you know, like, in love with her. I mean way before I met her."

I froze, waiting to see the construction workers erupt into a homophobic frenzy, but to my surprise, they seemed unfazed by Nina's revelation. They were hanging on her every word.

Spike's face slowly turned from bright pink to crimson, and

this delighted two elderly women sitting at one end of the counter.

"So what happened then, dear?" one cried. "Did you ever track him down?"

Nina almost levitated off her stool. "Not until I just happened to go to the library. Who knew? Oh, my God. He was like, a freaking recluse. Nobody knew anything about him. I mean, like he did book signings but never anywhere anybody had ever heard of. They were only in little foreign countries or something. Like, I mean, one time he had a signing in a drugstore in Nevada. I mean, do people even live there? Hello?"

She dropped back onto her stool. "Oh, but he was like a God. He was cool. I mean—" she looked at the construction workers "—I wanted to be his virgin bride or something, you know? Or maybe bear his children? I mean, I'd be famous then, too, you know, like I'd be the other half of his super-intellectual children."

Jake and I slid into a vacant booth and watched the show.

"Nina," Marti said, apparently now on first-name terms, "I can't believe Fred May is your hero. He's such a…"

"Yeah," Nina sighed. "A nerd."

"Woody Allen looks like the Terminator compared to Fred May," Marti added.

Nina rolled her eyes. "Well, yeah, but that's 'cause Fred's dead now. Nobody looks good dead."

One of the construction workers blew his soda all over the counter and collapsed in a heap into his buddy. The entire diner was laughing, or trying not to, but Nina was oblivious.

"I think I'm jealous of a dead guy," Spike said.

Nina looked stricken. "Oh, baby," she said. "Now, that was a long, long time ago. I don't sleep with him anymore."

"What?" It was hard to pin down how many of us asked that question.

Who was Fred May and when was he Nina's boyfriend? I thought back and couldn't remember any pimple-faced boy by that name.

Nina had the good grace to blush. "Not like that!" she said. "I always slept with his most recent book jacket under my pillow. He was my hero!" Her face fell, and for a brief moment I thought Nina was about to cry. "I just can't believe he's really gone. He was so like, young. I mean, forty-two is young to die of a heart attack, isn't it?"

Everyone sitting at the counter nodded and for a moment the diner fell silent. How did Nina do this? She never met a stranger. Everywhere she went, Nina drew them in, regardless of her appearance, her sexual preference or, God help us, her opinions.

Nina sighed and seemed to brighten. "Well," she said, "at least now I know he lived in Surfside Isle. I can always come here and just, you know, feel him in the air."

One of the construction workers leaned toward Nina's end of the counter and said, "I worked on his house when he redid his kitchen."

This prompted a flurry of comments from the others, all vying for Nina's attention with remembered pieces of personal information about her beloved. Jake and I might've gone unnoticed had Marti not looked up and spotted us.

"You two need menus?" she called.

This drew Spike's attention and she in turn nudged Nina, who reluctantly gave up her passionate discussion and moved to sit with us by the window.

"Well, it just goes to show you," she said breathlessly, "the universe has a cosmic reason for everything. I was supposed to come here to get stuck in a boring old library. How else would I have found out about Fred…?" Nina stopped, frowned at me and said, "Hey, what happened to you?"

Spike's expression mirrored Nina's. "It looks like somebody punched you."

"Slapped," I corrected. "The Concerned Citizens Against Sleigh Repossession paid me a visit. It's not as bad as it looks," I lied, "but I think we'd better all watch our backs."

"All this because you repossessed his sleigh?" Spike asked. "That doesn't make any sense."

I shrugged, wincing because even that small movement hurt, and told them everything, from my encounter with Joey Smack's people to the phone call from Mia.

"She's got an old family picture?" Spike asked. "Well, maybe it'll save us some time. So far, I have a list of all the boy babies born in Surfside Isle between 1959 and 1962. I figured this would give us a range to work with since Mia thinks he's around forty. Then I started cross-checking the parents' names with death records." Spike looked apologetic. "I figured it would be a piece of cake, but even after I narrowed down the list to two possibilities, it didn't give me what I needed. I'm going to spend some more time searching this afternoon."

Marti walked up to the booth carrying fresh drinks for Nina and Spike. She looked much less tired than she had the night before and there seemed to be a fresh sparkle in her eyes. I wondered what had happened between her and Tom after I'd left the diner in search of my beach cottage.

"These two already ordered," she said, and then stopped, noticing the welt on my face. "What happened to you?"

Her eyes flashed suspiciously to Jake, then back to me.

"He do this?"

"No. I had a little run-in with a pair of steps. I tripped and fell down the steps to the boardwalk."

Marti's eyebrows shot up. She looked hard at my face, frowning, apparently deciding whether or not to believe me.

"I'm recommending the special," she said finally. "Homemade vegetable soup and tuna sandwiches. You want menus?"

Jake shook his head and gave her the thousand-watt-smile

treatment. "If you say the special's the best, I wouldn't have anything else."

Marti rolled her eyes and gave me a pitying look. "I'm watching you," she told Jake. Turning to me she said, "And you gotta work with this guy?"

"It's like chicken pox," I told her. "Once you have it, you're immune for life."

Jake wasn't listening. His attention had been drawn to the front of the diner where Tom stood talking to a uniformed police officer.

"Excuse me a sec," he said, and left us to stare after him.

"I don't know," Nina murmured. "I've heard cases of people getting chicken pox twice, you know."

I turned my attention away from watching Jake and caught Marti staring at me again. She crooked her head in Jake's direction.

"You know, I believe I've heard the same thing about that chicken pox. You sure you're not itching, Stella?"

I felt my cheeks begin to burn. "Nope, I've got the antibodies. That chicken pox won't strike me twice."

Marti flipped her order pad shut. "Yeah, and there's plenty of people who'll tell you lightning doesn't strike the same place twice, too, but I don't never see them outside in a thunderstorm. There's pressing your luck and then there's asking for trouble."

She nodded toward Jake again and sighed. "Better check your vaccine," she murmured. "I don't think there's a dose strong enough for what he's carrying."

Marti walked back toward the kitchen, chuckling to herself. When she drew even with Tom she stopped, touching his arm in a gesture that left no doubt about the change in their relationship. His answering smile took my breath away.

"Now, that is love," Spike said. "Wonder how long they've been together."

"About sixteen hours," I said. "I was here when it happened."

Nina slid a little closer to Spike. "I love happy couples. They're just so…I don't know…happy, you know?"

Spike nodded, sipped her diet soda and leaned a little toward Nina. Happy. Everybody was happy, I thought, and that was nice, except when you had work to do and happiness became a distraction.

"Nina, what did you find in the archives?"

My cousin looked for a moment like a startled scarecrow. Her short, spiky blond and pink-tipped hair stuck out in wild tufts that framed her face and she wore faded denim overalls and a plaid flannel shirt. I could only imagine how the local librarians had reacted to Nina's arrival on their usually tranquil scene.

"Oh, yeah, that… Well, I didn't really spend too much time with those," she said. "I mean, not at first. First I told this really nice old lady all about what I was looking for and she's the one who said her son was forty-four now and maybe she could just call him and he'd know something."

"So did he?"

Nina shook her head. "Nope."

"So that's when you searched the newspapers?"

Out of the corner of my eye I saw Jake point to our booth and watched as he and Tom began walking toward us. Their progress was slowed by Tom's popularity. It seemed they could only move a foot or two before someone else stopped to greet Tom. At this rate, they'd arrive as we were finishing.

"Oh, no," Nina said. "I didn't get a chance to look at the old newspapers. The librarian, Mrs. Otis, made a couple of phone calls and before you knew it, there we all were, eating Mrs. Kinsky's streusel cake. Then Mrs. Otis said it was too bad Freddie May died a couple of years back because he used to be the high school yearbook editor and he was all the time writing these short stories about the town's history and his friends and stuff. So I said, not the Fred May that wrote action-adventure books for kids, and they said, yeah, that's him, Freddie May."

Nina was glowing. "The rest is history."

"So you never got to the newspaper archives?"

"Nope."

I felt my spirits sink below the tabletop. I was going to wind up spending hours in a damn library doing the background work myself while Jake would find some way to hit the streets without me.

"Mrs. Kinsky said everybody knew Fred would make it big one day. He was just, you know, different. While everybody else was out playing on the beach, Fred was writing scary stories."

I was only half listening, but it was enough to hear her say, "That's how I found him. Fred wrote about it. I don't think it'll be too hard now that we know his name."

I stopped watching Jake and focused on my cousin. "Now that we know whose name?"

Nina sighed impatiently. "Mia's brother, dummy. Isn't that who we're looking for? Doug Hirshfield, Fred May's best friend. His parents died when their house burned down."

"What makes you think Doug Hirshfield is Mia's brother?" I asked.

Nina rolled her eyes. "Because he had two sisters and because Fred's family adopted him."

"What happened to his sisters?" I asked.

"Stella, follow along here, all right? Who cares? Mia's one of the sisters and her sister is the other. Listen, Doug Hirshfield is the only boy anybody knows of who was born in Surfside Isle, is around forty, had two sisters, has dead parents and was adopted. He's the guy."

I had to admit there was a good possibility that my cousin had cracked the case in a single morning of gossip and coffee cake, but the facts still had to be checked.

"Where's Doug Hirshfield now?" I asked.

Nina shrugged. "We just don't know," she said. "Mrs. Kinsky thinks he never came back after he left for college, but Mrs. Otis said she's not so sure. She thinks we should ask Fred's mom."

Spike was apparently hearing this for the first time. "You didn't tell me about Fred's mother," she said. "She still lives here?"

Nina straightened proudly in her seat, reached into the pocket of her flannel shirt and withdrew a folded slip of paper.

"I wanted it to be a surprise," she said. "I knew Stella wouldn't think I could do it." She waved a note card in my direction like a signal flag. "I may not do it your way," she said, "but I always get the job done. I have here Mrs. Angela May's address. We can go see her right after lunch."

"See who?" Jake asked, pulling a spare chair up to the end of the booth.

"Fred May's mama, that's who," Nina answered.

"Now, that should be an experience you won't forget," Tom said. "She was always a character. I can't imagine she's changed too awful much."

Jake made the introductions and Tom straddled the extra chair, his long legs positioned awkwardly under the table in an attempt not to trip the passing waitresses. He was the right age to have known Fred May and Doug Hirshfield.

"Nina thinks Fred May's adopted brother could be the man we're looking for," I said.

Tom nodded, but he was distracted by the persistent buzzing of the pager attached to his belt.

"Damn thing won't leave me alone this morning," he muttered. "Damn reporters, like flies on shit."

He flipped open his cell phone, punched a number and when the person at the other end of the line answered, began talking without so much as a hello.

"Listen, you tell them sons of bitches that we'll do another press release at five o'clock and not before."

He listened to the voice on the other end of the line, shaking his head as he did and waiting for the tirade to end before continuing.

"I know. I've been doing the same thing since we ID'ed her. Now you tell them people this ain't TV and I ain't Elvis. I don't know what she was doing here. I don't know any more than what I already told them and I can't get more information to give out if they don't leave me alone to do my job."

He flipped the phone shut, crammed it back into its holster and sighed.

"You know, I'd rather it have been Jimmy Hoffa's body we found than Rebecca DeWitt. At least with old Jimmy, you knew it was a Mafia killing straight up. This thing's a mess."

Marti arrived with our food and Tom forgot all about his current frustrations. He hopped up in an attempt to help her, nearly knocked the tray out of her hand, and proceeded to turn beet red, all the while apologizing and unloading bowls of soup.

Marti had suddenly become every bit as klutzy as her new boyfriend, stammering and blushing like a schoolgirl.

"I don't know what's the matter with me," she murmured, but no one believed her.

Once the plates were safely on the table, Jake made an attempt to bring Tom back down to earth.

"So who was Rebecca DeWitt?" he asked.

Tom shook his head and frowned, no longer the smitten boyfriend. "It's not so much *who* she was as it is the circumstance and the timing. Becca DeWitt was Fred May's literary agent and she apparently died on the two-year anniversary of his death. So the gossipmongers are going crazy thinking she committed suicide because she couldn't live without him. I tried to tell them that it's next to impossible to tie your own hands behind your back, but they just won't listen. Now they're trying to come up with some new scenario and I don't have time to fool with them."

"Oh, my God." Nina gasped. "That is like, so completely tragic." Tears sprang to her eyes and she stared at Tom without seeing him. "It's like some cosmic-fate thing, you know? I mean, what if life had no meaning after Fred's death. I know *I* was depressed for weeks!"

Tom bit forcefully into his sandwich, probably so he wouldn't say anything to Nina. His eyebrows were knit together in a solid black line that darkened his features into a thundercloud of frustration.

"Tom, do you know a Doug Hirshfield? I think he's a local," I said, hoping to change the subject.

Tom's pager went off again. He snatched at it and read the text message without the same amount of irritation as he'd shown before lunch.

"Well," he said, snapping the pager shut, "that's the end of my lunch hour. The M.E.'s waiting in my office." He smiled ruefully at me. "Doug Hirshfield? Can't say I know the name."

He pushed his chair back and stood, the smile on his face even including Nina.

"Pleasure meeting you, ladies," he said. His smile broadened as he looked from Jake to me. "Hope you get your man, Stella."

Marti came up behind him, in time to hear his comment and throw in her two cents' worth.

"Oh, I don't think Stella's the type to leave empty-handed," she said.

Marti chuckled and walked off with Tom.

"She doesn't miss much, does she?" Jake asked, watching Marti's retreating figure.

I ignored this and turned the focus back to our case.

"All right," I said. "We need to pay a visit to Fred May's mother and we need to make sure Joey Smack doesn't decide to bother Aunt Lucy."

"Do you think he sent Aunt Lucy the flowers?" Spike asked. "I've been thinking about it and I can't figure out how an old man would find your aunt here. Joey Smack's more resourceful. He's already found you. He'd be more likely to bug a vase of flowers, too."

Jake was nodding as she spoke. "Certainly a possibility."

"I just can't help wondering why he thinks we still have the sleigh. I told him his damn sled is back with Lifetime. Why doesn't he just go down and pay for it?"

Jake frowned. "Maybe he thinks we took something else. Maybe it's not the sleigh he's after."

"What then—Santa Claus? That's all we took—Santa, the sleigh and a few reindeer. I left the entire load with Lifetime. I didn't see anything else, and I wouldn't have taken anything but what was on the repo order. The guy's got a screw loose."

My cell phone rang and I dug through my coat searching for it. Aunt Lucy's voice, sounding thready and frightened, crackled in my ear.

"Stella, I need you. Can you come home?"

Jake and I pulled into the driveway three minutes later. Spike and Nina were a close second, having remained just long enough to throw bills on the table to cover our lunch tab.

I pulled the Glock out of my waistband, held it down at my side and took the steps with Jake right behind me. Aunt Lucy met us at the door, her face ashen, lips compressed into a tight, worried line.

"What happened? Are you all right?"

Jake brushed past the two of us, scanned the living room and kitchen, and looked back at Aunt Lucy, waiting.

"Your grandmother called," she said, looking at Jake. "Someone broke into our house last night. They cut the phone lines, but the security system went into bypass mode and alerted the police department anyway. By the time they reached the house, whoever it was had gone, but not before they tore the house apart."

I felt my chest tightening. "Did they find the lab?"

Aunt Lucy's lab was a state-of-the-art chemist's dream, installed behind a hidden door in the basement by her friends at the CIA so she could tinker away on top-secret formulas without traveling to Washington, D.C.

Aunt Lucy shook her head. "No. Apparently nothing was taken."

I felt relief wash over me. As long as Aunt Lucy was safe, there were no problems.

"That's not the problem," she said. "Sylvia said this morning three large white panel vans arrived from Disaster Master. They're in our house now, cleaning up, painting, and repairing anything that needs it." Aunt Lucy took a shaky breath and continued. "When your grandmother went to see what was going on, the men said the bill had been taken care of—they assumed by the home's owner."

I nodded, and Jake broke in. "But you're not home to have called them. You didn't know."

Aunt Lucy sank into a chair by the front door. "I thought maybe my insurance agent had found out and sent them. He's good like that, but he didn't. I called him and he didn't know. He's in Westchester. He wouldn't have heard about a burglary in Glenn Ford. He says even if he had, he would've waited for me to call him and he wouldn't have used Disaster Master. He says they're too expensive."

Spike and Nina had slipped in while Aunt Lucy was talking, and stood around her looking worried.

"Did Sylvia call the police?" I asked.

"No, she called Jake's cell phone and got me. I told her to call the police, but by the time they showed up, the men were gone. The police called Disaster Master and they said yes, they'd received an order."

"With a check?" Spike asked.

Aunt Lucy shook her head. "Cash. A middle-aged guy in a cheap sports jacket. That's all they remember."

I looked at Jake and raised an eyebrow. What in the hell was going on? Joey Smack broke into Aunt Lucy's house and then, in a fit of contrition, had it fixed?

"He called," Aunt Lucy said. "I don't think it was Joey Spagnazi who did this."

"What? Joey Smack called? Here?"

Aunt Lucy nodded and looked at the wall phone hanging in the kitchen. "The phone rang right before I called you," she said. "The man asked for you, and when I said you couldn't come to the phone, he laughed and said he was sure you were having trouble walking." Her eyes darkened and for an instant my aunt seemed to struggle with her emotions.

"He said... He said...you would have trouble breathing if you didn't return his property."

"Damn! What is the matter with that guy?"

The wall phone rang and we all jumped. Jake crossed the room in three strides, jerked the phone off the hook and barked, "Who is this?"

He listened, frowning. "What delivery? We didn't order... Well then, who did? What?" He listened. "Where are you? All right, but I want to talk to you when you get here."

Jake hung up, turned to my aunt and said, "You didn't ask Guinta's Market to deliver any groceries, did you?"

Aunt Lucy looked as if she couldn't quite understand him. "Why would I do that? We're here, not home."

Jake smiled, but the smile never reached his eyes. "Well, that's just it. The guy on the phone said he was making a delivery from Guinta's but not to the Glenn Ford house. He's coming here, says someone paid to have him drive the order to the beach. He even has the address, so whoever sent him knows where you are."

Aunt Lucy lost her composure and panicked. "No! That's impossible! I didn't even tell Sylvia where I was going!"

"That leaves us with your friend, Marie," I said. "Don't worry, honey. I'm sure there's a simple explanation for all of this. I'll call her."

Aunt Lucy didn't seem to hear me. "Benito!" she called. "Where are you?"

She looked around the room, looking for Lloyd and growing increasingly agitated. Spike, noting this, walked quietly into the kitchen and poured my aunt a glass of Chianti.

She carried it over, knelt down in front of my aunt and gently wrapped the woman's fingers around the tumbler.

"Take a couple of sips," Spike encouraged. "We'll find him. Did he go outside?"

Aunt Lucy raised the glass to her lips, drank then nodded. "Oh, yes," she said. "That's right. He went outside a little while ago. He'll be back soon. I bet he's fishing."

I looked at Jake and knew he was as worried about Aunt Lucy as I was. The tone in her voice made me wonder if she was expecting a flesh-and-blood version of my uncle to walk back through the door and not a four-legged canine. She seemed one step further away from her tenuous hold on reality.

Spike stayed by Aunt Lucy's side, softly reassuring her as Jake and I slipped out the front door to talk and wait for the mysterious delivery from Guinta's Market. We sat on the steps, side by side, and listened to the pounding of the surf on the beach. The temperature had climbed into the lower forties but there was no breeze and the sun warmed my face, fooling me into thinking that winter might actually be on its way out.

Jake slipped his arm around my waist and it seemed natural to rest my head on his shoulder, if only for a moment. It was as if we suddenly fit together, held fast by the current crisis and the knowledge that we were the ones responsible for fixing it. All the superficial posturing fell to the wayside when the chips were down. We could fight about our pride later; for now, we'd be one strong team.

"You know," I murmured, "if we hadn't pissed Joey Smack off, this trip might've been a vacation. I mean, I think we'll find Mia's brother pretty quickly. If it wasn't for Joey Smack, we'd be enjoying ourselves."

Jake chuckled. "If it wasn't for Joey Smack, you'd be running back to Glenn Ford the minute we found our client's brother. The others wouldn't be here. You'd be all alone with me, and we both know that's more than you can handle."

I pushed off his shoulder and looked up at him. "Aren't you tired of that line yet?"

He was saved from answering me by the arrival of the Guinta's delivery van. It rolled slowly around the corner, searching for the house number, and pulled up into the narrow driveway behind Jake's pickup.

A skinny man in work pants and a gray zip-up jacket stepped out of the driver's-side door, a cigarette dangling from his lips, and proceeded to the back of the van as if he hadn't seen us.

The two of us watched him, but Jake dropped his arm from my waist and both of us slid our right hands behind our backs, touching our guns, ready to pull them out if the delivery wasn't what it seemed. Joey Smack had his fingers in a lot of pies around Glenn Ford. It would've been nothing for him to commandeer a delivery van and show up gunning for revenge.

When the driver emerged from behind the van, we both relaxed. He carried a large cardboard box loaded to overflowing with produce and assorted grocery items.

"Lucy Valocchi?" he asked.

"This is the place," I answered.

Jake and I were both standing now, and Jake moved down the steps to take the box. After a brief examination of its contents, he set it down on the top step and dug in his pocket for tip money. He peeled a twenty from a small wad of bills and handed it to the driver.

"Tell me everything you know about this order," he said.

The skinny man looked briefly at the bill before slipping it into his pants pocket, took a last drag on his cigarette and then ground it out in the dead grass.

"All I can tell you is this old guy comes in and fills a cart full of groceries, then he asks to see the manager. I only know this much on account of I was in the office clocking out when he come up. The old dude asks Johnny if we can do a special delivery for him and Johnny says he don't know, it depends."

The man patted his jacket pocket, found what he was looking for and pulled out a pack of cigarettes.

"The guy says he needs to send this order to Surfside Isle and right off, Johnny says we don't deliver that far and besides, his driver's off duty and he doesn't have anybody else. Now, I'm his driver, so I figure maybe the guy's gonna make it worth my while. I mean, he don't look flashy, but the guy's got money. I can tell that much by the way he's acting."

"What do you mean?" I asked.

"Well, some guys flash their money. They wear a lot of gold. They drive hot cars and talk loud. They treat the little guy like shit. Really rich guys don't do that. They wear expensive clothes, all right, but they don't talk about it. They just act like they know they'll get what they want because if it comes down to it, they'll pay you right. This dude was like that. So I said, I'm off duty, but I might be looking to take on a side job. How much you payin'?"

The skinny man paused, tapped out a cigarette and stuck it in his mouth.

"He says I'll pay you two hundred dollars."

The driver fished in his jacket pocket again, pulled out a lighter and lit his cigarette before continuing.

"And I was right about the guy, too. He paid cash for the

groceries, handed me two one-hundred-dollar bills and drove away in a beat up Land Cruiser."

Jake frowned. "You ever see him before?"

"Nope, and I bet I never do, too."

"How come?" I asked.

The skin around the man's eyes crinkled as he squinted up at me through the cigarette smoke.

"Well, for one thing, he wasn't local. His car had Maryland tags. And for another, he didn't look like he was in town to stay. There was a suitcase in the back of his Cruiser. I only know that 'cause he was parked right near the van, and I was watching the guy. I mean, it's not every day somebody like that comes into Guinta's. Besides, Benny Valocchi was a good guy. I don't want anybody making trouble for his widow. I gotta make sure this dude's on the up-and-up. I mean, money's nice, but it ain't everything."

I nodded and smiled at the man. "I appreciate you looking out for my aunt," I said.

"Think nothin' of it," he said. "Besides, from the way the old guy talked about your aunt, I think he was on the up-and-up. I asked him if he was related to your family and he said no, but he knew your aunt was on vacation. He said she was particular about her cooking. She didn't use just anything, so he wanted her to have what she was accustomed to. I thought that was nice, looking after her like that."

Jake pulled a card out of his wallet and handed it to the driver. "If you happen to see him again, give me a call, all right? Even better, if you catch his tag or—"

"Gotcha, chief." The skinny man stuffed the card into his pocket, turned to leave and stopped. "Hey, there's nothing wrong about that dude, is there? I mean, I wouldn't have taken the job if I'd thought he was—"

"No, I'm sure he was just trying to do us a favor," I said. "We just want to know who to thank, that's all."

The man seemed reassured and smiled for the first time. "That's good. I wouldn't want no harm done. You know, I got a family, too."

I nodded and smiled. The driver hitched his pants up with a nervous twitch and walked back to the van. As we stood watching, he cranked the engine and left, leaving us with a box of groceries and lots of unanswered questions.

Jake shrugged. "What do you make of that?"

I was rooting through the box, examining everything with a cautious eye. No bugs this time, just my aunt's favorite olive oil, fresh basil, tomatoes, semolina flour and assorted spices.

"I think he must know her," I said. "He told the driver he bet Aunt Lucy hated to be without her usual cooking supplies. They're all in here, like he knew she left in a hurry and he knew what she'd be wanting. That's weird." I straightened up and turned to Jake. "Actually, it's more than weird, it's spooky."

Jake didn't cook, at least I didn't think he did, so the fact that someone knew these peculiarities about my aunt didn't seem that strange to him.

"So far, we've got an old guy who tails your aunt to our office, serenades her from the back of a flatbed and sends her flowers…"

"With a bug on the vase," I added.

Jake nodded. "If he's the one who added the bug. Then he sends her groceries."

"But only the exact items she already has in her kitchen."

"So maybe he's the one who broke into the house," Jake said. "Maybe it wasn't Joey."

"Or maybe he knows Aunt Lucy, and she's forgotten."

Jake's expression softened. "Stella, have you considered the idea that maybe your aunt knows who he is and doesn't want to tell us because it might seem she's being unfaithful to your uncle's memory?"

"No, that wouldn't fit. She thinks Lloyd is Uncle Benny. She wouldn't cheat on my uncle."

Jake picked up the box of staples and started up the steps. "Stella, your aunt's a very smart woman. Granted, your uncle's death threw her for a loop, but do you really think she believes your dog is her dead husband? I mean, I could see her pretending that, maybe even half believing it, but really, do you think she's that delusional?"

I followed him, thinking about what he was asking and realizing that I just wasn't sure. Aunt Lucy was brilliant, but she was also eccentric. It would comfort her to believe Lloyd was Uncle Benny. On the other hand, maybe that was all it was; like a toddler with a baby doll, a comforting stand-in.

Aunt Lucy wasn't in the kitchen when we returned. Spike and Nina were sitting at the kitchen table, Aunt Lucy's empty Chianti glass between them.

"She's lying down," Spike whispered. "I think she'll sleep if we're quiet."

Jake put the box of groceries on the counter and joined us at the table.

"I made coffee," Spike said. "I thought we could use a little added brainpower."

Nina's eyes were red-rimmed and I knew she'd been crying, probably worried sick about Aunt Lucy. I reached over and patted her hand while Spike found mugs and brought the coffee to the table. We needed to stay focused, I thought. We needed to take charge so the unknown wouldn't feel so overwhelming.

"Okay," I said. "Let's make a plan."

"Stella, I really don't feel like doing a mission statement right now," Nina murmured.

Jake hid a grin behind his coffee cup. "I think she's just talking about a short-term plan, like maybe for the afternoon."

I nodded. "I don't think Aunt Lucy should be left alone

again, not with Joey Smack on the loose and her secret admirer scaring the hell out of her."

"Why don't you and Nina go look up Fred May's mother," Jake said. "I'll stay here with your aunt. I can call the local florists, just on the off chance one of them delivered the flowers."

Spike said, "I'll go look for Lloyd. He hasn't come back yet and I know your aunt will worry."

Nina's eyes were huge, worried orbs. "Do you think that's safe? I mean, look what happened to Stella!"

"I think Joey Smack's looking for Stella and Jake, but not us. I think I'll be all right. Besides, I have all that Krav Maga training. I don't think Joey's people want to mess with me."

Nina didn't seem any less worried. "That's martial arts—those guys have guns."

Spike nodded. "I'll be very careful, baby."

"All right then," I said, standing. "Let's get going. Her place is on Apple Street, 2912 Apple, in case anything happens or you need us. The sooner we leave, the sooner we'll be back."

Spike pulled a pen out of her pocket and wrote down the address on the only paper handy, a scrap of paper towel. "Got it," she said.

Nina seemed torn, but Spike urged her up. "That's right, baby. Go see old Freddie's mama so you can tell me all about it. Of course," she said, with a sly grin, "I will try not to be jealous of your other love."

Nina tried to smile back. "Oh, baby," she whispered. "If you only had a clue!"

I hustled her out the door then, knowing she'd cave if we didn't keep moving. I kept asking questions, making her search for directions and watch the road signs all the way across town. When we reached the address written on Nina's folded-up index card, I turned and tapped the piece of paper.

"Are you sure this is it?"

Nina stared up at the low-slung brick building. "It has to be," she answered. "It says 2912 right there on the front door."

The sign in front of the building said 2912 all right, but it also said Ocean Bay Nursing Home.

"Shoot! She's probably comatose."

Nina fumbled with her door handle. "Stella, you're stereotyping. Mrs. Kinsky says she stops in to visit at least once a week. Come on."

Nina sailed right up to the front door, rang the bell, waited for an attendant to open it and marched us both up to the front desk.

A large woman sat behind the desk reading a paperback entitled *Destiny's Dark Desire.* The cover left no doubt as to the book's contents. A half-naked pirate held a blonde captive in his arms. I looked at the reader, imagined her in the pirate's arms instead of the blonde and knew why she wasn't happy to be interrupted.

"We're here to see Angela May," Nina said. "Is she still in room 131?"

The attendant sighed, looked at a sheet of paper attached to a clipboard and nodded.

"Cool," Nina said. "Thank you." She turned to me. "Come on!"

We started off down the hallway with Nina in the lead. I followed her, feeling uncomfortable and ill at ease. I don't like nursing homes; they make me think about death. They smell of urine and disinfectant—at least the ones I'd been in always did. This one wasn't as bad, but I knew if I sniffed hard enough, I'd pick up the scent.

We passed a woman in a wheelchair. Her left leg had been amputated just below the knee. She wore a pale housecoat and she had gray, wiry hair and a dull, disoriented look on her face. She grabbed at Nina, stopping her, and I froze.

"Help me," the woman muttered.

Nina knelt down beside the wheelchair, took the woman's hand in hers and smiled. "Whatcha need, sweetie?"

The woman said it again. "Help me."

"Okay!" Nina said cheerfully. She stood up, still holding the woman's hand and nodded toward the chair. "Push. We'll walk down to the nurses' station and see if we can't find someone for her."

Nina patted the woman's hand and walked along beside her while I steered the chair. When we reached the station, Nina spotted a woman in a bright smock, gave her a bright smile and said, "My friend needs a little help, I think."

The nurse looked up from her chart work and gave Nina a smile that was every bit as bright. She walked over to her patient, and just as Nina had done, knelt down, touching the woman's knee as she spoke.

"What do you need, Mrs. Colson?"

The tiny woman babbled something incoherent and the nurse nodded. She looked up at us. "Sometimes she gets lost," the woman said. "It's all right." She looked back at Mrs. Colson. "Come on, honey. Let's go to your room."

Nina watched their progress for a second then started back down the hallway.

"Do you know where we're going?" I asked.

"Yep. I'm just following the signs." Nina raised an eyebrow. "You don't like this, do you?"

"Not even a little bit."

Nina shook her head. "Stella, try and look at it this way, they don't want to be here, either. They're lost and scared. They just need a little reassurance, that's all. A touch or a hug."

"I hope I never end up here," I muttered.

Nina's eyes glittered. "Wouldn't we all? Being old isn't easy, especially when our culture doesn't value age and wisdom." She stopped in front of a closed door. "Here we are."

She didn't hesitate, tapping lightly and listening to the sounds of a TV blaring from inside.

"Mrs. May?"

Nina opened the door a few inches and poked her head inside. An elderly woman with snowy-white hair sat in a wheelchair. A large TV flickered a few feet in front of her and Oprah looked out at us, a broad smile lighting up her face.

"Do you believe that? Honey, I was just amazed!" Oprah gushed.

Nina stepped into the room, walked up to the chair and placed one hand on the woman's shoulder.

"Why, honey," Angela May said. "I didn't hear you come in. Turn that thing off and sit down." When she saw me she said, "You brought a friend. Isn't that lovely! Pull up a chair, darlin'."

Nina spotted two folding chairs against the wall and handed me one.

"Maybe you should let me handle this," she said softly.

"Good idea," I whispered.

She smiled at Mrs. May, opened her seat and placed it in front of the woman's wheelchair. I followed her lead but stayed slightly off to the side, making Nina the focus of the elderly woman's attention.

"My name's Nina," she said. "I came to see you because I'm trying to find Doug."

Mrs. May nodded. "How is school, dear?"

Nina smiled. "School is good, but I can't find Doug. Do you know where he is?"

Mrs. May's face fell and tears came to her eyes. I shot Nina an "Oh, shit!" look and muttered, "Maybe we should go."

Nina reached out to touch Mrs. May's knee. "Don't cry, sweetie."

"He's dead," Angela May said. "Didn't you know? We lost Dougie."

Nina shook her head slowly. "No, honey, Dougie's not dead."

Mrs. May shook her head vehemently. "Yes, he is! They told me Fred died, but he didn't die. He came to see me yesterday. Doug died."

Nina changed the subject. "Did Mrs. Kinsky come to see you this week?" she asked.

The transformation was instantaneous. "Oh, darlin', I love her! I love her! I love her! She is so good to me! She brings me cake!"

Mrs. May's voice rose and the words came rapidly in a staccato cadence that seemed stuck in her head. "I love her! I love her!" she repeated.

Nina wasn't fazed by this. "I know you do," she said. "You love lots of people, don't you?"

Mrs. May's smile broadened.

"Do you love Fred?" Nina asked.

"Oh, yes, I do! I do!" Her face clouded. "He can't be dead! I won't have it! Never!"

"Shh," Nina soothed.

"I will kill her! I'll kill her, I will!"

Nina looked at me, puzzled. "Who, darling?"

"His wife! Dolores! I will kill Fred's wife! I don't like her! Fred is not dead! He is not!"

Mrs. May was growing more agitated, her voice rising until I thought someone would certainly hear her and come running.

Nina tried distracting the distraught woman. "What lovely violets," she said, pointing to a windowsill full of flowering plants.

Mrs. May looked at them for a moment, muttering, "I hate her! Fred is not dead. Doug is lost."

Nina tried the photographs pinned to the cork bulletin board. She took one down and brought it over to Mrs. May.

"Look," she said. "There's Fred. See?"

Angela May took the picture, studied it carefully, then tossed it back in Nina's lap. "Not anymore! That Fred is gone! He is dead! He went away, he did! Doug went first and he will never come back. Never! I hate her! She made him go!"

Nina handed me the picture. A tall man with a beard and glasses smiled out at me, his hand resting on his mother's shoulder. Dead Fred, Fred is dead. I was catching Mrs. May's rhythmic speech. Dead. Dead. Dead. Poor Fred.

I walked to the corkboard and studied the other pictures. Two young men at the beach caught my attention. While Nina soothed the agitated Mrs. May, I carefully removed the photo and turned it over. "Doug and Fred, 1982," was written in scrawling script across the back.

I recognized Fred from his other picture. Doug stood on the left, tall like his adoptive brother, but fuller, more muscular, with beach-boy good looks and white-blond hair. A real charmer.

"Turn on *Cops!*" Mrs. May demanded suddenly. "It's three o'clock. Time to catch the bad guys! I love it! I love *Cops!*" Mrs. May smiled at Nina. "They will get Dolores," she said. "The cops, they will get her and I will kill her!"

I looked at the clock and saw that it was indeed three o'clock. Nina switched the TV on, fumbled with the remote and found Mrs. May's show. As we watched, a uniformed officer from Baltimore ran along a back alley, chasing a drug dealer.

Nina rose and motioned toward the door. "I think we should leave," she said. "I don't think she can tell us anything else. Maybe if we come back tomorrow, she'll be more alert."

I looked at the tiny woman, engrossed in her favorite reality show, and shook my head. Somehow I didn't think time was going to help Mrs. May. Time was collapsing in on her, blending the past with the present and slowly fading her memories like black-and-white photos left too long in the sunlight.

Soon it would all be erased, every treasured moment and every painful nightmare. Life would end as it began, with a vast, blank screen.

I followed Nina out of the room, softly closing the door behind us and trailing my cousin from the building. We stepped out into the brilliant sunlight and I inhaled deeply for what seemed to be the first time in hours.

"I hope that never happens to me," I said.

Nina frowned. "I think you should stay focused on the present," she said. "We only have today. There's no guarantee you'll even be around tomorrow."

I pulled my keys out of my coat pocket and started off toward the car. "I know, I know, I could get hit by a truck and die."

Nina grabbed my arm, stopping me.

"No," she said. "I wouldn't worry about getting hit by a truck." She inclined her head toward the parking lot, raising her eyebrows and contorting her face into a spastic pointer aimed in the direction of Jake's red truck.

Cauliflower Ear and his short, fat accomplice leaned against the tailgate of Jake's truck with Spike sandwiched in between them.

"I see what you mean," I murmured. "Today is all that matters."

Chapter 9

Nina and I walked slowly toward the truck. Spike seemed to be standing between her two captors patiently, but the little man had a gun to her side, taking choice out of the equation.

"Your Krav Maga on the blink again?" I asked.

Spike sighed. "Yeah, it broke down when these two goons made me an offer I couldn't refuse."

I raised my eyebrow and smiled, hoping it irritated Spike's keepers as much as they were irritating me.

"And what might that be?" I asked Cauliflower Ear.

He deferred to the little guy with a grunt. The short man glared at me and raised his gun arm slightly, making sure I knew there was a weapon trained on Spike's side. I also noted the fresh white gauze bandage, courtesy of our earlier encounter.

"Look at this," he said, and handed me a Polaroid picture.

Lloyd was tied to a wooden table leg. At his feet lay a newspaper, the front page faceup to show that it was today's paper.

"Mr. Spagnazi would like to make a deal," the short man said.

I felt my body go numb. My mind began to fill with murderous impulses and images. It was all I could do to keep my face carefully neutral.

"What sort of deal?"

"The sort that winds up with him getting his property back."

"I told you, I don't have the damn sleigh!"

The man shook his head impatiently. "Mr. Spagnazi already has the sleigh, you know that. He wants what was inside the sleigh, stupid."

"Joey Smack wants Santa Claus?"

The short guy jabbed Spike hard with the gun muzzle making tears spring to her eyes. Nina lunged toward him and I caught her as Spike yelled, "Don't!"

"Joey Smack don't give a rat's ass about no freakin' Santa Claus!" he said. "Joey wants a white Christmas. He wants his snow back."

"His cocaine," Spike explained, like I wouldn't know.

"I don't have Joey's cocaine," I said.

Cauliflower Ear smiled. "And you don't got your dog, either," he said.

I cocked my head and looked at him. "He speaks," I said. "Tell me something. Was it an effort stringing all those syllables together?"

Cauliflower didn't seem to understand the question, so I turned my attention to his keeper.

"I can't describe in enough detail or with enough passion how badly I'm going to fuck you up," I said. I kept my tone cool and even, but inside my heart was banging against my chest.

"I'm seeing a dog-fur rug," the man said, "spread out in front of the fireplace. Maybe I'll lay you out naked there. Do a little roadwork on ya. Let you find out what a real man's all about."

I let my gaze fall to his crotch and laughed. "Let me know when you find one, Shorty." The man's face colored nicely. "Where does Spagnazi want to do the exchange?" I asked.

"Joey's busy," the little guy said. "He's got employee problems and other shit to attend to. I'll handle the trade-off."

"Fine," I said. "I'll need twenty-four hours and a guarantee Lloyd won't get hurt. In fact, I'll need to know he's fed, warm and happy before we do any kind of deal."

"Jesus Christ," the short guy said. "It's a fucking dog!"

"And you're a fucking moron," I said.

"We'll be in touch," the short man said.

He shoved Spike toward us and backed away. Cauliflower jumped behind the wheel of a white Lincoln Town Car, started the engine and pulled up beside his boss. The short man waved his gun toward the three of us and hopped into the passenger seat.

"Keep your phone where you can hear it," he called from the open window. "Otherwise, the dog's a rug!"

With a loud squeal of burning rubber, the Lincoln bounced the curb and shot off toward town. Nina sobbed and pulled Spike into a hard embrace while I tried to make out the license plate on the car. When that proved fruitless, I studied the photograph of Lloyd. He appeared to be sitting in the kitchen of an abandoned house. There was no other furniture in the room, just the table, and while substantial, it had certainly seen better days.

The floor was a checkerboard of tile squares and reminded me of my elementary-school cafeteria. Faded, dingy café-style curtains hung over an ancient porcelain sink. Holes in the room indicated the spots where the stove and refrigerator had once stood. It could've been any older home left to fall into disrepair, in any town, perhaps not even in Surfside Isle. The only thing vibrant and alive about the photo was Lloyd, and he didn't seem at all happy.

"You all right?" I asked Spike. "I thought for sure they were going to keep you as their hostage."

She nodded. "I think my being an assistant district attorney scared them. I was on my way to the beach when they came at me from a side street. They wouldn't have had a shot if they hadn't started yelling about Lloyd. When I saw the picture, I knew I had to bring them to you."

"Hey, don't beat yourself up about that," I said. "You did the right thing. I just can't figure out how they ever got close enough to Lloyd to catch him, that's all."

"Food?" Nina said.

I thought of Lloyd, sitting at Aunt Lucy's table, gobbling down bacon and eggs each morning or slurping spaghetti for dinner. Lloyd lived for food and if the food had been drugged, or even if it hadn't, Lloyd would be an easy mark.

My cell phone rang as I pulled out of the nursing-home parking lot.

"Hello, beautiful," Pete said.

I was not in the mood for Pete's simpleminded flirtatiousness.

"Find anything yet?"

Pete sighed. "Stella, there's more than one Mia Lange out there, and a few of them have criminal records, but I can't tell for sure until I have a social or a birth date."

I was driving through town now, keeping an eye out for a white Lincoln, on the off chance Joey Smack's henchmen had been dumb enough to park it in front of an older home in need of renovations.

"How about a ballpark guesstimate of her age?"

Pete exhaled loudly on the other end so I'd know he was going to a lot of trouble for me, and said, "Better than nothing, I guess."

"All right—somewhere between thirty-five and forty-five."

"That's the best you can do? You don't know anything else about this woman?"

Spike and Nina were silent, listening with undisguised interest.

"Hold on," I said, pulling into the parking lot of a beach-wear store. "I've got a cell-phone number, will that help?"

I fumbled through my purse and came up with Mia's contact numbers and gave him the cell-phone number.

"No home number?" I could tell Pete thought I'd only done a half-assed job and it bothered me.

"Well, actually…"

I started to explain that Jake had been the one doing the initial paperwork and we'd been interrupted by Joey Smack's revenge team, but remembered that I didn't owe Pete an explanation. It didn't matter what he thought of me.

"Yeah, Pete, that's all I got. I mean, I have her sister's home phone, but that won't help you."

Pete sighed. "Give it to me anyway," he muttered. "You never know."

I read off the numbers and waited patiently for him to finish writing.

"What's Jake's birth date?" he asked.

"You wish!" I answered and broke the connection.

"I knew there was something fishy about her!" Nina said. "What did Pete say? He's not coming up here, is he? I mean, I think that would be disaster, not that he's not a nice guy maybe, but you know, with Jake and you being…"

Her voice trailed off in a squeak as Spike pinched her.

"Well, aren't you?" Nina finished.

I pulled out onto the road again and stared straight ahead. Maybe if I ignored her…

"Stella, aren't you and Jake, you know, starting something?"

"Nina," Spike cautioned.

"Well, they are. Pete would just mess it all up. He's got negative energy. But…"

She paused and I was grateful for the momentary silence, even if it only lasted a few seconds.

"Well, technically, I suppose you should call him back and tell him about Lloyd. I mean, he is Lloyd's father."

"What? Nina, Lloyd's a dog. Pete just acts like one. He's not Lloyd's anything."

"Well, Lloyd belonged to Pete before you took him, didn't he?"

I turned onto Forty-eighth Street and prayed I didn't kill Nina before I could park the truck.

"Technically," I said, "Lloyd belonged to Pete's ex, Tracy. She left him behind when she left Pete, so Lloyd was only staying with Pete. Since Tracy abandoned him and Pete didn't really own him, Lloyd was really his own dog. I offered him the chance to leave Pete and he was grateful. So I guess I don't owe Pete shit!"

"Oh," Nina said, nodding. "So Lloyd's like an emancipated minor, only he's a dog."

"Exactly."

I turned into the driveway, threw the truck into Park and escaped. Jake opened the front door and practically pounced on us as we started up the stairs, zeroing in on Spike.

"What happened to you? I thought you were looking for Lloyd," he said. "When you didn't come back I ran down to the beach and you were gone. I was about to call the police."

Spike looked over Jake's shoulder into the house.

"Is she still sleeping?"

When Jake nodded, Spike began filling him in, keeping the story short and emotionless. She didn't go into how scared she'd been, even though the fear lingered in her eyes and her hands shook just slightly as she described the way the two men had forced her into their car.

"You told them we had the cocaine?" he asked when Spike finished.

"What choice did I have? They've got Lloyd. It buys us some time to try and find him."

Jake nodded. "I would've done the same thing."

The four of us were standing at the foot of the steps leading into the house, shivering as the day slowly pulled the sun down across the horizon. Our shadows leaned across the dead grass like black ghosts and the only color came from the sun's scarlet descent into the ocean.

"Can we go in now?" Nina's teeth chattered as she spoke and she wrapped her arms across her slender body in an attempt to keep warm.

We started up the stairs. Nina froze, her hand on the doorknob, and turned back to look at me.

"What are we going to tell Aunt Lucy about Lloyd?" she asked. "I mean, do we, like, say he was here but he left again? We don't tell her about those guys taking him, do we?"

Spike frowned. "I don't think we should upset her any more than we absolutely have to," she said.

"Well, dogs do run off sometimes," I said. "It's not that unusual. Let's just play it down, like it's no big deal."

Behind me Jake whispered, "You're dreaming." And I knew he was right. Aunt Lucy was a lot of things—elderly, frail and overwhelmed—but she was certainly not stupid.

I left the others downstairs and climbed the steps to my room. I needed a shower and clean clothes. I needed to think while hot water ran across my shoulders. I needed a plan, some way to feel back in control.

I was looking for bath towels when Nina found me. She held two plastic shopping bags in her outstretched arms and she was grinning.

"Spike said she thought you were up here and I figured you might want to take a shower."

I looked down at the wrinkled clothes I'd worn for two days, sniffed at my shirt sleeve and nodded.

"I bet I smell as bad as I look," I said.

"Well, here you go! This should help."

I took the bags and must have looked puzzled because Nina added, "Remember? I picked up some stuff for you at Handy Mart this morning." She gestured to the bags. "I tried to buy the stuff you use and all, but it was Handy Mart and they don't have the best selection."

"Oh, Nina, that's sweet."

"Well, we may not have a corporate mission statement yet," she said, "but we do have petty cash and a credit card. Now we have corporate shampoo and toothpaste, and you have uniforms." She shrugged. "Well, jeans and stuff, but it is a business expense and everything I bought was on clearance. I saved the receipts."

I grabbed two towels from the hall closet, thanked my cousin, took the bags, closed and then locked the bathroom door behind me.

"Stella?" Nina called through the door.

"Yeah?"

"Hand your dirty stuff out to me. Spike and I are going to run a load so we don't run out of clean clothes."

I stared at the door. What was this? Nina was becoming the organized corporate administrator, on top of the details and anticipating our every need.

"Thanks!"

I stripped, handed the dirty clothes out to her and was pulling the shower curtain back to start the water when Nina called to me again.

"The shampoo's already in there," she said. "And the toothpaste and your new toothbrush are in the medicine cabinet. Oh, and I put some fresh razors in the shower, too."

Damn! Who knew ditzy Nina could be so totally efficient? I hopped in the shower a grateful woman, stood under the strong stream of water and began to feel as if our bad luck was about to change. After all, we didn't really have any huge problems here. What we had was a series of small complications.

The missing person's case was so easy I wondered how Mia and her past investigator had come to such a dead end.

We were only hampered by the repercussions of Joey Smack's repossession case, and surely Jake and I could clear that up. As for Aunt Lucy's admirer, well, he was probably harmless. Weird but harmless.

I emerged from the shower smelling like mango and vanilla; warm, relaxed and back in the game. Then I opened the Handy Mart bags.

"Nina!"

No answer. I opened the bathroom door, peered out into the hallway and heard the sounds of voices and a washing machine drift up from downstairs.

"Nina!"

It was pointless. She either couldn't hear me or didn't want to. I slammed the door shut again and returned to the bags. What in the hell had she been thinking?

I pulled out the padded red satin and lace bra, the matching tiny lace thong panties, and stood staring at them. I reached back into the bag, hoping against hope that she'd thrown those two items in as a joke, and found the same thing in black and then in purple.

Nina had to know I didn't wear stuff like this. I didn't wear padded bras. I wore cotton, not satin. And I never, ever, wore thongs! If God had meant for us to floss our butts, well, it wouldn't have come in the form of underwear.

I pulled out the jeans. Low-rise, boot cut, button-up, dark denim. I groaned. I did not have the hips for low-rise jeans! The tops were spandex—okay, cotton with spandex added— but they were also V-neck and fitted. Nothing in the bag was me. Where were the turtlenecks, the pullover sweaters and the tailored shirts?

I groaned. What choice did I have now? I turned away from the oversize mirror and started dressing. I held my breath as I pulled on the jeans and picked the black V-neck blouse in the vain hope that the dark color would somehow offset the padding in my satin and lace bra. When I'd finished, I turned around to face the music.

"Oh, this is a complete disaster," I muttered, studying the woman in the mirror.

The woman staring back at me was definitely uncomfortable. The cop was gone. I reached for the tube of hair gel, squirted some into the palm of my hand and stood studying the new me as I ran my fingers through my hair.

It wasn't that the clothes didn't fit, exactly. They did. Maybe they fit too much. The jeans hugged my hips. My breasts stood at a phony attention and the shirt did nothing to hide the fact that I now had cleavage. Detectives and cops needed to be able to blend into the scenery, not stand out.

I reached for the hair dryer and couldn't find one. I looked under the counter and in the linen closet before realizing there was no hair dryer. I looked back into the mirror and swore. Great. The only way to control my hair was to dry it with a big brush and pull it back into a ponytail. Without a hair dryer, my hair would curl and frizz, taking on a life of its own.

"Get a grip!" I said to the mirror. "Lloyd is out there, scared, and you're in a bathroom whining about your hair? Please!"

I was bigger than my hair, I reminded myself. I watched as the first few whips of hair began to spring into curlicues that flew away from my skull like miniature bottle rockets. All right, so maybe nothing was bigger than my hair, but it was certainly not my most important worry.

I turned away from the mirror, hung up my towel and left the steamy bathroom. Lloyd needed me. Aunt Lucy needed me. It was time to get to work and kick some serious ass. I stopped by the bedroom, grabbed my gun and attempted to stick it in my waistband. The cold metal hit exposed skin and tight denim before I realized my usual hiding places wouldn't work.

"Shit!"

I stomped downstairs and into the kitchen where everyone had gathered to watch as Aunt Lucy made dinner.

"Jake, do you have an extra pancake holster? Hell, I'm not picky. Do you have any extra holster?"

Jake looked up, opened his mouth, and just as quickly snapped it shut. Nina watched, grinning, and Spike's eyes widened ever so slightly.

"You didn't buy a hair dryer?" I asked Nina.

"No, they're bad for your hair, and some studies have suggested that they alter your brain chemistry."

I glared at her. "Those clothes," I said.

"Were all on sale, so don't go getting mad because you think I spent too much!"

"Spent too much?" I was sputtering.

Nina held up her hand like a traffic cop. "Stella, you never do anything nice for yourself. You've put all your time and energy into your work. You don't have to thank me."

"Thank you?"

"Just pretend you were on *Ambush Makeover* and I was your stylist. I know you don't have time to do it for yourself. I was just trying to bring more positive energy into your aura."

Aunt Lucy turned away from the stove to study Nina's handiwork.

"No brush?" she asked.

I rolled my eyes up toward my hairline. "It wouldn't help. Don't you remember how my hair was when I was in high school? It hasn't changed. I just need a hair dryer and a flat iron to tame it."

Spike leaned her head to one side and studied me. "I like it natural," she said.

"Yeah, wait an hour and see what happens."

She leaned her head to the other side and frowned. "I bet I'll still like it. Makes you look younger, less like a cop."

"My point exactly," I said. "I like looking like a cop."

Jake didn't say a word. He sat staring at me as if I'd suddenly grown two heads. It was beginning to irritate me.

"Well? Do you have another holster or not?"

"Yeah, I'll go look in the truck."

He seemed relieved at having a reason to step outside, as if the discussion of clothing and hair dryers had made him claustrophobic.

Aunt Lucy turned back to the stove and was stirring a large pot of something that I hoped turned out to be edible and not another cleanser.

"How is she?" I mouthed silently to Spike.

Spike nodded once and lifted her hands in a "Who knows?" gesture. "I think she's okay," she answered.

"I'm fine," Aunt Lucy said.

"How did you do that?" I asked.

"Hood vent, it's stainless. You think I got eyes in the back of my head?" She reached for the tumbler of Chianti that sat next to her spoon rest by the stove and kept on stirring the pot.

"Don't worry about me," she said. "I'm all right. Just find Lloyd. After supper, you and Jake. Find him and bring him home."

Chapter 10

I was beginning to question the wisdom of my vocational choices. My law-enforcement career had come to an untimely end, mainly because the police department in tiny Garden Beach, Florida, hadn't been big enough to hold my cheating, lying, no-good boyfriend, my slut-for-brains partner and myself. Okay, so there was also the issue of my inability to restrain myself from discharging my service revolver into the walls of our trailer after discovering my no-good boyfriend in bed with my slut-for-brains partner. Still, my behavior was unprofessional and indicated to me, and probably others, a questionable future in police work.

At question now was my career as a know-it-all, do-it-all private investigator and repo artist. It seemed to me, as soon as I put out one fire, two more started. Nothing was simple. Take for example, Lloyd. Joey Smack's henchmen weren't rocket scientists. They were bumbling idiots, and yet they had Lloyd and I didn't. Before I could find Mia Lange's brother,

I'd have to find Lloyd and satisfy Joey Smack. This was no way to run a company, let alone an investigation.

I was thinking all of these things while the five of us sat around the dinner table eating in relative silence, acutely aware of Lloyd's absence. It was a relief when the meal finally ended.

"I'm going for a walk."

"I'm coming with you," Jake said.

Aunt Lucy nodded, gathering plates from the table as she began cleaning up.

"Walk, ride, whatever," she said. "Just bring him back with you."

No pressure. "Just bring him back with you." Sure. Piece of cake.

We shrugged on our coats. I added a scarf, gloves and a hat, and we were out the door, walking as if we were being chased, because in a way, we were.

"This is ridiculous," I told him. "There's no way I'm going to come up with cocaine for Joey Smack. We've gotta find Lloyd."

Jake was walking, head down, hands in the pockets of his jacket, his forehead creased in a dark frown.

"That won't take care of the problem," he said. "That'll just piss Spagnazi off more. I'm gonna have to go see him."

I stopped dead on the pavement. "You can't do that. The guy's a fruit loop. He won't listen to you."

Jake's expression was grim. "I'll make sure he does."

Macho posturing. Now, what was that going to accomplish? "Jake, the repossession business is not about customer satisfaction. It's a given, the repo-ee is always gonna be pissed off. I say we tell the cops and let them handle Joey Smack, after we get Lloyd back, of course."

We were walking again, both too restless to stand still. The sound of the surf pounding against the beach roared louder as we reached the parking lot and headed for the darkened sand beyond it. The clouds had vanished and overhead stars dotted the blackened sky.

"Stella, what makes you think Spagnazi's gonna listen to the cops?"

I shrugged. Right now, I just wanted my dog back. I wanted to earn our ten-thousand-dollar retainer and I wanted my life back on a normal, even keel. Of course, it never had been exactly normal, but still, I could dream.

We ducked under the boardwalk and emerged onto soft sand that became firmer as we drew closer to the water. We walked without speaking for a few minutes. I studied the oceanfront houses, most of them darkened and boarded up until summer returned, and imagined a perfect world, where I lived at the beach in some quiet, remote area, and never had to worry again about Joey Spagnazi.

We both froze as a black form broke out of the darkness, running across the sand in a streak of silvery, muscled movement. Fang bore down on us and Jake moved instinctively to shield me from her. I stepped away from him and knelt, waiting for her to reach us.

"Don't move, Jake. It's all right."

The huge animal stopped a few feet short of us, lifted her lip and growled low in her throat at Jake.

"It's okay, puppy. He's with me." I stretched out a hand and stroked Jake's leg, then extended it in the dog's direction. "Come here, baby," I murmured. "He won't hurt you."

"Baby?" Jake whispered. "You call that thing Baby?"

"Actually, I call her Fang. Baby's just a term of endearment. Isn't that right, baby?"

Fang whined softly and drew a little closer, gradually reaching my side but never taking her eyes off Jake. I stroked the soft fur along her neck, felt her hot breath warm the side of my face, and gently stroked Jake's leg again with my free hand.

"Fang, this is Jake. Nice Jake." I stroked his leg, aware of the tension in the solid muscle that ran the length of his thigh.

Fang gave Jake a cursory sniff and stepped closer to more thoroughly inspect him. Jake turned his hand and extended it to her.

"Good girl," he murmured. "Good girl."

Fang whined, turned back to me, and snatched my coat sleeve in her powerful jaws, the movement sudden and without warning. I gasped, instinctively pulling back, and felt her tug hard to hold me. She backed up a step, and when I didn't move, she dropped my sleeve and ran off a few steps, barking in short yips.

"Did she hurt you?" Jake murmured. I saw his hand sliding slowly toward the back of his pants and stopped him.

"No. Wait."

Fang came back, reached for my coat sleeve and pulled.

"She wants us to come with her."

I stood and when I did, Fang dropped my arm and repeated the process of running off a few steps, looking back and barking.

We started after her, but Jake stopped me, pointing to dark splotches in the sand.

"What?"

"That's blood," he said. "Look. See how she's favoring her front right leg? I think she's hurt herself."

I watched Fang trot forward and saw the limp.

"Oh, God. I bet she did that this morning when she helped me. Oh, poor Fang."

I hurried after the dog, but when I moved faster, so did she.

"Fang, stop." I called softly. "You're hurt. Let me see your paw."

Fang trotted on, ignoring me, heading across the sand to the abandoned Victorian house where she seemed to live.

"Maybe she's going back under the porch," I said. "Animals do that when they're hurt. They go back to their lair. Maybe she'll let me look at it there."

We followed the huge animal across the beach, across the dunes to the house, but instead of running through the lattice-work and underneath the porch, Fang veered right and disappeared behind the building.

"Fang."

An answering bark came from the darkened rear of the house. Jake pulled his gun from his back pocket and slid it into his jacket pocket.

I reached one hand down to check the slim pancake holster that rested securely against my left side, felt the reassuring bulge of my Glock and followed Fang into the darkness.

Her barking drew us to her, up the back steps and onto the porch. As my foot hit the porch, a piece of wood gave, throwing me off balance.

"Stella, wait."

Jake reached into a pocket and pulled out a small Maglite. A brilliant spot of white illuminated my foot, and then the rotting wood flooring in front of us.

"Step over there," he said, pointing with the flashlight to a seemingly intact board. "But go easy. This whole porch is probably dry-rotted."

Fang's bark came, louder this time, and along with it a familiar answering bark that had me half running to cross the rotted floor.

Jake's light hit Fang's fur and he moved until the beam caught her standing at the back door in a pool of broken glass and blood. Fang had tried to rescue Lloyd, lunging at the frame until the wood splintered, and shattering the back door's glass window.

"Fang, come here," I cried. "You'll cut yourself more. Let us do it."

Jake rushed in front of me, reached the door and quickly

swept the doorway with his foot, removing the larger glass shards. He started to kick the door open and stopped, gasping as the pain from the wound in his side stopped him.

"Allow me," I said, stepping up beside him.

"No, you—"

Too late. I gave the door a swift, hard kick and felt the old wood splinter through and give way. We were in. Jake went through first, illuminating the room in front us with the slender beam of the Maglite.

Lloyd was in the far left corner of the kitchen, just as he'd been in the Polaroid. He was tied to a leg of the kitchen table, only now the table lay on its side. The rope around Lloyd's neck had pulled short, forcing the poor dog's head down close to the floor and preventing him from moving more than a few inches.

I pulled my pocketknife out of my coat pocket, pushed past Jake and knelt by Lloyd's side.

"Oh, baby," I murmured. "Here."

I cut the thick, plastic cord and Lloyd was free. Fang stood over him, whining and licking his face with her long pink tongue. Lloyd grinned immediately, his discomfort forgotten.

For a few minutes, everything was forgotten as Jake searched the house and I stood guard in case Lloyd's kidnappers returned. When he returned, I tried to help Fang.

"Easy, sweetheart," I murmured, gently taking Fang's injured paw in my hand.

She growled low in her throat, but didn't pull away. Jake held the light and I examined her blood-and-sand-encrusted foot. A shard of glass glittered back at us from the thick pad of her foot.

"Let's take her back to Aunt Lucy," I said. "Go get the car."

Jake shook his head. "I'm not leaving you here. It's too risky."

"I'll be fine. Fang's foot is a mess. I need tweezers and bandages."

Jake wasn't budging. "Do what you can now so she can walk without making it worse, then we'll all go back to the house."

I examined the paw again and sucked in my breath. The cut around the glass shard oozed blood. I felt my stomach erupt into fluttery twinges and my skin began to tingle painfully.

"Do you want me to do it?"

Jake moved to take Fang's paw. The dog growled louder, then barked viciously, teeth bared, lip lifted.

"Okay, okay, easy, girl!" He backed off.

I looked around the dimly lit kitchen, spotted bottled water Joey's men had used to fill Lloyd's water bowl, and nodded toward it.

"I need that. You see any paper towels?"

Jake ran the light around the room. No such luck.

I pulled my knife back out of my jacket pocket, looked into Fang's eyes and began speaking to her as if she could understand me.

"Baby, I need to take the glass out of your paw and clean you up a little bit."

The dog stared at me, her eyes liquid and soft. She licked the tip of my nose.

"All right," I said. "This will probably hurt a little."

I searched my pocket for tissues. None. I needed gauze. I needed something to use to stop the blood and clean the wound.

Jake placed the water by my side, fished a lighter from his pocket and took my knife. As he ran the blade through the blue and orange flame, I took off my coat and reached up beneath my shirt.

"Don't look," I told him.

He looked up.

"What are you doing?"

"Jake, keep your eye on what you're doing and don't look at me."

He lowered his head and I pulled my arms out of my stretchy top, hoping to undo my bra and remove it without having to take off my shirt.

With cotton, it's easy. With spandex, it's impossible. The shirt held me like a straitjacket. Finally I gave up, pulled it off over my head and dropped it on top of my coat. I fumbled with my bra clasp and felt it give. The lacy fabric fell forward into my hands and I heard Jake's breath escape in a whoosh.

"I told you not to look."

The knife lay next to the water jug and Jake sat back on his haunches studying my body.

"What are you doing?"

I grabbed my shirt and pulled it back over my breasts, glaring at Jake as I did so.

"The bra is padded," I said. "I'm going to use it to clean Fang's paw. Give me the knife."

He reached down, picked the Spyderco up carefully by the handle and said, "Watch out, it's hot."

I rolled my eyes at him and took the knife, handle first, from his fingers. I picked up the bra and slit the left side of the cup.

"What are you doing?"

"Taking out the padding."

"Damn. Was that your best bra?"

I gave him a withering look, pulled out the pads and turned to Fang.

"Only the best for you, sweetie."

Ten minutes later, Fang was a new woman. The glass was removed, the cut cleaned of grit and sand, and a black satin bandage was wrapped securely around her paw, held in place by bra-strap bows.

"Looks much better on you, girl," I murmured.

Jake sighed. "Let's get going," he said. "I don't want to risk spending any more time here than we have to."

I looked over at Lloyd. As I'd worked on his girlfriend, he'd paced anxiously in the background, whining every now and then, and padding up close to watch over my shoulder.

"Lloyd, let's take Fang home. She needs some medicine for that cut. Why don't you tell her that and see if she'll follow us."

"Stella, you don't—"

I rose to my feet, pulled on my coat and raised an eyebrow at Jake. "No, actually I don't, but on the off chance Lloyd does understand what I'm saying, I thought I'd explain."

Fang did indeed follow us home, trailing behind Lloyd in a straggly caravan that wound the three blocks back to our beach cottage. When we reached the foot of the front steps, she stopped, hesitating until Lloyd barked softly.

I looked at Jake and smiled.

"You see? A little communication is all it takes."

Jake ignored me and opened the front door. Aunt Lucy, Spike and Nina were sitting at the kitchen table playing Scrabble but they stopped and rose to their feet as we entered.

The look on Aunt Lucy's face when she saw her beloved Lloyd—the relief, the genuine joy—was worth more than Mia Lange's ten-thousand-dollar retainer. For a moment I almost conned myself into believing our new professional endeavor was well worth the effort. We had restored happiness to my aunt's worried heart.

Of course, that was before reality intervened and burst my bubble.

"Who's this?" Aunt Lucy asked Lloyd.

She nodded toward Fang.

"Lloyd's friend. You know, the dog that—" I stopped, realizing that I hadn't told Aunt Lucy about Fang, and from the look on her face, it didn't matter.

"You brought another woman home with you?"

Lloyd froze, tongue lolling out of his mouth, the joyful homecoming momentarily compromised.

"Aunt Lucy, this is Fang. She saved Lloyd. If it had not been for her, Lloyd might've died. He was, um, caught…by a…um…trapped and, well…she led us to him. Look, she's hurt."

The thundercloud of my aunt's jealousy passed as quickly as it had arrived and she moved toward the huge animal.

"Wait!" I said. "Let me introduce—"

It was a wasted breath. Aunt Lucy went to Fang and Fang allowed it without hesitation.

With gentle hands, Aunt Lucy took the dog's injured paw in hers.

"I'm sorry," she whispered. "I thought Benito… Let me see this."

Nina and Spike stood frozen by their chairs, their attention riveted to the giant wolf-dog.

"What a sweet puppy," Nina cooed.

Spike looked at me. "How did you find Lloyd?" she mouthed silently.

I pointed to Fang and smiled. Spike nodded and the exact explanation was tabled for a later time.

Aunt Lucy barked orders, sending us scurrying for her first-aid kit, healing salves and of course, the Chianti. When she'd poured a small bowl of water for the dog she turned to her audience.

"Would you like a crowd standing around your examining table?"

Jake grabbed the Chianti jug and motioned toward the stairs.

"Ladies, if someone will grab the glasses, we can take this meeting upstairs."

Which is how we all wound up sitting in my room drinking Chianti and plotting our next course of action. After two glasses of wine the decision-making process became easier. Nina would return to the library in hopes of finding Doug

Hirshfield. Spike would return to the courthouse and search for any records pertaining to the Hirshfield family. If Doug Hirshfield was not Mia's missing brother, Nina and Spike would begin pursuing the other names Spike had garnered in her earlier search.

Jake was going to stay with Aunt Lucy and contact some of his "government resources" about our Joey Smack problem. When the picture of Mia's sister arrived by overnight express, I would take that to Nina so she could show it to her new pals and try to track or confirm the identity of Mia's family that way.

By the end of our third glass of wine, Spike's eyes grew heavy and she leaned her head on Nina's shoulder. Nina reached over and stroked her hair gently.

"Baby's tired," she murmured. "Come on, honey. Say nite-nite to the nice people and let's go crawl under the covers."

With a sleepy smile, Spike let herself be led off to bed, leaving me alone with Jake and the Chianti. The room seemed to shrink, and my double bed was suddenly too close to his. When Jake leaned forward to pour more wine in my glass, I pulled back.

"No more for me. I'm a working girl."

Jake smiled. "Wouldn't want you to drop your guard," he said.

I frowned, held up my glass and studied it. "On three little juice glasses of wine? I hardly think so."

Jake nodded. "My point exactly."

"All right," I said, extending the glass. "One more."

He didn't move. "You sure? I wouldn't want you to say I got you drunk and had my way with you."

"Yeah, right. Four little juice glasses and I'm toast? Sorry, kid. I was raised on Uncle Benny's Chianti."

Jake leaned forward and filled my glass. He flinched slightly as he moved, favoring his side.

"Does it hurt much?"

Jake smiled. "Nah, pain builds character."

"Liar. Let me see."

I stood up, put my glass on the nightstand between us and waited for him to pull up his shirt. When he didn't, I reached out, took his wineglass and placed it on the table beside mine.

"Pull up your shirt, Jake."

"It's fine, Stella. Your aunt gave me one of her salves to put on the wound. I swear, it's almost healed."

"Prove it. Show me."

Jake met my gaze and held it as he slowly stripped his T-shirt off over his head. I watched, forgetting to breathe, as his lean, muscular torso came into view; a neat, white square bandage covering the hole in his side.

"I guess that's fair," he murmured.

"What?"

Jake chuckled. "Well, I imagine the look on my face was about the same as the one I see on yours."

I jumped, looking away from his body and reaching for my Chianti. I forced myself to take a long, slow, deliberate sip of wine before I turned back to him. When I did, I was back in control.

"Look on my face?" I echoed. "I was looking at your bandage." I put my hand on his shoulder, felt the rock-hard muscle beneath smooth skin and pushed him away, back onto the bed.

"Let's see how it's doing."

I reached down and ripped the adhesive-taped bandage away. The amorous look on Jake's face vanished.

"Ouch."

I smiled coolly. "Pain builds character, right?"

I made myself look at the healing injury and not at his face. It looked as if Jake's side had almost completely healed, which was impossible because he'd only been shot two days ago.

Our eyes met and Jake shrugged. "You know your aunt. I don't know what she put in that stuff, but whatever it is, it works."

I crossed the room to the dresser, grabbed the box of gauze pads, adhesive tape and the silver tube of Aunt Lucy's miracle salve.

"She's a miracle worker, all right," I said.

I sat on the side of the bed and redressed his wound, avoiding his gaze but feeling it on my face as I worked.

I finished, made a move to rise, and found his hand tight on my arm.

"Put that stuff on the nightstand," he said. "We have unfinished business."

His tone left no mistake about his intentions. I struggled to pull my arm free, his grip tightened, and suddenly every inch of my body went on pleasure alert.

"Jake, I…"

"Put it on the nightstand."

When I still didn't move, he took the bandages from my hand and dropped them to the floor beside the bed.

"Look at me, Stella," he whispered.

He reached out and took my other arm, turning me toward him. I inhaled and steeled myself for what would come next. I looked at him and waited.

"I want to make love to you, Stella," he said. "I want to undress you slowly. I want to run my fingers and tongue over every square inch of your body. I want to tease you until you think you might lose your mind. I want to bring you to the edge of more pleasure than you've ever allowed yourself to feel, and then stop. I want to build you up over and over again until you beg me to take you…because…"

"Jake, stop. No. I can't."

Jake reached a hand up to stroke the side of my face, his fingers trailing gently down the side of my neck, and sliding around to cup my head firmly as he pulled me toward him.

"Yes, you can," he murmured.

"No…"

The word came out in a half whisper and stopped as his lips met mine. I was so weak. I felt my body come alive, craving his touch. I moved without thinking, taking what I wanted, exploring him, tasting him, and letting my tongue wander, losing myself in the sensations.

Jake slid his arms on either side of my body and rolled, flipping me beneath him with a fluid movement that suddenly put me at his mercy. He kissed me again, gently, and let his tongue wander as mine had, down the side of my neck and into the sensitive pocket between my neck and collarbone.

My body was on fire, swelling and responding to each flick of his tongue on my skin. With one hand he captured both of my wrists, pulling them above my head and holding them fast. I struggled to free them, wanting to touch him again, and found I could not move.

"Jake, let me…"

He rose up on his elbow, rolled slightly away from me, but never loosened his grip on my wrists. His free hand moved across the fabric of my blouse, sliding across the slinky material to encircle the tips of my nipples.

I gasped, caught my lower lip between my teeth and felt my back arch to meet his fingers.

He stopped then, staring into my eyes with a longing that took my breath away.

"I want you, Stella," he whispered. "But I won't take you until you're absolutely certain you want me, on my terms. I won't move any further until you ask me to. I heard you today when you said you want a commitment and I respect that. I just can't offer you one."

My brain took over, my heart ran away and my body screamed. Shit. Reality once again reared its ugly head. Jake could give me everything I'd ever imagined in a lover, everything but a future.

He stared down into my face. "What do you want, Stella?"

My brain said, "Tell him you have to go now."

My heart said, "But he's the one!"

And my body said, "Oh, come on. Quit thinking so much. What's an orgasm between friends?"

I heard a sigh escape my lips. I tried to reach for him, then remembered that he held my arms.

"Let me go and I'll show you."

Jake smiled and shook his head.

"No. Tell me. Say the words."

I felt a well of frustration come to a boil inside myself. I didn't want to say the words. I wanted to do something without thinking. What was wrong with this guy?

"Come here," I whispered. "Kiss me. Let my hands go so I can touch you."

Jake shook his head, not moving.

"Nope. That's your way. You'll put it back on me. You'll turn the attention away from you and on to me. So when I lose my mind to your incredible touch, you can say things got out of hand. You can say we made love, but you didn't mean to. It'll become a mistake."

He shook his head again. "Not this time, Stella. This time you ask for it. This time you tell me what you want."

I felt tears start, hot behind my eyes. Damn this man. Why couldn't anything with Jake Carpenter be simple?

"So you want a guarantee that if we make love, I won't be hurt when you walk away?"

Jake shook his head. "Not necessarily. I can't control how you feel. All I can do is tell you I can't offer you anything more right now than today. If you can handle that, fine, but otherwise, I don't want to hurt you."

His grip loosened on my wrists and he pulled away, not touching me. I closed my eyes, wishing I didn't have to open them and find him looking at me. What had started out as a revenge fantasy in my head was becoming a disaster in which

I got even, but signed a liability waiver against feeling bad afterward. The entire thing between Jake and me had started when I'd wanted to wound him for leaving me. Now, here he was basically saying, go ahead, just don't let it hurt you. Damn. What kind of revenge sex is that?

Furthermore, it sort of irritated me that he could maintain such control. And who was he to take care of me anyway? Who did he think I was, some sheltered little thing with a big heart and no protective shielding?

"You know, Jake, I'm not the little girl you used to know. I can take care of myself."

He smiled softly. "I know you can, Stella, but I also know you run away when you're hurt. I don't want you to run away again."

My heart rose at those words, only to fall when he finished his thought.

"We've got a business to think of, and your aunt to protect. I don't want something to happen between us that could ruin the agency."

The revenge fantasy returned. He didn't want to ruin his new livelihood; that was the motive behind his hesitation.

"Oh, Jake," I whispered. "You don't know me at all, do you?"

I stretched out one finger and ran it lightly down the center of his chest. "Come here," I said.

He caught my finger and stopped me.

"Say it, Stella. Tell me what you want."

I felt the words rise up in my throat and die before I could speak them. *Love me, Jake. Love me and never let me go.*

He cupped my chin with his finger, raising my head to meet his gaze.

"Tell me what you want."

Another woman's voice seemed to come from my mouth. "Hold me, Jake. Just hold me."

"That's it," he whispered. "Come here."

He took me into his arms, pulled me close and held me tight against his chest. I closed my eyes and sank into him, every muscle in my body letting go and relaxing into the warm safety of his arms. It felt strangely like home.

We lay there, neither of us saying a word. His breath was warm on my hair and my hand rested on his chest, feeling the strong pounding of his heart beneath it. I felt myself letting go, drifting contentedly, and was surprised when he moved.

"Don't go anywhere."

Jake rolled to the other side of the bed, got up and turned off the light. As my eyes adjusted to the darkness, I saw him begin to undress. He tossed his jeans onto my vacant bed, and then slid his boxers down over his thighs.

I held my breath, drinking in the silhouette of his body against the pale light that shone through the bedroom window. I studied him, memorizing the way muscle blended into muscle, drinking in and savoring each new revelation as he began to walk slowly toward the bed.

"Give me your hand," he said.

He pulled me up to stand in front of him, stroked the hair back from my face gently and began undressing me. My shirt went first, then my jeans, button by button. He knelt to pull them off and I placed a hand on his shoulder for balance. His hands ran the length of my legs, knee to thigh, and stopped at the slender lines of my thong panties. He hooked a finger under each thin fabric strap and slowly pulled them down and off.

"Oh, Stella," he breathed. "You are beautiful."

He rocked back, studying my body in the moonlight for a long moment before he stood and pulled me to him. I felt him harden against me and move, pulling me down onto his bed.

He pulled back the blanket and left me lying there before him; exposed, shivering with anticipation more than cold.

"Jake, please…"

He rolled close to me, up on one elbow, the index finger

of his free hand poised above my body, hovering between my chest and my stomach.

"Please what, Stella? Tell me what you want."

"Make love to me, Jake. Now."

A soft chuckle escaped into the darkened bedroom. "No, baby, you're not ready. First things first. What do you want first? Take it one minute at a time."

"Kiss me."

Jake leaned forward, rolled between my legs and lowered his head to brush my lips with his own. The kiss was gentle at first, then searing as the heat between us built to a crescendo. His tongue left trails of fire across my skin as it wandered slowly down my neck.

"Please, Jake, touch me," I whispered.

"Where?"

I moaned. "Everywhere."

I reached for him, running my hand across his flat stomach, determined to turn the tables on him. My hand moved, following the swirls of hair that thickened as I worked my way lower.

He stopped me, grabbing my wrist in his iron grip and raising my fingers to his mouth. He kissed each fingertip, gently sucking them, one by one, into his mouth.

"That's enough for now," he said softly.

"What do you mean?"

He pulled me to him, wrapped me against his body and ran his hand down my back.

"The old Stella just came out, looking for a way to control the process. It's your way of telling me to stop. You can't let go with me, at least, not yet."

"That's not true!" I protested. "I just wanted to reciprocate."

"And I told you that wasn't an option yet. You hide behind your control. When we make love, nobody will be hiding behind anything."

"You misread me," I said.

"Are you comfortable?" he murmured.

Comfortable? I was in agony.

"Yes," I lied.

"Good." He stroked my hair. I struggled to free my arms, but he stopped me. "Shh. Go to sleep, baby."

"What? But..."

Jake's whisper, hot against my ear. "You said hold me. I'm holding you."

"But that was before you..."

His hand ran the length of my back sending an electric current of desire through my body.

"I know. But I choose to believe the woman who asked to be held. I am holding you, your skin against mine, until you feel safe. Until it's time to move on to the next level."

"Jake, really, I'm..."

He chuckled and I felt every inch of him against my skin. I knew he wanted me as badly as I wanted him.

"Right side or left side?" he whispered.

"For what?"

"Do you sleep on your right side or your left?"

I had to think before I could answer. "Left."

"Turn over."

I could not believe this man.

"What?"

"You heard me, turn over."

Jake rolled me away from him, spooned me against his body and slipped his arm across my belly, his hand gently cupping my breast.

"Good night, Stella," he whispered.

"Please, Jake..."

He nuzzled my neck. "Shh."

I closed my eyes, willing the burning in my body to subside. Minutes later I heard his soft, even breathing and knew he'd managed somehow to drift off to sleep. I lay in the darkness wondering what it would feel like to sleep with Jake Carpenter every night. What would it be like to fall in love with a man who cared enough to read my heart before he took my body?

Chapter 11

When I opened my eyes, Jake had vanished. Sunlight streamed through the bedroom window and I was naked. I closed my eyes as sleep half tugged me back into a vague midnight memory.

We had been sleeping. I had moved, rolling from my left side onto my right, and was lying with my head on his chest. His strong arm held me in place, but in my dreams he was touching me, his fingers exploring my body, slipping between my legs and sliding deep inside me. I moved, fitting my body to the rhythm of his hand, moaning as I drew closer and closer to the edge of climax.

I felt him, hard against my inner thigh, and reached out to feel the thick, solid length of his erection. The skin was soft against the steel bulk of him and I sighed. He moved in my hand and I tightened my grip, feeling the friction of his mounting desire match my body's swollen, wet response.

I remembered the sound of Jake's moan, loud in my ear, and

the feel of my nipples hardening in anticipation. I felt my dream blending with reality, felt myself coming up from the depths of unconsciousness into the cool night air of our bedroom and realized he had removed my fingers with a tortured groan.

I heard myself moan, "No," as he pulled me back down onto his chest.

"Go back to sleep, baby. We must've forgotten the rules while we were sleeping."

"But I was so close."

"You were?" A brief silence, then, "Close your eyes, baby. Keep on dreaming."

I felt his fingers touch my skin again, sliding deep inside me, moving slowly, rhythmically building my body's response. I couldn't stop. I knew I should, but I couldn't.

His voice, hushed in my ear, whispered, "Let it go, Stella. Come to me."

His fingers were everywhere, sliding slick against each sensitive nerve ending, teasing, promising, but never hurrying. I felt myself hesitate, reluctant to let go, poised on the edge of explosion and release, but unable to give myself over to the ecstasy.

He read me. He read my body and ran his tongue the length of my torso. I forgot to breathe. He bypassed his fingers, nipped gently at the tender skin of my inner thighs and began teasing me. His tongue moved closer and closer. The anticipation built.

"Please, Jake!" I cried finally. "Please."

Again the whisper. "Tell me what you want. Say the words."

"Oh, Jake."

"Say it, Stella. I can't until you do."

"Taste me, Jake. Please."

His tongue moved the few remaining inches and I lost track of anything other than the blinding need I had for his

touch. He gripped my hips with his hands and pulled me to
him. I moaned as I came with an urgency that drove all conscious thought from my head.

The memory made me sit up, wide-eyed, and look around
the sunny room. Had I been dreaming? Had I reached for him
in the night? Had he taken me beyond any prior point of com-
parison and then, what, gone to sleep? Had we made love or
had it been all about me, with no fulfillment for him? Surely
I would've remembered making love with Jake?

The door creaked open and he walked in, two coffee mugs
in his hand.

"You're up. Good. I brought you some coffee."

He walked around the bed, set the mugs down on the nightstand and bent to kiss me gently on the lips.

"How'd you sleep?"

I stared up at him. He was dressed, wearing a T-shirt and
jeans, and seemed not to notice that I was naked. It was almost as if nothing had ever happened, which plagued me, because now I wasn't sure. What exactly had gone on?

"You all right?"

I nodded. "Sure."

"Good. We've got a lot to get to today. See you downstairs."

He turned and was almost out of the room before I found
my voice.

"Jake?"

He looked back at me. "Yes?"

"About last night…"

He walked back to the bed, rounding to my side and sat
down on the edge.

"Did we…" My voice trailed off because I wasn't sure exactly how to phrase the question.

"Baby, last night was wonderful. I loved holding you." He
leaned over and patted my hip. "Now, let's get a move on, all
right?"

"Wait. I mean, did we?"

Jake frowned. "Did we what? I told you four glasses of Chianti was too much."

"Not that. I mean… I know we didn't do *that!* I mean, did you…did we… Or, did we?"

He looked puzzled. "Stella, honey, drink the coffee. I had no idea you were such an airhead in the morning."

"Never mind. I'll see you downstairs."

He smiled, but I thought I saw something else in his eyes, a glint of pleasure at my confusion perhaps?

"See you downstairs," he said, and was gone.

By the time I'd showered, dressed and finished my coffee, I'd managed to convince myself that I'd been dreaming. I'd taken my desires and fulfilled them with a dream, pure and simple. It was the only way I could work with Jake and still function.

I walked downstairs and found the others eating breakfast. Lloyd sat at his customary place at the head of the table but Fang was nowhere in sight.

"Oatmeal?" Aunt Lucy asked. "I got brown sugar and raisins, too."

I nodded, noticing Lloyd was eating eggs and bacon.

"Fake eggs," Nina said, shaking her head. "I don't know how he eats them."

I looked around the room. "Where's Fang?"

"You didn't hear her last night?" Jake asked. The twinkle was definitely there in his eyes.

"No. I didn't hear a thing."

Jake nodded. "Well, she was down here scratching at the door and moaning. Must've been around four. I came down and let her out. I hate to see something trapped when it needs to be released."

Definite twinkle. I felt my cheeks begin to burn.

"Fang's claustrophobic?" Nina asked.

"Nah, she probably wanted to go sleep where she's most comfortable. Once she got to feeling better I'm sure she was ready for a good night's sleep."

His eyes met mine and I choked on my coffee. The door-bell rang and Jake became all business, reaching for his Sig-Sauer as he walked to the door and cautiously opened it.

"Express mail," a female voice said.

There was a brief exchange and then Jake walked back to the kitchen, a large cardboard envelope in hand.

"The picture," I said. "Great. Open it."

Jake took out his knife and slowly slit the top of the enve-lope and reached inside to pull out a small photograph, its edges curled with age. He stood, examining the picture for a long moment before handing it over to me.

"Well, this shouldn't take too long," he said. "We can track these people through the real-estate records."

I took the picture from him and stared down at the family standing in front of their beach house. Two young boys, one tow-headed, the other dark, stood in front of a man and woman. They stood smiling out at the camera, their Victorian beach cottage in much better repair than it had been last night when we'd recovered Lloyd.

"I don't believe it," I said, passing the photo along to Nina. "Look at those two little boys. That's Fred May and Doug Hirshfield, isn't it?"

Nina squinted, frowned and studied the photograph intent-ly. Spike leaned over and looked, too. Nina nodded.

"That's them, all right," she said. "I'd know that face any-where, at any age."

"Even better," Jake murmured. "Now all we do is find Fred May's long-lost brother. Piece of cake."

Spike frowned. "Stella, didn't you say that Mrs. May said Doug is dead?"

Nina answered for me. "She gets a little confused, I

think. Fred's the one who died, but I think she doesn't want to accept that, so she says Doug is dead and Fred is missing."

Made sense to me. Now all we had to do was find Doug Hirshfield, and that was standard P.I. routine work. If the man had a driver's license or a social security number, we'd have his location by the afternoon.

I looked at Jake. "So do we go back to Glenn Ford and run a computer search or do you call one of your buddies?"

Jake's Delta Force background and CIA contacts made getting need-to-know-only information a whole lot easier to obtain. It was another good reason for having Jake as a business partner and not using him for more personal pursuits and needs.

A detailed vision from my late-night dream popped, unwanted, into my head and I was momentarily breathless. It had to have been a dream; no human male could ever please a woman so completely. I'd probably heard Fang scratching and moaning, incorporated the sounds into my own wet dream and that was that. Right?

"Ready to go?"

Jake's voice startled me. I looked up to see him standing in the entrance to the kitchen with his jacket on and my coat in his hand.

"Go?" I echoed stupidly.

"Don't you think we ought to check in with Tom and let him know about last night?"

"Why would we—"

Jake interrupted before I could make a total fool of myself.

"We should tell him about Joey Smack's men taking Lloyd and how we broke into that house to find him. Someone's liable to report a break-in, you know. I wouldn't want him going through all the trouble to find burglars or vandals when it was just us."

I exhaled slowly and nodded. What was wrong with my

brain this morning? Of course we needed to talk to Tom. He might even be able to help us locate Doug Hirshfield.

"Coming," I said, and blushed all over again.

Spike got up with me and said, "I'll lock the door behind you. Don't worry, we've got this end of things covered."

She nodded slightly in Aunt Lucy's direction as I met her gaze.

"Thanks, Spike. Call us if you need us."

I followed Jake out into the frigid January morning, blinking at the brilliant sunlight as I watched him simultaneously unlock the truck, climb up into the cab and dial a number on his cell phone.

He cranked the engine and pulled out into the street.

"Hey, baby," he said. "Call me." He clicked the phone shut and turned on the radio.

"Checking in with your harem?" I asked.

Jake's eyebrows rose and his mouth twitched with a suppressed smile.

"Jealous?"

I felt heat flooding into my face and gave myself a huge mental bitch slap. What possessed me to say that?

"Nope, not at all. Just making conversation."

Jake's mouth twitched again as he slowed the truck down in front of Marti's Café.

"Well, lucky for you Tom's at the diner and you won't be needing those witty conversational skills after all."

He pulled into a parking space in front of the tiny restaurant and cut the engine. Tom's unmarked police car sat two car lengths behind us. Inside, Tom sat at the counter in his usual place, his head bent in deep conversation with Marti and a uniformed officer.

All three of them looked up when we walked in, and while Tom and Marti smiled a greeting, not one of them looked at all happy. The young uniform slid off his stool, said his goodbyes and walked past us, nodding to Jake as he passed. Tom called after him.

"Make sure you lock that up in the safe, Cal, okay?"

"Gotcha, Detective."

Tom patted the stool beside him, smiled up at us and said, "Have a seat."

I took the stool next to Tom and smiled when Marti arrived with two fresh cups of coffee.

"Anything new with your homicide?" Jake asked.

The smile vanished from Tom's face and his eyes darkened. "Yeah. Son of a bitch. Turns out she was pregnant, about twelve weeks along."

"Poor thing," I murmured. "Guess Nina was wrong about her."

Marti heard me, but the other two were talking about the forensic details.

"How was your cousin wrong?" she asked. "I didn't think that girl was ever wrong about anything."

I smiled at her. "Well, she may act like a dingbat, but Nina certainly seems to have a gift for uncovering the truth. I hate having to tell her she was wrong about Rebecca DeWitt."

Marti was distracted for a moment by a customer who stuck out his mug for a refill. When she returned, I continued.

"Nina had it all figured that because Rebecca was her beloved Fred May's literary agent, she committed suicide on the second anniversary of his death. Her being pregnant negates that theory in my opinion. It proves she was in love with someone else and wouldn't have killed herself over Fred, especially if she was carrying another man's child. She had too much to live for."

Marti shook her head. "Who'd have figured you for a romantic?"

"What do you mean?"

"What if she slipped up, got pregnant in a drunken stupor to a one-night stand, and killed herself because she realized she'd ruined her life and all was lost? Now, do you want the daily special or something from the menu?"

I stared at her, slack-jawed.

"It's French toast today," she added.

"Marti, her hands were duct-taped behind her. How do you commit suicide with your hands tied?"

"First things first," she said. "French toast or something else?"

"French toast."

Marti nodded. "Good choice."

She scribbled on her order pad, slipped the paper onto the counter of the pass-through window behind her, and turned back around to find all three of us watching her.

"She didn't kill herself, honey," Tom said.

Marti raised an eyebrow. "See? That's a man for you. Come in on the last half of something and think you got the big picture. I never said Rebecca DeWitt killed herself. I was merely offering Stella here, an alternative."

She looked at me. "Becca DeWitt was Fred's literary agent, not his girlfriend. Besides, she was dating some other guy. That's why she was down here so often, even with Fred May dead. She'd come to see this other fella."

"Who?" I asked.

Marti shrugged. "I don't know. What do I look like, *People* magazine? I just know people saw her around every now and then. 'Course, everyone knew her on account of Fred. I heard she was seeing some guy."

Tom leaned forward a little, turned so we could hear him without any of Marti's other patrons overhearing.

"I tried to follow up on that. A few people remember seeing her with a man, but I get twelve different descriptions and not one name. I don't know if this mystery guy has anything to do with her death or not. We think she may have been the victim of a robbery. We found her car yesterday. It was abandoned off I–95. Rebecca's wallet was missing."

"They killed her and dumped her body in the ocean?" I asked, incredulous. "I didn't think car thieves went to all that trouble."

Tom shrugged. "They don't usually, but it could've been the easiest way to get rid of her. If she died here, then they could've driven over the canal bridge, thrown her body off and kept on going. The M.E. puts time of death around 4:00 a.m. Low tide peaks around 6:00 a.m. Current would've been going out and the body would've ridden with it."

Jake frowned. "So a car thief who also fishes or knows the tidal charts takes this into consideration before he jacks your victim? That doesn't make sense."

Marti arrived with two orders of French toast and bacon, plopped the second one down in front of Jake and said, "You looked like you could use a little sweetening this morning. Eat up."

Tom held his cup out to Marti for a refill and when she reached to take it, I noticed their fingers brush in a quick caress. When she took the coffeepot farther down the line of customers, he returned to Jake's question.

"I'm not saying he was a smart car thief, just lucky. And I don't think he meant to kill her, either."

I put my fork down. "Now, how can you know that?"

"Preliminary autopsy results show she was dead when she hit the water. She had a stroke." Tom pulled a notepad from his shirt pocket and studied it. "Stroke due to carotid dissection. Apparently that can happen to anyone at any age. Now, the attack probably added enough stress to trigger the stroke, but nobody outright killed the woman."

Marti passed by, filled my cup and shook her head. "Fry the bastard anyway, just on principle," she said, and walked off.

Tom smiled after her. "Wouldn't want to piss her off," he murmured.

"I heard that." Marti called over her shoulder.

Tom's grin grew wider and he shook his head ruefully. "Shoulda found that woman years ago."

Jake smiled, saw me look at him and winked. "Well, sometimes they're just not ripe for the picking. Maybe it's better that you found her now. Imagine how wild she must've been ten years ago."

"Oh, please," I said. "How would you know?"

Tom's cell phone rang, preventing him from answering. I heard him say, "Good. That's what I wanted to know."

He listened intently for another moment, his head cocked to one side, staring at Marti but clearly focused on his conversation.

"But you're fairly certain it's his work?"

There was another pause and Jake shot a questioning glance in my direction. Tom snapped the cell phone shut and sat staring at his empty plate for a moment. It was all I could do not to grab him and say "What?" Instead, I focused on Marti's amazing French toast.

Indirectly, perhaps, a case could be made for my curiosity. DeWitt had been Fred May's literary agent and Fred May's adopted brother could be the man we were looking for.

"The car thief obviously didn't read much," he said finally. "There was an unpublished Fred May manuscript under the driver's seat of Rebecca DeWitt's car. She was sitting on a gold mine and her attacker never even knew it."

"I thought Fred May was dead," Jake said, pushing his empty plate aside.

Tom nodded. "He is, but apparently he was one hell of a prolific guy. This makes two complete novels that've turned up since his death."

Marti caught Tom's eye and winked. He blushed and gently pushed his coffee cup out toward her, a signal that didn't mean he wanted coffee. She slowly began working her way back toward us, stopping at each filled seat to check on her customers or to tease them gently about one thing or another.

"How do they keep finding his work?" Jake asked.

"Well, you know, he was from here, so there's his home place and then there's the house where he lived. I suppose there were papers and stuff in both homes."

Marti was three customers away, talking with an elderly couple about homemade applesauce. She seemed mesmerized by their conversation, and yet I could tell she was also watching the kitchen staff, listening in on what bits of our conversation she could catch and monitoring her other customers. She proved this by jumping right into our conversation a moment later.

"You know they found the first book when they put Fred's place on the market."

"Who found it?" I asked.

Marti shrugged. "I don't know. Either the Realtor or maybe Rebecca. She's the literary agent for his estate, so she'd probably be the one to go through all his papers. I don't think his wife would've found them." She frowned. "I think they were separated or something by the time he died."

Marti shook her head and smiled. "Anyway, all I know is that kind of thing happens all the time. Guess his mom won't have to worry about her nursing-home bills."

Jake was getting restless. He'd finished his coffee and shook his head when Marti offered more.

"Tom, I need to talk to you about something. Think we could step outside?"

When the two men left, Marti turned to me, eyebrow raised in a question mark.

"We broke into a beach house. Jake just wants to confess before some Realtor comes to show the place and calls the cops."

This stopped Marti. She cocked her head, eyes twinkling, and grinned.

"Needed the privacy, huh?"

I could feel my cheeks reddening. "No, nothing like that."

I dropped my voice to a whisper. "Someone took my dog and locked him up in the kitchen of this old house. Get Tom to tell you about it later."

Marti's look changed to one of concern in an instant. Her eyes darkened and she frowned.

"Is your dog all right?"

"Lloyd? He's fine. He's fallen in love with a beach dog and spends all his time drooling and watching out the window for her."

Marti smiled. "Love'll do that!" Her gaze flickered to the window that ran the length of the café and she chuckled. "I guess I've been doing a fair amount of looking out the window and drooling myself."

I spun around on my stool. Tom was outside, leaning against his unmarked car, listening intently as Jake talked, his back to us. There was something in the way they stood that sent a tiny shiver of anticipation through my body. Foolish as it probably was, I liked watching strong men. I liked the unselfconscious way they stood, the way they seemed to assume they could handle anything that came their way, including women.

Oh, God. I was becoming one of *those* women, the kind who squeezes their man's arm and squeals over their strong muscles. No. Impossible. I would not get turned on by something as stereotypical as brute force and testosterone. Still, there was a part of me that liked knowing Jake could handle me, the same way I could handle him.

"Shut up!" I whispered, apparently out loud, because Marti said, "What?"

"Nothing," I said, spinning back to her. "I think maybe that drooling stuff is contagious, that's all."

She laughed and I stood up, put the money for our meal on the counter and decided I'd spent enough time thinking about romance and way too little time doing something that was actually productive.

"Marti, do you know anything about Fred May's brother?"

"Doug?"

I nodded. "Yeah, does he still live in the area?"

Marti frowned, thinking hard. "You know, I don't know. Seems to me he took off right out of high school. Went to college somewhere far off, or into the military. I don't know. Why don't you ask his mother?"

I shook my head. "Tried that. She's got Alzheimer's or something and really couldn't help us."

"Did you ask the nursing-home staff?" she said. "Wouldn't they have his name and number? I mean, if something happened, the nursing home would call the family."

I nodded. "They can't give out that information, but there are other ways we can try to get it." Of course, those ways weren't legal, but I wasn't going to tell Marti that.

My cell phone chirped deep inside my purse. I caught the call on the fifth ring, nodded a hasty goodbye to Marti and stepped out into the frigid winter morning.

"I was about to hang up," Pete said. "I don't like voice mail."

Jake looked up as I walked past and I shook my head at him, indicating there wasn't trouble at the house.

"What did you find out?" I asked.

There was a slight pause, Pete's way of being dramatic without a drumroll.

"There is no Mia Lange in that age range," he said.

"What do you mean?"

I reached Jake's truck, heard the doors unlock and looked back to see Jake pocketing the remote.

"I'll be there in a minute," he called.

"What I mean is, I've searched every way I know how to, legal and illegal, and there is no Mia Lange over the age of eighteen or under the age of fifty-six. I think you've got a bogus client."

I climbed up into the cab of Jake's truck, pulled the door

shut against the blustery wind and leaned back against the passenger seat.

"I kind of thought that's what you'd say."

"I traced her sister's phone number, if that helps," he said. "It's registered to Carla Bucknell. I haven't found a criminal record on her yet, but she does have a driver's license and I got her address. You want that?"

I took down the information mechanically as my mind scurried to figure out all the possible implications of having a phony client.

"I do have some good news for you, though," Pete said.

"What?"

"Your friend Jake hasn't been arrested since he was eighteen and picked up for drinking underage."

I hung up on Pete and watched as Jake shook hands with Tom and started toward the truck. I gave him just enough time to open the door and start up into the cab before I pounced on him with Pete's news.

"Mia Lange isn't Mia Lange," I said.

Jake looked at me, unfazed. "Who is she then?"

"I don't know, but she isn't who she said she was. Doesn't that concern you?"

Jake stuck the key in the ignition, started the truck and pulled away from the curb.

"Not really," he said finally. "I thought something like that was up when she paid ten thousand in cash."

"Why didn't you say something?"

Jake shrugged. "Stella, I figured it would all come out eventually. It wasn't any big deal. The client isn't required to tell us the truth, the whole truth and nothing but the truth. They pay money for services rendered. Unless they ask us to do something blatantly illegal, or unless we just don't feel like taking the job, we're paid to do our job without checking their moral barometer."

Jake sighed and seemed irritated. He was staring out at the street, frowning, and the little muscle in his jaw was twitching.

"I don't know about you," he said, "but I'm not independently wealthy. My auto-body shop burned to the ground, remember? I can't earn a living unless I'm working."

"But what if—"

"Stella, you know what your problem is? You think you're still a cop. You think like a cop, you act like a cop. That makes you paranoid by nature and a stickler for following the rules. Well, private investigators have a different set of rules. They don't have to play fair."

I couldn't believe what I was hearing. "You mean you don't care who this woman is, or why she wants to hunt down her alleged brother, you're just going to take the money anyway?"

"Exactly. If I find out she's looking to harm the guy, sure, I'll do something about it, but for now, I'm taking the money."

Jake pulled up in the driveway of the beach cottage and looked over at me.

"Come on, Stel, loosen up. I'm not a criminal. I just happen to know the world a little bit better than you do. I've seen things you couldn't even imagine, so if our client wants to hire us under an assumed name, so be it. Doesn't mean she's up to no good. I figure she might be looking for the father of her illegitimate kid. Maybe she's embarrassed about it, or maybe he's an old flame. It could be anything, Stel. It's not always sinister."

I shook my head. "I didn't like her from the start. I can't imagine what she's trying to run on us."

We got out of the truck and started up the steps to the cottage.

"If it makes you feel any better, I asked a friend to check her out."

"What friend?" I asked, thinking about his earlier phone call.

Jake smiled. "Always the cop investigating."

"Asshole."

"Jealous?"

"You wish."

We would've continued this legendary debate, but the arrival of yet another delivery van stopped us. This time the company was local, Vigo's Floral Ecstasy, the sign on the side read. The van was lime green, with pink-and-orange swirls rippling across the panels in hallucinogenic swirls. A huge gold crown encrusted with multicolored lights topped the vehicle, and tiny flags flapped violently from their posts at each corner. It was a hippie flashback of the worst variety.

A tall, skinny kid with a nondescript goatee slid out of the driver's seat, walked to the back of the van and produced another flower arrangement.

"Yo," he said, shuffling up to us in jeans that sagged below his navel. *"Qué pasa!"*

I saw Jake's hand creep toward his gun and didn't move to stop him.

"For me?" I said, reaching to take the arrangement.

The kid shrugged. "Why not? There's no card. Knock yourself out."

Jake handed the kid a dollar. "Back at ya."

The boy looked at the dollar bill the way I used to look at a penny handed to me by a well-meaning elderly relative.

"Peace," he muttered.

"Whatever," Jake answered. "Who sent these?"

The boy held out his hand. Jake took the hint and dropped another dollar into his outstretched palm. The kid looked at the dollar, sighed and looked back at Jake.

"Don't know."

"You wanted money to tell me that?" Jake asked.

The boy grinned. "I figured you were making a charitable donation."

Jake snatched the bill from the kid's hand and pocketed it.

"Whoa, dude," the boy said. "Did you see those trails?"

Without another word, the kid turned, flinging his hand out in front of him, then following its path with his eyes. He swung back up into the truck and pulled away, still moving his hand back and forth in front of him as he zigzagged down the street.

"See anything?" I asked, holding the pot out for Jake's inspection.

He searched the flowers, felt along the rim and bottom of the pot, and finally stepped back, shaking his head.

"No bugs."

"Okay, let's go."

We started up the steps. The front door opened and Aunt Lucy stood framed in the doorway. Her face paled as she studied the flowers.

"Where did those come from?" she asked quietly.

"Pretty, huh?" I said, ignoring the question. "A spring arrangement, I think. There's red tulips, daffodils, violets and something else."

"Lilies of the valley," she said softly. "I don't want them."

She turned and walked away from us as we followed her into the house. She kept on walking, back into the kitchen where beakers and test tubes once again littered the countertops and table surfaces.

"They don't have a card attached," I said.

Aunt Lucy looked up at us. "He knows I know," she said cryptically.

Jake frowned. "You know what?" he asked.

Aunt Lucy sighed, clearly irritated. "Get rid of them. I don't want them in my house."

"Oh, how beautiful!" Nina exclaimed. She walked across the living room and stood at the edge of the kitchen, studying the arrangement.

Aunt Lucy took the vase from my hands, crossed the room to the back door, flung it open and hurled the colorful bouquet out into the backyard.

"Enough is enough," she cried, turning to face us. "Don't you see what he's trying to do?"

A tear snaked its way down her cheek as she looked from one to the other of us in a mute appeal that I couldn't understand. It was clear she was both angry and frightened, but of what?

I moved, going to her and wrapping her into an embrace. Beneath my fingers I felt her trembling frame shake and for a moment thought of a wounded bird with hollow bones.

I stroked her back. "Come sit down, honey, and tell us about it. Let me help you."

I looked over her shoulder at Nina. "How about a nice cup of tea, Aunt Lucy? I think we could all use a good cup of tea, right, Nina?"

Nina nodded, gulped and said, "I was just about to make some ginseng."

Aunt Lucy raised her head, a shadow of her normal self returning at the mention of ginseng.

"Don't give me that crappy twig stuff," she said. "I want English breakfast tea. It's up in the cabinet."

I led Aunt Lucy to the table while Nina bustled about preparing the tea and Jake moved equipment out of the way at the table. Spike had slipped silently into the room and was efficiently gathering sugar, milk and lemon slices.

"What's going on, Aunt Lucy?" I asked.

Lloyd, on cue, walked into the kitchen, collapsed in a heap at Aunt Lucy's feet and licked her ankle. Instead of being pleased, Aunt Lucy began to cry softly.

"I never told you," she murmured to the dog. "I wanted to, but I thought at first it was you. After that, it was too late. It wasn't often, maybe once a year, sometimes on my birthday, sometimes in January. I just— I don't know, I…"

Aunt Lucy shook her head. She looked up at me, her eyes pleading.

"You understand, don't you? I mean, I didn't know what

to make of it. I didn't want to make too much of it because what if there was some perfectly reasonable explanation, like a secret friend from church, or our insurance agent remembering me, or something…"

Her voice trailed off and she sat staring at her hands.

"Aunt Lucy, someone's been sending you flowers for a long time?"

She nodded, clearly miserable and ashamed.

"I should've told Benny, but I didn't think it was so bad, really. And what if I'd been making a big deal out of nothing? It wasn't as if they arrived regularly. For years there weren't any at all. But then, after Benny…was gone…after I started selling my formulas on TV, they started again. Only now, there are cards and more flowers and the groceries. I don't know how to make him stop."

Nina brought a mug of tea to Aunt Lucy and set it before her.

"Who is he, Aunt Lucy?" she asked softly.

My aunt reached for the mug, cradling it to warm her hands, and stared, unseeing, into the brown liquid.

"I have no idea," she said.

I took a deep breath. "Never a card? What did you mean when you said, 'He knows I know'?"

Aunt Lucy brought the mug to her lips, took a tentative sip and carefully set the cup back on the table before she answered.

"The flowers, they're always the same ones, red tulips, violets, daffodils and lilies of the valley. I finally figured out he was sending me a message with them. Flowers have symbolic meaning, you know."

"Oh, wow," Nina breathed. "I, like, totally get this man, you know?"

Spike pinched her arm and shook her head in warning.

"What?" Nina whispered. "I don't think it's so bad."

"What is he saying, Aunt Lucy?" Jake asked.

Aunt Lucy drank a little more tea and seemed to steady herself. "Daffodils are a symbol of unrequited love. Violets say, 'I'll always be there, watching out for you. I'm faithful.' Red tulips are a declaration of love. They also mean 'believe me.' And lilies of the valley say, 'You've made my life complete.' They symbolize a return to happiness."

I shook my head. "Someone sends you flowers for years and you have no idea who it is?"

Aunt Lucy shook her head vigorously. "If I did, I would've put a stop to it years ago. In fact, I thought he'd given up. I didn't receive any flowers for over twenty years, then, a couple of months ago, they started again."

"That is so weird," Nina said.

Aunt Lucy looked around the table at us all. "You've got to believe me," she said. "I would never be unfaithful to my Benny." She looked down at the sleeping dog by her feet. "Benito," she murmured, "you do believe me, don't you?"

Lloyd opened one sleepy eye and smiled at my aunt. Good dog, I thought, good, good dog.

Aunt Lucy, temporarily satisfied, stood up and stepped away from the table. "I believe I'll go lie down," she said. "I'm very tired."

"Good idea," Spike said. "I'll carry your tea."

Aunt Lucy nodded and followed her down the hallway, looking for all the world like a tired, overwhelmed child.

While Aunt Lucy slept, the rest of us tried to make sense of her predicament. This was next to impossible. Flowers arrive annually for a few years, then stop, and then pick back up again over twenty years later. Nina closed her eyes and smiled dreamily.

"I am sensing someone from her past," she murmured. "Someone who loved her and, oh, my God." Her eyes popped open. "He died. Now, his son carries on the tradition."

I rolled my eyes. "Nina, what gave you that idea?"

She shrugged. "I don't question, I intuit. It's a gift, Stella.

You should try it. Just close your eyes and let your mind clear." She closed her eyes again. "Now, what is your brain telling you?"

We all stared at her. "Baloney!" I said.

Nina's eyes opened. "You're hungry?"

Jake interrupted. "I think your aunt's TV show started this. Maybe he hadn't thought of her in years and then, there she was."

"If it's even the same person," I added. "What if the two events aren't related at all? I mean, this most recent series of gifts goes beyond an annual flower arrangement. Now he's sending groceries."

Spike came back and wrapped her long slender fingers around her coffee cup and regarded us with a troubled look.

"Do you think he's dangerous?" she asked.

Jake said no, but I wasn't so sure. "Well, he's escalating. His gifts keep getting larger. He tracked her here. How could he have done that?"

Jake was frowning now. "I don't know about that one," he admitted. "It is strange that this guy found us."

"Well, if he's a nut he'll have to take a number. We've got enough psychos hunting us to populate a mental ward. All we can do is keep our guard up and make sure she's safe."

"What about your case?" Spike asked.

"Well, there are a few complications," I began. "For one thing, our client isn't who she says she is."

"But that's not uncommon," Jake added.

"Told you she had bad karma, didn't I?" Nina said to Spike.

"So you're still working for her?" Spike asked. The expression on her face clearly showed her disapproval.

I shrugged. "I figure we find this missing brother of hers, but before we tell her about it, we make her tell us who she is."

Jake sighed. "Look, we've got ten thousand dollars, cash. I've got a call in to a friend of mine. If she can't find out who we're dealing with and assure me that this is on the up-and-up, I'll be the first one to hand the money back, minus expenses and our daily fee, of course. For now, we need to keep looking."

Nina leaned back in her chair with a satisfied smile. "Does anyone at this table still doubt the need for a mission statement?" She slowly shook her head. "I think not."

I looked at her. "I think you need to go back to that library and see if you can't find out something about Doug Hirshfield, like where he lives, or what happened to him after high school. This time you might consider at least looking in those archives."

"Has anybody looked in the phone book?" Spike said, pulling the book out of a drawer.

"Been there," I answered. "He's not listed."

"Oh, well, it was worth a shot," she said, putting the book away.

"Okay, how about this," I said. "I'll take Nina back to the library so she can work her magic with the librarians *and* the archives. And I'll go to the nursing home and see if I can learn more there."

Spike frowned. "They won't release any information to you, you know. There are laws…"

I smiled at her. "I know all about the laws. I'm just saying Mrs. May might be more clearheaded today." But I was thinking the staff might be more careless if there was a distraction or two.

I saw the gathering thundercloud of disapproval on Jake's face.

"Of course," I added, "if you think we should do this another way, I can…"

The storm blew over. "No, what I need to do I can do here while I'm keeping an eye on your aunt."

Spike sighed. "I can go with you to the nursing home, if you'd like," she said. "Maybe you can find out what you need to know without, you know, breaking any laws."

I smiled at her. "You're a sport, Spike. Trust me, the trauma of your former career as an assistant district attorney will one day fade into oblivion and you will be just as corrupted as the rest of us are."

Spike raised an eyebrow. "I sincerely hope not," she said. "I intend to change the system from within."

"Virtuous," I said, "but sometimes impractical. However, I will do my best to stay within the legal limits and confines of the law, for your sake."

I crossed my fingers under the table.

Nina jumped up, looked at us still sitting around, and said, "Well, let's get a move on. The library closes at five, you know."

I looked at my watch. "Nina, it's only eleven. We haven't even had lunch yet."

Nina smiled. "I know. But developing relationships takes time. I need to bond with my women."

I started to say something sarcastic but stopped. Nina had turned out to be a highly skilled investigator. Her methods were strange, but they were, so far, very productive.

Spike and Nina went upstairs to gather up their coats and bags. Jake was leaning in the kitchen doorway and when I started past him, he reached out and grabbed me, pulling me close with a strong grip that said he meant business.

"Listen, you be careful," he said. "Joey Smack is gonna be pissed about us taking Lloyd back. And until we know more about our client…"

"I thought you said…"

"Never mind what I said. I'm checking her out."

I wanted to close my eyes, just for a moment, and step into his arms. The musky scent of him was intoxicating. I could feel him wanting me, could feel the raw energy that seemed to course between the two of us, and knew without a doubt that we would not wait much longer.

"So you're saying I'm right, we do need to check her out," I murmured.

Jake's hand cupped my chin as he raised my head to meet his lips. My eyes closed. My skin tingled with the anticipation of his lips on mine.

"You are such a smart-ass," he whispered. "Always have to be right."

I brought my hands up to touch the sides of his face, felt the rough stubble of beard, and pulled him to me, kissing him hard, not caring that he knew how badly I wanted him.

A low moan escaped from somewhere deep inside his chest and he gripped my shoulders. His tongue slipped inside my mouth, tasting me, exploring and promising. Only the sounds of Nina's and Spike's footsteps on the staircase kept us from losing complete control.

Jake pushed me away, still gripping my shoulders, and looked deep into my eyes.

"Be careful," he said. "I have big plans for you later. I wouldn't want you to mess them up by getting yourself in a jam."

I felt my stomach flip over as a shiver of anticipation reached every nerve ending in my body.

"Don't worry," I whispered. "I might just have a few plans of my own."

"Do you now?" His eyes twinkled and a grin tugged at the corners of his mouth.

"Oh, most definitely. If I were you, I'd rest up."

His eyes darkened dangerously. "Maybe you should be taking your own advice," he murmured.

Chapter 12

By the time the others reached the living room, I was standing at the door, keys in hand, and Jake was nowhere to be seen.

Nina gave me a knowing grin. "You are so not subtle," she said, giggling.

I felt my face redden. "Shut up."

I opened the door and was halfway out when I heard her tell Spike, "Look at her. She has beard burn on her cheeks. Five dollars says they get married."

Spike's answer was lost as I ran down the steps to Jake's truck. This was no time to be thinking about Jake Carpenter. We had work to do. I forced myself to return to cop mode, relying on the skills I'd built up over the past years to switch my mind back into a fighting, ever-vigilant professional attitude that had saved my life in the past and would protect all of us now.

But even after I dropped Nina at the library and drove to

the nursing home, I could feel Jake's body on mine and taste him on my lips. My mind was on the case at hand, but my body belonged to him.

Spike's anxiety was what finally pulled me all the way back to the reality of our situation. She practically levitated off the truck's bench seat, her body humming with paranoia.

"Don't worry," I said. "This'll be a piece of cake. Doug's phone number is probably written down on a piece of paper next to her bedside table."

But of course, it wasn't. First rule of private investigation: If it was right out in plain sight, if it was easy, they wouldn't have hired you.

"If it isn't, we'll just go to plan B," I added.

Spike frowned. "Plan B? Is plan B legal?" she asked, her tone edging into that of a professional attorney on the job.

"Sure it is," I said, mentally crossing my fingers.

I pulled into a parking space.

Spike hopped out of the truck, headed for the front door of the nursing home. I knew without asking that she didn't have any faith in my ability to find Doug's address, but that didn't matter. Results were the only thing that mattered.

The two of us slipped down the hallway, easily anonymous in the bustle of lunchtime preparations and medication checks. We couldn't have picked an easier time to visit Fred May's mother. Carts carrying covered trays rolled slowly down the corridors. Nurses wearing brightly patterned scrubs sorted through drawers on other carts, pulling out pills and pouring water into cups. Spike and I plastered smiles on our faces and walked as if we knew where we were going, which, in fact, we did.

I stopped outside of Mrs. May's door and looked at Spike. Inside we could hear the sounds of the TV blaring out a game show.

"She's a little hard of hearing," I cautioned.

Spike's eyebrow lifted. "So whatever we ask her will be broadcast down the hallway?"

I shook my head. "Just ask if she's seen Doug lately. That wouldn't be out of place."

"But she doesn't even know me," Spike protested.

I smiled. "Spike, she doesn't know anybody. She won't know she doesn't know you. Just tell her you're a friend of Doug's."

Spike looked as if she was about to bolt and run, but from inside the room an announcer yelled "Come on down," and I shoved her through the doorway.

Mrs. May was absorbed in her program, her wheelchair pulled close to the set, her eyes glittering with excitement as a model in an evening gown spun a giant wheel.

"Hey, sweetie," I said, touching the woman's shoulder. "Remember me?"

Mrs. May looked up at us, momentarily confused, then smiled.

"Why, of course I do, Maisy," she said. "Where have you been?"

I crouched down beside her wheelchair and pointed to Spike. "I brought an old friend of Doug's by. I thought you'd like to tell her all about how he's doing."

This brought an unexpected reaction. Tears formed in Mrs. May's eyes and her face crumpled.

"I can't, honey," she whispered. "He's dead."

Spike took over, edging me out of the way with a sharp look of disapproval.

"Here, sweetie," she said. "Here's a tissue."

She patted Mrs. May's arm softly and I stepped back. Mrs. May had told us the same thing yesterday, only I thought she was confused. Now I wasn't sure. Had both her sons died?

I stepped over to the bedside table, looking for anything that would tell me who to contact in case of emergency, and found nothing. I slowly slid the drawer open and began inspecting its contents. Nothing. A hairbrush. A picture of an elderly man, probably Mr. May, and a small box of tissues.

I slipped over to the dresser and pulled open the drawers one by one as Spike talked to Mrs. May about the game show. Again nothing. There was no indication that Mrs. May hadn't dropped into her room from Mars, bringing only pictures and no identifying papers or documents. I had only one other option, her medical chart.

I signaled to Spike. "Be right back," I whispered.

Her eyes widened with alarm. "Wait, I'm coming with you."

"Spike, I'm going to the nurses' station. It's the only way…"

Spike nodded, her lips compressed into a tight line. "I know. I'm coming with you. I'll distract them or something. Besides, if I don't come, you might get caught, then where would I be?"

"In the clear comes to mind."

Spike scowled. "Well, I can't let you get locked up. Nina'd kill me."

I grinned at her. "And that scares you? I didn't think anything scared Spike Montgomery."

Spike smiled, just a little bit, but nonetheless, it was a smile. "I didn't say it scared me. I just like to keep her happy, that's all."

I shook my head and walked out into the hallway. Up until now, I'd assumed Nina did far more worrying about what Spike thought and felt than Spike did about Nina. Obviously I'd been wrong. No great surprise; lately I'd been wrong about quite a few relationship issues.

We approached the nurses' station as if we owned it, Spike following my lead. The charts sat right behind the desk on a rolling rack, arranged in rows by room number. A few charts lay open on the desk where someone had been writing. People were everywhere, bustling up and down the hallway, in and out of rooms, but not behind the nurses' station.

I slipped around the counter, walked to the rack and grabbed the chart to room 131. Easy as pie. I stood for a second assessing the risk, determining my next move, and decided that walking off with the chart might call more attention to myself than just standing still and reading it.

I leaned against the counter using Spike for cover and began to rifle through the pages near the front.

"May I help you?"

A tall, thin man wearing a multicolored scrub top stood just in front of Spike, bending his body like a Gumby doll in an attempt to see past her to me.

Spike matched his contortions, leaning in closer to the counter and said, "No, I think we've got everything we need."

"Who are you?" the man asked.

"Who are we?" Spike echoed. "No one told you?"

This took him aback for a second. I flipped to the emergency-contact page and caught my breath. Doug Hirshfield wasn't dead after all. He was apparently quite well and living right here in town.

"Um," I said, poking my head around Spike's thin shoulders, "I could use a pen and a piece of paper. How about that notepad?"

I indicated a notepad by the man's elbow and was amazed when he turned and handed it to me.

"Marge Adams," I said, smiling. "Blue Cross, Blue Shield?"

Spike nodded, catching on. "Chart audit," she whispered. "Routine but completely unannounced. Regulations, you know."

The man nodded, fingers toying with the ends of his stethoscope nervously. "How's it look?" he murmured.

I scribbled the address and phone number down hastily while Spike fielded the question.

"Well, according to the HIPPA guidelines, there may be a few problems. For one thing, these charts just sitting out here where anyone could read them…"

"Oh, man. I knew it."

I pinched Spike's side softly. "Done," I whispered.

"We'll be in touch with the results in a few weeks," Spike said calmly. "Thank you for your patience."

As we walked away I could hear the guy behind us hastily rolling the chart rack back against the far wall.

We kept our pace brisk but unhurried, heading toward the exit and freedom.

"I hope that was worth it," Spike said.

"Completely. Hey, where'd you get all that stuff you were spouting back there?"

Spike shrugged and the beginnings of a smile tugged at the sides of her mouth. "It's just attorney stuff," she said. "I know a few phrases that pertain to almost every area of the law, just enough to make it sound like I know more than I do."

"Well, thank God," I said, passing through the exit and into the relative safety of the parking lot. "'Cause we got Doug Hirshfield's name and address out of that little dog-and-pony show."

"So is that where we're going now?" The excitement in Spike's voice was obvious. She'd had one adventure and was ready for more.

"Nope. Next we check in with Nina, and then we talk to Jake and see what he's found out about our client. You know, there's always the possibility that Doug Hirshfield isn't even the man we're looking for."

"But I didn't find any other record of—"

"I know, but we need to approach this thing cautiously. We don't even know who our client is yet."

Spike sighed, disappointed, and climbed up into the cab of the truck.

I started up the truck and pulled out of the nursing home's parking lot. I was as anxious as Spike to find out more, but there were too many other questions to answer first.

"Why don't you call Nina on her cell and see if she's ready to be picked up. Maybe she's found out something interesting."

Spike pulled her phone out of her bag and began dialing. I drove slowly in the direction of the library, casually inspecting the homes we passed and trying to imagine Surfside Isle in the busy summer season.

"Already?" I heard Spike say. "Okay, we'll be there in a minute." Spike laughed. "I know, that's a new world record for you, isn't it?"

Spike flipped the phone shut and turned to me. "She says she's done, and not only that, she has something to show us that will bust this case wide open."

"'Bust this case wide open.' She actually used those words?"

Spike laughed. "Yeah, she watches a lot of TV. But she sounds pretty excited, even for Nina."

I made the turn onto the block where the library was and caught a flash of white in my rearview mirror. As we rolled to a stop and Nina came walking toward the truck, the white Lincoln Town Car swung into view.

"Spike, tell Nina to hurry. We've got company."

Spike threw open the door and yelled, "Nina, run!"

Nina froze for a moment, eyes wide, and then turned her head slightly, aware now of the white car. She broke into a run, crossing the short distance to the truck and half hurling herself up into the cab. I tromped on the gas pedal and we were off, the Lincoln close on our tail.

"Is it Joey Smack?" Nina cried.

I glanced in the rearview mirror and spotted Cauliflower Ear at the wheel. "Yep," I answered. "Hold on."

I wrenched the wheel hard to the left, cut a sharp U-turn and tore off away from the library and closer into town.

"How're we going to lose them?" Spike asked.

"We're not." I said. "There's no way to lose them. The island's too small."

I shot past Marti's Café, cut right, rounded the block and came out in front of the courthouse.

"Now what?" Nina yelled.

"Watch."

I turned left again, cut behind the courthouse and made a beeline for the low-slung white brick police department. The Lincoln was barely a car length behind us.

"He's sticking a gun out the window!" Nina screamed.

I drew even with the police department, jumped the curb and drove right up to the double glass doors that marked the department entrance.

The look of surprise on Cauliflower Ear's face was priceless. He turned, said something to his short friend and the gun was abruptly withdrawn from view. Cauliflower gunned the engine, the Lincoln shot off, only to come to a screeching halt halfway down the block. The street was blocked by Tom's unmarked police car.

The driver's-side door was open and Tom was crouched behind it, a shotgun aimed directly in the path of the oncoming car.

"Oh, shit. Hold on."

I floored the truck into reverse, laying tire across the pavement of the street as I blocked the Town Car's retreat.

"Get out." I screamed. "Get inside the building."

The three of us piled out of the vehicle as Cauliflower Ear's car headed back in our direction, doing 35 mph in reverse. I pulled out my Glock, used the hood of the truck for cover while Spike half dragged Nina across the sidewalk and into the police department.

Tom and I had the street blocked. There was nowhere for the two goons to run, but they were armed and anything could happen.

The Town Car stopped. There was a hasty consultation between Cauliflower and the short man, followed by the short guy losing his temper and lashing out at Cauliflower's already mangled ear.

Tom reached for a megaphone and spoke into it.

"Get out of the car, now. Put your hands in the air where I can see them and get out slowly."

He looked around, turning the bullhorn in my direction, and then spoke into it again.

"Jake, that you?"

I smiled to myself and waved my gun at him over the hood of the car, knowing he couldn't hear me and also knowing he'd assume I was Jake when he saw the gun.

"I'm calling for backup," he said.

Like we needed backup.

The Lincoln's two front doors slowly opened. Cauliflower emerged from the driver's side, hands in the air. On the other side, the short guy also emerged from the car, but I could see the bulge in the back of his suit coat and knew he had other plans.

Cauliflower started to lie facedown in the street, but as I expected, the little man decided to run.

"I got him," I screamed, and took off, leaving Tom to cover Cauliflower.

Behind us I heard the door to the P.D. slam open as the promised backup began arriving.

For a short, beefy guy, the little man could run. He flew toward the courthouse, leaping a short fence as if it were a hurdle and continuing on. It took me almost fifty yards to catch up to him, and another five to bring him down.

I hopped on his back and we went crashing to the ground. There was a loud grunt as he hit, the air whooshing from his lungs and leaving him breathless. I sat on him, the muzzle of my Glock flush with the back of his skull, and thought for a moment about revenge.

Then the cop in me took over. I reached for the gun in his waistband and pulled it out, the adrenaline rush making my hands shake just slightly. I heard Tom issuing instructions, heard the sound of footsteps approaching and felt a slight twinge of regret that it was all over with so quickly. A deeper pain edged at my heart and for a moment I was almost breathless with the realization: I missed being a cop, missed it more than I'd ever realized.

"Stella," Tom cried. "I thought you were Jake."

He knelt by my side, pulled out his cuffs and was about to take over when I stopped him.

"Please," I said, meeting his eyes. "Allow me."

Without a word, Tom handed me his handcuffs and I snapped them onto the little man's thick wrists. I hopped off his back, tugged my prisoner to his feet just as I'd done a thousand times before and turned to see the look of acknowledgment on Tom's face.

"Hard to leave the job, isn't it?" he asked softly.

I nodded, feeling tears clog my throat and making speech impossible.

"I appreciate the assist," he said. "Wanna tell me about it over a cup of joe?"

I nodded again, this time embarrassed by the lone tear that escaped, snaking its way down my cheek. I brushed it away before the little guy could see it, but Tom didn't miss a thing.

"All right," he said. "Let's get this dirtbag inside and go have lunch with Marti."

He didn't wait for me to answer. He walked his prisoner toward the front door of the police department and handed him over to a young boy in a uniform. I figured the kid couldn't have been out of high school, but he was wearing a gun and a badge and seemed to have a handle on his captive. All I knew was that for that one moment, I would've traded places with him and maybe never looked back.

Spike and Nina rushed out of the building with Tom following behind them.

"I called Jake," Nina said. "He said to tell you not to mess up his truck and call him when you can."

"Don't mess up my truck." Typical Jakespeak for, "Be careful."

I smiled, looked behind them to see Tom standing in the doorway and called, "We'll meet you up there, okay?"

Tom threw up his hand. "Won't be more than a few minutes."

Taking a statement in a diner was certainly not standard police procedure, even in a town as slow and small as Surfside Isle, but I knew why Tom was making the exception. It was his way of acknowledging a fellow officer, even if I wasn't on the job anymore. It was his way of acknowledging my grief, by letting me talk to him about his two new prisoners just the way he'd talk to another detective. It was damn nice of him.

We climbed back into the truck and I turned the cumbersome vehicle back around and headed for Marti's.

Spike sat next to me, content to ride silently for a moment before asking in her quiet, steady voice, "You all right?"

I nodded. "Fine. Really. It was no big deal."

"All in a day's work, huh?" she murmured.

I looked at her, saw she'd read me, and nodded. "Yep."

She reached over and covered my free hand with one of her own, squeezing briefly before letting go.

"I know just how you feel," she said softly. And I was sure she did.

When we reached the diner, Marti met us at the door, menus in hand, grinning.

"Tom called," she said. "Told me he was meeting some pretty women for lunch. If I'd 'a known it was you, I wouldn't have stuck those thumbtacks on the seats."

She ushered us to a secluded booth and announced, "The special today is beef tips over rice. I highly recommend it."

"I'm not having lunch," Nina said, her chin tilted a bit defiantly.

"No?" Marti asked, no longer surprised by anything Nina said.

"Nope. I'm going to start with dessert. The way my day's gone, I figure I should eat dessert first, in case something happens and I don't get time for the good stuff." Nina frowned at us. "You know," she said. "There are no guarantees in life. It could all go *poof!* in an instant."

Marti nodded. "Well, in that case, coconut cake is the specialty of the day, and—"

"I highly recommend it!" we all shouted, laughing along with her.

"Does this mean you're all having cake?" Marti asked.

We nodded in unison.

"All right then," Marti said. "I'll have to join you. Be right back. Coffee?"

Another choral nod from the three of us and Marti disappeared into the kitchen.

"Oh, I almost forgot," Nina cried, and reached deep into her purse. "I found the most amazing things."

As we watched, Nina pulled a sheaf of copy paper from her purse, carefully unfolded it and slid one of the papers around to face my side of the table.

"See? There's your information. Tells you everything you need to know."

I pulled the paper closer and studied it. It was a small, one-column-wide article entitled, Local Man Earns Ph.D.

"It was buried in the 'Hometown Spotlight' section," Nina explained. "I almost missed it."

I scanned the article and learned that Doug Hirshfield had gone from earning his B.S. in physics at Yale to Columbia, where he'd managed to earn his Ph.D. in biomechanical engineering in 1992.

"Then what happened to him?"

Nina slid the second piece of copy paper toward me. A

small box revealed that Doug Hirshfield, of Quantico, Virginia, had attended the fiftieth wedding party held in his parents' honor in 1993.

Nina's smile disappeared as she added, "But I don't know where he is now. Nobody knows. I asked all of my friends at the library, but nobody had any idea. They said he never did anything but study as a kid, so they figured he was off working for some university or something."

I looked at the articles again. Quantico, Virginia, was the home of the FBI, wasn't it? What were the odds one of our top-secret agencies had need of the services of a biomechanical engineer? Quite good I thought.

"Don't worry about it, honey," Spike said. "Stella got the address from the nursing home."

Nina's eyes widened. "Fred's mom was feeling better?"

Spike and I shook our heads and smiled.

"No." Nina breathed, turning to Spike. "Oh, baby, I am totally impressed. You broke the law to help my cousin? Oh, that is like, such a turn-on."

Spike's cheeks colored and I couldn't stop a giggle from escaping.

"Oh, wait. There's this, too," Nina added. "Look."

Nina slid one last piece of paper in my direction. The article was entitled, Local Author Celebrates Another Bestseller, but it wasn't the article that caught my attention. Beneath the text was a photograph with the caption "Fred and Tonya May at Korean Embassy Dinner." I studied the picture, noting the couple standing beside the Korean dignitary. They were dressed for a black-tie affair, with Fred in a tux and his wife in a strapless, sequined gown.

I picked up the paper and held it closer to the light from the outside window, seeing now what had excited Nina. The woman in the photograph had long blond hair, but there was no mistaking her identity. Mia Lange, our phantom client, stood smiling out at me from her place beside her deceased husband.

"Holy shit."

Nina nodded, beaming as Spike took the paper from my hands and looked for herself.

"Mia Lange?" she breathed.

"The one and only." Nina grinned. "Before they separated."

I gaped at her, openmouthed. "Separated?"

Nina enjoyed her triumph of knowledge. "Yep. Divorce was final two weeks before he died. Here."

She slid one final piece of paper across the table. It held the one-line newspaper listing of Fred's divorce from Tonya.

I sat back against the seat and saw Tom enter the diner. Marti met him, tray in hand, and nodded toward our booth.

"We're going to have to make this the shortest lunch in the history of humankind," I said, stuffing the papers in my purse. "I can't wait to show this to Jake."

"What about Tom? Should we tell him?" Spike asked, her voice pitched low so he wouldn't overhear.

I shrugged. "I'd rather talk to Jake first. Something tells me we might not have all the pieces of the puzzle."

My head was spinning with all the possibilities. Mia Lange was really Tonya May, Fred's wife, and Doug Hirshfield was her brother-in-law and not her brother. So why would Tonya May be unable to locate her former brother-in-law? And since she wasn't looking for a kidney for her ailing sister, why was she looking for Doug?

I felt my stomach tighten and it was all I could do to wait for Tom to reach the booth and slide in beside me. I felt as if somewhere a clock was ticking and if we didn't reach it in time, horrible things might happen. I knew this feeling was irrational, that I had no basis in fact to support this, but felt panic growing inside myself anyway. Something was wrong, bad wrong, I just knew it, but there was nothing I could do.

Instead, I needed to sit patiently, hear what Tom had to say and answer his questions. Everything would fall into place eventually, investigations always did. You worked the clues a step at a time and in the end, patience paid off. It was just hard to see that now.

The real names of Joey Smack's enforcers were unimportant. The fact that they had rap sheets long enough to paper an entire neighborhood merely meant that Joey was taking his current gripe seriously enough to send his very best. However, since they seemed to have been frequently arrested, their skill was somewhat in question. How good could you be if you were continuously arrested?

Tom took their arrests seriously, as I would have had I been in his place, but to me, it was just another snag in an already crazy investigation. I was so anxious to reach Jake I barely heard what Tom had to say about Cauliflower Ear and the little man.

Spike, Nina and I wiggled and squirmed our way through lunch, and when we were at last free to go, we had to fight to keep from running out the door of the diner.

"This is going to blow Jake's mind!" Nina said as we drove down the street to the beach house.

"What in the world?" I cried, spotting the house. "Look! What is that?"

Ahead of us, parked in the center of the driveway, was a black sedan with government plates and dark, tinted windows.

Chapter 13

The three of us climbed down out of the truck and circled the black Ford. Spike met my eyes with a concerned frown.

"Things just get stranger and stranger," she muttered.

"Might as well go see what's up," I said. "We won't find out by standing around out here."

Nina was already heading for the front door. She looked especially Ninaesque today. Her blond spiky hair was frozen into stiff spears that stood out at angles all over her head. She wore pink platform sandals that laced up her ankles, and in a nod to the frigid temperature, she had added purple-and-gray striped socks. She wore a fairly conservative suit, for Nina; tight black leather miniskirt and matching black biker jacket, complete with an emblem on the back proclaiming her to be a member of the Triad Leather Club. The outfit was a recent acquisition from the local thrift store.

I watched her ascending the steps and thought of the un-suspecting government agent inside and smiled. This would be interesting. And then I remembered Jake's phone message to his government friend, the one he'd called Baby, and wondered if the mystery woman had taken it upon herself to deliver her information on our client in person.

Nina's body shielded me from our guests. I heard voices as we stepped into the living room, but couldn't see anything until Nina abruptly moved out of the way and left me face-to-face with Jake's friend "Baby."

Baby was the kind of woman who makes other women want to resign from their gender. You look at her and think, why bother? She was tall, maybe five-eight, with long, straight black hair and ice-blue eyes. Her complexion was flawless. She didn't wear makeup, she didn't need to. Her eyelashes were indecently long. Her nose was straight, perfectly shaped and pointed, like an arrow, to full, kissable lips. She even smiled.

She wore her standard-issue government suit as if it had been custom cut to fit her sleek, flawless body. Even the bulge of her gun beneath the suit jacket somehow managed to look like a come-on. Long, muscled legs, the bearing of an athlete—it was all there in one perfect package. I wanted to hate her, but why bother?

"Stella," Jake said, "this is Sheila Martin."

I shook her hand, felt the strength of her grip, and felt my heart plummet about twelve thousand feet. Surely Jake was in love with her. What man in his right mind wouldn't be?

"And this is Barry Kincaid," he said, his tone hardening just enough for me to pick up the warning in it.

Barry Kincaid was invisible next to Sheila Martin. He was tall, handsome, clean-cut and a mere two-dimensional object next to his dazzling companion. He was the type of agent you send in to do surveillance, while Sheila was a Mata Hari seductress.

Jake took the lead. "Stella is my partner in the agency," he said as we all sat down. "I think she should hear this."

Barry Kincaid cleared his throat softly, looked at Spike and Nina, and seemed about to say something, but Jake interrupted.

"They're also investigators with the agency. They need to be here, as well." Jake's tone said end of discussion.

Sheila looked at Jake and smiled. When he smiled back, I saw their history as clear as if they'd shown me the video. When she turned and smiled at me, it was a business smile, the kind that doesn't extend to friendship but wouldn't preclude it, either. Nicely neutral.

"Jake called earlier and asked about Douglas Hirshfield. When I called him back and he told me a little bit more about your investigation, I figured we might need to come up and talk."

I nodded, waiting for the shoe to drop.

"We believe your client is a person of interest to this agency," she said.

"A person of interest," Spike said. "That means she's under investigation?"

Good old Spike, never show your hand. Good girl. Spike wasn't telling what we knew, merely setting Sheila up to give us more than she probably intended.

"It's no big deal," Barry Kincaid interjected. "We just think…"

His voice trailed off as Sheila looked at him.

"We just think it would be better if you dropped the investigation. I know you wouldn't want to compromise a possible matter of national security."

Her smile was so smooth. You almost couldn't help wanting to please her.

"What about Doug Hirshfield?" I asked. "Wasn't that why you called her, Jake? I mean, how did you realize Mia Lange was an object of interest to your agency if she's using an assumed name?"

I saw the corners of Spike's mouth twitch. Score one for our team, I thought.

Barry tried to field the question. "It's one of her aliases," he said. "We recognized it."

Hmm. One of her aliases, eh?

"So you were looking for her?" I asked.

Sheila laid one restraining hand on Barry's knee, but it was too late. "No, we knew where she was, we just don't want her—"

"You don't want her to find Doug Hirshfield?" I finished for him. "Why not?"

Sheila looked at Jake, as though maybe he was supposed to rein me in, but Jake was looking at me, a puzzled expression on his face.

I frowned, questions flooding my head. Why wouldn't Fred May's widow know where her brother-in-law was? Why wouldn't she look for him herself? Maybe she knew he didn't want her to find him. Maybe she didn't want him to know she was looking. Why?

I smiled at Sheila. "Does our client pose a danger to Mr. Hirshfield? I mean, I could understand you wanting us to stop helping her if she posed a danger."

Sheila's expression grew serious. "I'm sorry. I can't tell you anything more. It would compromise our investigation."

"But you're shadowing her, right?"

Sheila looked wary now. "We can't always be everywhere at all times. We wouldn't want to create a situation of unnecessary risk. I'm sure you understand."

So it seemed to me that Mia wanted to hurt her former brother-in-law from Quantico, the same town these folks came from. Why would Mia want to hurt a government scientist? Had he possibly done something to her? Had he hurt someone she loved and this was payback?

I considered Fred May. Would Mia care if Doug had hurt Fred? Mia and Fred had been separated at the time of Fred's death. Had Doug done something to cause the separation?

Or, more likely, I thought, had Mia done something and Fred reacted?

Furthermore, why would the government care about a war between brothers? The government would only care if something happened to compromise security. Bingo.

I straightened in my chair, leaned forward and smiled at Sheila.

"I'm thinking it's like this," I said softly. "Doug Hirshfield works for the CIA. Maybe Mia had an affair with Doug, and in the process learned something you didn't want her to know, or took something Doug was working on."

The imperceptible flinch from Sheila meant I'd scored a direct hit. Jake was now staring at me as if I'd once again played a wild card without consulting him. Oh, well. I couldn't help that, at least not now.

"I'm sorry, Ms. Valocchi," Sheila said. "We're not at liberty to discuss that."

I smiled. "So Mia hired us to put you off her trail, and if we don't help her, she won't find him. But what if she does? Are you protecting him? I mean, she seems to know he lives here. And why would she want to find him if she already has what she wanted?"

Sheila was silent.

"If she's the object of an investigation, if she has something you want, or knows too much, then you must be looking to prosecute her. You'd have her safely locked away then, unless you people still assassinate civilians."

I went on quickly, not waiting for the reaction to my incendiary remark. "Ah," I said, leaning back in my chair, "I bet Doug's a witness. And since you haven't arrested her yet, Mia must have taken something and you don't know where it is."

"You're wrong," Sheila said, her smile just a bit hesitant. "But you have a wonderful imagination, doesn't she, Jake?"

She turned to him, the smile a thousand watts of pure seduction, and I'll admit it, I felt a distinct twinge of jealousy.

"Okay, Ms. Martin," I said, "let's just lay all our cards out here, shall we?"

The two agents were more than a little uncomfortable, but it took a cop's eye to see it: the dilated pupils, the shallow but increasingly rapid respirations, the mild agitation that showed in the way Barry Kincaid shifted his feet ever so slightly, but constantly.

"Mia Lange may be using an alias now, but she was also Fred May's wife. Fred May, the author of bestselling espionage novels, the man who circled the fringes of the intelligence community and hobnobbed with diplomats. Add to the mix his adopted brother, Doug, a biomechanical engineer working for the CIA on top-secret projects. You read about these things all the time, government workers selling secrets to foreign agents. How hard would it have been for Mia to gain access to her brother's home?"

Sheila shook her head. "That's all speculation," she said. "It makes wonderful fiction but very poor reality. Doug Hirshfield was a brilliant scientist, but hardly the intelligence guru you're making him out to be."

"Was?" I echoed.

Sheila's eyes darkened. "Was. He died almost three years ago. He had a stroke. So you see your speculations are groundless."

"Then why is Mia looking for him?" I asked quietly.

Sheila shrugged. "I have no idea. Perhaps she doesn't know he's dead. I believe she and Fred were already separated when Doug died."

"You think she wouldn't have heard?" Jake asked, entering the discussion.

Sheila met his gaze. "It was hardly a big news event. It might not have even made the local papers, let alone reached Tonya May. Beyond that speculation, I can't say. But I would appreciate it if you didn't tell your client. I really couldn't stop you, but you would be doing our investigation a terrible disservice as well as placing others at risk."

"Wait a minute," I said. "Doug is listed as Mrs. May's next of kin," I said. "Who pays for her nursing-home care if Doug's dead? Why is he listed as an emergency contact? Why does he have a local address?"

Barry Kincaid smiled to himself but remained silent.

Sheila said, "We pay her bills. Mrs. May has Alzheimer's. She wouldn't know her own children. We provide the nursing home with what they need in order to continue providing Mrs. May with care. It prevents unnecessary questions."

Sheila stood, signaling Barry Kincaid to join her, and looked around the room at the rest of us.

"In this time of political unrest," she said, "our national security is of utmost importance. I'm sure you all appreciate this. I would also appreciate it if you kept what I've told you to yourselves. Lives would be at risk if this information became common knowledge. I know you wouldn't want that to happen. I know you meant well by taking your client's case, but I guess you were just too good."

Sheila smiled and turned to take Jake's hand.

"I'm just grateful you called and we could talk. Hopefully, you will respect our wishes, even if you don't fully understand the reasoning or the logic behind it. If Mia Lange calls, I suggest you tell her your investigation led to a dead end and offer to return her retainer. Don't worry, we'll reimburse you."

Jake seemed dazed almost. He nodded, but I could tell his thoughts were far away.

The two agents left. As the door closed softly behind them, Nina breathed an audible sigh of relief.

"So like, do you think they're real?" She looked around the room, hopped up and crossed to the mantel, lifted a pottery vase and peered deep inside.

"What are you doing, baby?" Spike asked.

Nina spun back around. "Just checking. I thought maybe somebody nominated us for a new reality TV show or something." She stiffened, pulled her mouth down into a straight, hard line and fluffed imaginary hair. "Our national security is at risk," she mimicked. "Please. They don't really talk like that."

Spike frowned. "Well, Nina, now, I don't know. Have you turned on CNN lately? They all talk like that."

I looked at Jake. "So what did you think?"

He stretched and stood. "I think you've got some explaining to do," he said. "What was all that about Mia being Fred May's wife?"

Nina and I spent the next ten minutes updating Jake while Spike busied herself putting the teakettle on to boil and cleaning up the leftover lunch dishes. Lloyd emerged from Aunt Lucy's bedroom, signaling her impending arrival, and Jake asked one final question.

"How did you know that Mia—Tonya—whatever her name is, had taken something from Doug?"

I grinned at him. "Lucky guess. I mean, it's not such a stretch, is it? She asked us to find a man who's practically family to her. She instructed us not to approach him or tell him she was looking for him. Why? Her husband divorces her. Why? Doug died right before they separated, if you believe your friend Baby. If that were true, why wouldn't Tonya know about it? I just figured Tonya doesn't believe he's dead, or else, she wants to make sure he is. If she stole something from him, something valuable and top secret, he'd know. He'd be able to pin the theft on her. That's why I think she wants to find him. I think she wants to know he's dead or else kill him herself."

Nina couldn't contain herself. "Then it *is* a matter of national security," she said. "And we can help."

Spike shook her head. "No, now, Nina, I think we should just leave this to the experts."

Nina scowled. "Yeah, what good have they done, huh? They're just following her around. I think we are the perfect people to set a trap for her. I think we should tell her we've found her brother and see what happens."

"What do you think will happen, Nina?" I asked.

She smiled. "Well, if it's a good trap, she'll come down and try to kill the decoy. Wouldn't that prove she has something to hide? Wouldn't that give the CIA something to work with?"

Jake shook his head. "I don't think so, honey. I think it would only confuse matters."

I was sitting at the kitchen table, doodling on a piece of paper while I tried to sort out fact from fiction. The government said Doug Hirshfield was dead. Our client seemed to think he wasn't. What did either party have to gain from lying to us? If we believed Doug Hirshfield was dead, there would be no more reason to search for him. If we didn't look for him, we wouldn't work for Tonya May. If we didn't work for her, she wouldn't find her ex–brother-in-law, or at least, she'd have to start all over again and that would keep Doug hidden.

If we believed Doug Hirshfield was alive and that Sheila Martin was lying, then we had to believe we had made the government uncomfortable by looking for him. And why would Tonya May pay ten thousand dollars to a private investigator if she knew, or even had reason to believe, her brother-in-law was dead? Did she just want to be sure? If so, why not give us his name and shorten the process?

The questions rumbled around in my head like clothes in a Laundromat dryer. It was all out in front of us, in plain sight, but who could tell what was what? Furthermore, didn't we have an obligation to make sure Doug Hirshfield wasn't in danger? If he were alive, would the government be watching out for him? Surely they would, but had we now jeopardized his safety by coming so close to finding him? And were we even close?

I looked up and found Jake watching me. It was as if he read my thoughts and for once agreed with me.

"You want to check it out, don't you?" he said.

I nodded. "I don't like feeling stupid, like the wool's been pulled over my eyes. I want to know who's been playing me, and then I want to do something about it."

Spike walked over to the kitchen table and stood beside Jake. She was frowning and obviously needed to say something.

"What is it, Spike?"

She shook her head. "I'm not sure. I've been trying to recall exactly what Jake's friend said about Mrs. May. When you asked why Doug's name was listed as his mother's next of kin, didn't she say that they'd been paying the bill, doing it because they didn't want to upset Mrs. May or raise unnecessary questions?"

I thought back and nodded. "Yes, that's what she said."

Spike's frown deepened. "That's what I thought," she said. "There's only one small problem with that statement."

We all looked at her, waiting for the former assistant district attorney to make her case.

"A problem?" Jake prompted.

"Yes," Spike said. "Fred was still alive when his brother allegedly died. Why wouldn't his name be on the record as next of kin? Wouldn't that be the most logical solution? Why would the CIA ever be involved when Doug's attorney should've administered his estate?"

Spike looked at us, her eyes darkening into bottomless black pools of concern.

"You're right, Stella," she said. "Doug Hirshfield isn't dead."

In the momentary silence that followed, Aunt Lucy's footsteps sounded in the hallway. Discussion of Doug Hirshfield stopped, as all of us made a concerted effort to lift Aunt Lucy's spirits.

* * *

We spent the afternoon playing Scrabble around the kitchen table. As I pretended to focus on the game, an idea came to mind. I leaned over to Jake and whispered, "I've got a plan, but we need to wait for dark."

Aunt Lucy looked our way, and I smiled. "Just looking for *Q*'s," I said. If Aunt Lucy sensed the underlying tension that seemed almost overwhelming to me, she didn't mention it. When she'd finally whipped us all soundly, she stood up and looked at her assembled family members.

"Some people can sit around all day acting like they're retired. I have dinner to prepare, and if I remember correctly, you people are trying to find a missing person. Now, either something's changed, or you no longer need the money. Which is it?"

Nina flushed deep pink and busied herself putting the board game away. Spike and Jake deferred to me and I took a deep breath before attempting a plausible explanation.

"The, um, computer data bank that houses the information we're waiting on has lost touch with its server," I said. "So we're sort of on hold."

"Hmmph," she said. "And to think I actually thought those government agents had something to do with it."

"How did you know about that?" I sputtered.

Aunt Lucy just looked at me.

"I thought you were sleeping."

She sighed. "Your uncle here woke me up. So I listened. Big deal. I just think you ought to be about taking care of this mess and not fooling around playing Scrabble with an old lady! I'm fine. So I get a few boxes of groceries and some flowers from a nutcase? That was then, this is now. Life goes on. So quit holding my hand and do something productive. You people drive me nuts!"

That was Aunt Lucy, all right. Down, but never out. Back in the game before you knew it.

I smiled and patted her arm.

"We had to let the news settle a bit," I said. "We weren't baby-sitting you."

Lloyd moaned, begging to differ, I suppose.

"All right, so maybe we were a little worried."

Aunt Lucy shook her head and moved toward the refrigerator. "I'm starting to think your cousin was right about you. You do need a mission statement."

Jake was watching us and smiling. He loved to see me catch hell from Aunt Lucy. Finally, he took pity on me and spoke up.

"We've got a plan, Aunt Lucy," he said. "But we're waiting for it to get dark."

His eyes twinkled when he looked at me and I caught my breath.

I looked away, willing myself not to think about the two of us. Instead, I concentrated on the task ahead. It seemed fairly simple. We would go to Doug Hirshfield's house, see whether he lived there or not, and if he did, let him know that his ex-sister-in-law was on his trail. We could leave it at that, but at least then we could walk off with a clear conscience. We would no longer be responsible for inadvertently putting him at risk because of our own ignorance.

With all the government screwups these days, I figured a little help from the private sector would at least give Doug Hirshfield an opportunity to take matters into his own hands. And then I was going to address the matter of Jake's decision to accept this case without thoroughly checking out our client. Nina and Aunt Lucy were right. We needed a mission statement.

Chapter 14

"Let's see the address," Jake said.

We were upstairs in the bedroom we shared, pulling on the black sweats Nina had found at Handy Mart and layering T-shirts and socks beneath them in an attempt not to freeze when we went looking for Doug Hirshfield's house.

I'd been ignoring Jake, grabbing my clothes and then scooting down the hall to change in the bathroom. I couldn't allow myself to be distracted by the thoughts and images that kept appearing without warning in my mind's eye. I needed to stay sharp and aware. I needed to get this business over with and then think about having a personal life, maybe.

Jake seemed equally anxious to avoid the subject of last night. He'd stayed tight and focused throughout dinner and was no different now that we were alone.

He scanned the piece of paper I handed him, looked at the street map he'd spread out on the bed and seemed to arrive at a conclusion.

"It's about twelve blocks from here," he said. "I think we should walk it. I think we should take Lloyd, head for the beach and see if anyone follows us."

"So you think Baby doesn't trust you?" I asked, but I'd already drawn the same conclusion.

A tiny muscle in Jake's jaw began to twitch. He was irritated.

"I think she's good at her job," he said evenly. "I think if I were her, I'd watch us. I also think she'd watch Doug's house, if he's alive and living there. If we're not followed and the house isn't under watch, then we can turn around and come back home."

I took a deep breath and exhaled slowly. We would come back to the beach house and then what? I studied his profile as he searched the map. No doubt about it, if we were left alone in a room tonight, he would be mine by morning.

Stop that. No thoughts like that now.

I picked up my coat, turned away from him and headed for the door.

"I'll see you downstairs," I said and left.

When he met me in the living room a few minutes later, I'd reverted to my professional, hands-off persona. I felt in control again and ready to work.

Lloyd danced around our legs, half tripping us as we negotiated our way out of the house and down to the street. He sniffed, joyously happy to be out and on the run again. I watched him, sure he was sniffing for recent traces of his new love, Fang; envious that for her, life could be so simple.

"What're you thinking?" Jake asked.

"I'm thinking I don't see any signs of a tail," I said.

"You're sure?"

"Yeah, I don't see anybody. Why, did you pick something up?"

I looked anxiously over my shoulder, scanning the empty houses, trying to see whatever it was he'd seen, and failing.

Jake grinned and took my hand in his.

"I meant, are you sure that's what you were thinking," he said. "You looked sort of far away." I moved to grab my hand back and he tightened his grip. "Don't you think it looks better if we at least act like we're taking a friendly stroll?"

Jake stopped beneath the lone streetlamp on the block and pulled me into his chest. He cupped my chin with his hand, brought my face up to meet his lips and kissed me. It was not a stage kiss. It was deep, long and searching. It was a kiss that rekindled a hot flame inside my body and took away all thought of the winter temperature. I was suddenly on a beach in the Caribbean, too hot for comfort and yearning to strip off every stitch of clothing that prevented my skin from touching his. Damn. How did he do that?

When he pulled away, I gasped for breath, filling my lungs with cold air and trying desperately to maintain some sense of composure. My body was screaming for his touch and when he moved to continue our walk, I felt cheated.

"What was that?"

"Insurance," he answered.

"Against?"

Jake grinned. "It's double-indemnity insurance. If anyone's watching, they think we're two lovers looking for some time alone. If we're truly alone, it's a reminder of what I have in store for you later."

He took my hand again and kept strolling down the sidewalk, following Lloyd as if he had no other agenda. My knees were shaking, but my mind had already jumped to payback mode. Okay, so it was a game to him. Well, I could play every bit as well as he did.

"But, Jake," I said softly, "you don't know what your touch does to me."

He glanced over at me, uncertain. I widened my eyes and tried to look almost but not quite scared. He stopped and stared down into my eyes. My breath caught in my throat. My heart beat double-time as I reached for his collar and pulled his lips close to mine.

"I want you, Jake. I want to feel your skin on mine. I want to taste every inch of your body. I want to know what pleases you."

And then I kissed him, biting his lip and sucking it gently, feeling the response that came washing over me like a tidal wave.

I pushed him away then and smiled. "Gotcha," I murmured. "Just wanted to purchase a little bit of that insurance policy for myself."

The slight moan that escaped his lips was my reward. *Don't play with me, Big Man. I'm more heat than you can handle.* I cautioned him silently.

Lloyd suddenly broke into a run, sprinting for the beach at top speed. We hurried after him, the game forgotten as alarm bells began ringing in my head. When we crossed the dunes and the ocean came into view, I saw her. Fang was waiting for Lloyd down by the water's edge, her silver coat gleaming in the moonlight, head thrown back, throat exposed as she uttered a long, beckoning howl.

"Lucky bastard," Jake muttered.

I watched Lloyd rush to meet his girlfriend and had to agree with Jake. It was a dog's life all right.

The two of us trailed after the dogs, slowly making our way along the outline of the shore toward Doug Hirshfield's oceanfront home. We made a perfect picture to any outside observer, two couples enjoying a romantic romp along the beach, wrapped up in each other, not a care in the world.

The dogs circled back after we'd walked for close to ten minutes and stayed close, Lloyd following his Australian sheepdog roots to herd and Fang following him because it was probably a game to her.

"Shouldn't we be close?" I asked.

Jake nodded and pointed to a streetlight at the end of a street. "I've been counting. This should be it. His house should be the third one on the left."

I squinted, trying to see the details in the house. As we walked closer, I felt a twinge of disappointment. There was no sign that it was occupied. It looked like every other house along that row, closed for the season, windows boarded against the hurricanes of fall and the nor'easters of winter.

Fang broke away and ran in a straight line toward the house, looking back and waiting briefly to make sure we were behind her.

"How does that dog always know where we're going?" I asked.

Jake shrugged. "Maybe she doesn't. Maybe she's just running to investigate."

I didn't buy it. Fang was smarter than most dogs. I didn't think she ran without purpose and I didn't for a minute think she didn't know our destination.

When she ran up to the back door of the house and scratched at it, I knew she was trying to tell us something.

We stood in the shadows watching Fang whine and scratch, searching the surrounding lots and houses for any signs of surveillance. When my cell phone rang, I jumped.

"Hello?"

"Hey, beautiful," Pete said. "I've got news."

I looked at Jake, mouthed Pete's name and shrugged. "What?"

Pete's tone deepened. "Where are you?" he asked.

I sighed, exasperated. This was so like him. "I'm walking along the beach. So what is it you wanted to tell me?"

"He's right there, isn't he?"

Another long sigh. "Yes."

Pete chuckled. "So you can't tell me how bad you miss me, huh, baby?"

Oh. My. God. What woman in her right mind would ever take Pete seriously? And what had ever make me think I was going to be the one to change him?

"Pete."

"All right, all right. Don't get huffy now, baby. I was just playing with you."

"The news?"

"Oh, yeah. Well, remember when I said I hadn't found a criminal record on your client's sister yet?"

I stopped feeling impatient and began paying serious attention. "Yeah?"

"Well, I kept looking. She didn't have a record in Glenn Ford or anywhere else in Pennsylvania, but she does have one in New Jersey."

"Oh, really?"

Jake was inching closer to the beach house, leaving me behind to listen to Pete.

"Yeah. Petty shit mostly. A DWI, shoplifting to start and then she graduated up to a higher class of crime. They got her on embezzlement of a former employer. Looks like she was the bookkeeper for a dry-cleaning business. Anyway, she's on probation for another year."

So Tonya's sister was a petty crook, so what?

"Well," Pete said, "there is a little more."

The man just loved hearing me beg.

"What else, Pete?"

"She's working for a crook."

I was stamping my feet in the sand, trying not to freeze, and growing steadily more impatient with my former boyfriend.

"Pete, can you just cut to the chase? I'm freezing. How do you know she's working for a crook, and what's she doing working for somebody with a record? Isn't she breaking her probation?"

Pete chuckled. "I didn't train no slouch, did I?" he crowed.

"That's right, sweetheart, she's breaking her probation and they seem to know all about it. When I called, they gave me the name and address of the guy. When I ran him, he came back dirty. Now I'm thinking they would've done the same thing and checked their parolee's employer, but maybe that's just your bureaucratic machinery at work. Maybe they just haven't gotten around to busting her yet."

"What does this have to do with my client, Pete?"

I watched Jake disappear around the side of the house and felt my anxiety level slowly rise.

"Well, it all leads back to your client. You see, this Carla Bucknell has a sister, Tonya, and she has a record, too. Seems like she was a nurse for a while, only she got into trouble for taking the drugs she was supposed to be giving her patients. That cost her big time. No more nursing license. She refused rehab and they yanked her license. So you're working for a junkie, baby."

I sighed. So Tonya was into drugs; always a good motive for thievery.

"And your client's sister works for a guy who's got a rep-utation for supplying needy addicts with all the nose candy they could ever want."

How did Pete know all this?

"Who does she work for, Pete?"

There was silence as Pete enjoyed his moment.

"You do want me, don't you, baby?" he murmured.

"Pete! Tell me who she works for!"

"All right, all right. God. Your client's sister works for a mob guy named Joey Spagnazi. Ever hear of him?"

"Jesus."

"I'm good, baby," Pete laughed, "but not that good." The phone was muffled for a moment and in the background I heard a female squeal and then Pete saying, "Hey, come back here."

I flipped the phone shut, reopened it and cut the thing off

before slipping it back into my coat pocket. So while some things became clearer to me, others became hopelessly entangled. Tonya was a junkie. Her sister worked for the alleged largest supplier of cocaine in southeastern Pennsylvania. And he claimed we had something he wanted. This all had to tie into Tonya, but how exactly?

Jake, Lloyd and Fang rounded the far corner of the house and began walking toward me. When he reached me, he shook his head.

"Nobody's in there," he said. "I doubt anyone's been there in months. Let's go."

He started off but I grabbed his arm, detaining him.

"Don't you want to know who that was on the phone?"

Jake pulled the collar of his coat up around his neck, blew on his hands and rubbed them briskly together.

"I know who it was. Pete, right?" I nodded. "Well, what did he want?"

When I finished telling Jake everything Pete had told me, he uttered a long, slow whistle.

"Good work for old Pete," he said. "So Tonya's a junkie and her sister, Carla, works for Joey Smack. Hmm. Wonder how this all comes together?"

He started walking. "Come on, it's freezing out here. Let's go home and think about this where it's warm."

I swallowed hard and started after him, the words *someplace warm* echoing in my head.

Spike and Nina were waiting for us in the living room when we returned. Behind them in the kitchen, Aunt Lucy again tinkered with beakers and Bunsen burners. When Lloyd entered the house with Fang trailing behind him, Aunt Lucy looked up and smiled.

"So you brought your friend, did you?" she asked Lloyd. "Good. I have treats for you both."

Fang walked quietly to my aunt and nuzzled her hand.

Aunt Lucy bent to stroke the huge dog's head, murmuring gently into her ear as she did so. Lloyd, not wanting to be left out, nosed his way in between the two, insisting upon attention.

"Isn't that just like a man?" Spike murmured.

"Hey, I object, Counselor," Jake protested.

"Really?" I said.

Jake ignored me and headed for the jug of Chianti that sat out on the counter.

"Any takers?" he asked, and not one of us refused him.

The house was warm, the table lamps shedding a yellow glow that seemed to turn the shabby furniture cozy and make the entire atmosphere more like home. The four of us sat, sipping our wine, rehashing the evening's events, and agreeing that we probably hadn't caused Doug Hirshfield any danger by looking for him.

"He's probably miles away from here, in some government facility for safekeeping," Spike offered.

"I bet that Tonya's looking to kill him," Nina said. "I bet she lured him into bed with her and stole his government secrets. I bet she wants to kill him before he tells on her."

Jake smiled behind her back. Nina's analysis was simplistic, but probably true. Why else would Tonya be looking for him?

Jake built a fire in the fireplace and eventually we were all lulled into silence, listening to music that Nina picked out and played on the cottage's antiquated sound system. Spike pulled Nina back into her arms, cradling her against her chest as they lay on the couch watching the orange flames dance across the logs.

Jake filled my glass again, walked to the armchair where I sat and perched on its arm. Neither of us said a word for what seemed like hours. Then, when I'd finished my wine, he reached over, took the glass from my hand and placed it gently on an end table.

He stood up, reached for my hand and pulled me up onto my feet.

Without a word, he turned and would have started for the stairs had I not stopped him. If I followed him like this, holding his hand, wouldn't everyone know where we were going and what would happen after that?

He turned back, saw me glance at the others with a cautionary frown and nodded.

"You're right," he whispered, dropping my hand. "What was I thinking?"

My chest relaxed.

"Good night, everyone," he said. "See you in the morning."

I stopped breathing, saw Nina and Spike glance up briefly to offer their own good-nights and then return to their conversation beside the fire. Aunt Lucy was nowhere to be seen, and as Lloyd and Fang had also disappeared, I assumed she'd gone off to bed without me realizing it.

I felt my heart pounding in my ears, my feet seemed to blindly follow in Jake's wake and I found myself walking up the stairs behind him.

When we reached the upstairs landing I stopped, yanking him to a halt.

"What are you doing? They're going to think we're…we're going upstairs to… Jake, what will they think?"

He seemed unmoved by my protest. He smiled, enjoying my discomfort.

"Well, Stella," he murmured, "I suppose they'll think we're going upstairs to make love. And since that is what we're doing, they'd be right."

I felt my face grow hot and my ears began to ring.

Jake took me by the shoulders, turned me to face him, and looked deep into my eyes. "Stella, you're an adult woman. You lived with a man in Florida. Your cousin and her girlfriend don't exactly expect you to be a virgin. It's your life. It doesn't matter what people think. What matters is what you feel is right and what you want."

I nodded, my heart pounding in double-time.

"Stella," Jake said, tipping my chin up so that my gaze met his. "Do you want me to make love to you?"

I swallowed, wishing he wasn't forcing me to acknowledge my desire for him, wishing I could have him and still consider it a happy accident.

"Do you?" he whispered, his finger trailing a line of liquid fire down the side of my neck. "Do you want me to make love to you?" The finger slid down my chest, circled the side of my breast and rested gently on the tip of my hardened nipple.

"Yes," I answered.

"Good," he said, scratching the fabric of my blouse with his fingertip.

He moved his hand, encircling my waist, and brought the other hand down, sweeping me up into his arms and carrying me up the last few steps.

"Jake, put me down. What about your side? Jake!"

I am not a lightweight. Carrying me wasn't like you see on TV where the little pixie is scooped up by the burly pirate. Still, he made it seem effortless. He stepped into our bedroom, kicked the door shut with his heel and walked with me to the bedside.

"Don't move," he ordered.

"But I—"

Jake's eyes darkened. He sat down beside me on the bed, leaned over to kiss me, then asked, "Stella, do you trust me?"

I nodded, but he didn't seem at all satisfied with my answer. "I don't think you do," he murmured. "I hurt you a long time ago, but you carried it with you for years. You were still mad when you saw me for the first time in over ten years. Why would you trust me now?"

"Because I know you're different now," I said. "We were kids. I was…wrong."

He raised one skeptical eyebrow. "Really? Then why would you trust another man after Pete? He cheated on you. Why trust me?"

What was he doing, trying to talk me out of this? I frowned at him.

Jake sat back, watching the conflicting emotions spin their way to the surface. He leaned over me, his eyes melting into mine and said, "Stella, if I take you now, your way, you'll hide behind your little glass wall and only taste the surface pleasure. That's not enough for me."

I tried to rise up, but his hand held me down, giving me no other option but to face him.

"This is something, coming from you," I said. "Aren't you the King of One Day At a Time? Didn't you say you didn't want any commitments? Isn't this just a passing indulgence? Surely that hasn't changed?"

Jake didn't break his gaze. His eyes seemed to bore deeper into my soul, making me suddenly afraid to hear his answer.

"Stella Luna, you frighten me," he said at last. "You have a way of sliding under my skin and touching my heart. For some reason, you continue to stick with me and I don't buy that it's just good business. I think you know as well as I do that there is a bond between the two of us that has been there for years, waiting for its opportunity."

He was watching me, gauging my reaction to his words, and when he didn't see disagreement, he forged ahead.

"I don't know what that bond will become in the future, and I don't want to ever hurt you intentionally, but I do want to discover you. I want to bring out the woman I know is hiding behind the wall. I want to make love to you as you should be loved. I want to feel your body shed its defenses and give itself over to something far more intense than some redneck cop can provide. I just don't know if you're ready for that. I don't know if you can put yourself into my hands long enough to enjoy receiving."

"That's not true," I cried. From nowhere, hot tears sprang to my eyes and I wanted to disappear from his intense scrutiny.

"Isn't it? You ran from Glenn Ford after I hurt you. You ran back when Pete hurt you. Don't you think I see that?"

Damn him. The tears flowed in a steady stream down my face, across my neck, dripping onto the sheets behind me.

"Stella, shh," he soothed. "I'm not saying you're broken, or even that running is wrong. I'm saying I don't blame you for defending yourself. I'm saying I want to love you, but I don't know if you're ready. I don't want to be just another temporary fix, another sharp regret. If we make love and for some reason our relationship doesn't last, I would not want you to look back and feel regret."

Jake leaned down and kissed the side of my face, following the tear tracks down my cheeks with his lips. When he raised his head he was smiling gently, his eyes warm.

"Is this what you want, Stella? Is it really what you want?"

He stood up, still looking into my eyes. "I'm going to run downstairs and pour us both another glass of wine. I'll give you a few minutes to think."

He left me and for a moment I gave way to an overwhelming surge of grief and loneliness, crying silently into the pillow so no one would hear. How could he do this to me? How could he see through my skin and know me like that? How dare he force me to put my feelings into words when he already knew how I felt?

I sat up, brushed the tears away and made myself think. I thought of the panic I'd felt when he'd been shot, the panic that rose beyond normal concern for a partner and became an aching pain in my chest. I thought about the way he'd loved me in my dream or not-dream, without concern for his own satisfaction, only mine. I thought of the way he loved my aunt, with genuine respect and emotion, without expectation of reward or even acknowledgment. I thought of the pain and self-blame I'd seen in his eyes over my uncle's death. Jake was no longer the bad boy from high school. He had become the man I'd only seen beginning all those years ago.

And he was right. I ran from all pain, real or potential. I'd started when my parents died and I was still running. Jake wasn't trying to stop that. He was merely trying to offer a respite. He wanted to love me, without strings, without promises that might not ever be fulfilled. He wanted to pull me away from the past and into the moment. Jake wanted me to feel right now, without worrying about the future. "Love as if your heart has never been broken." Wasn't that how the saying went?

I sat there, turning the idea over and over in my head, feeling my heart lightening with each passing moment.

I heard him returning, his footsteps echoing down the hallway as he drew closer and came to a halt in front of the door. As I watched, the door slowly swung open, and he stood on the threshold, holding two glasses of my aunt's Chianti.

His eyes searched my face for a sign. A small smile grew as he walked toward me.

"So," he said softly, "have you made up your mind?"

I looked up at him and smiled, felt my heart swell and something deep inside me give way.

"Yes."

Chapter 15

Jake set the wineglasses down on the nightstand and reached deep into his jacket pockets. He pulled out two candles that I recognized from the living room and a pack of matches. He turned back to me, still smiling.

"Stella, do you trust me?" he said.

I nodded.

"Enough to turn your body over to me and not worry that I will hurt you?"

A quiver of anticipation ran the length of my body. "Of course."

His eyes darkened. "Good, because this is about you."

"Oh, I don't think so," I said. "Not this time." But when I reached for him, he gripped both my wrists in one strong hand and pushed me back onto the bed.

"Especially this time," he whispered, and pulled a short length of rope from his jacket.

"Where did you…?"

Jake smiled. "I'm a guy, Stella. I have a truck and a tool-box. What man wouldn't have a little rope lying around."

With a deft move he tied my wrists together, brought them up over my head and secured them to the bedpost behind me.

"Stella," he said, rocking back to look down at me. "If at any point you want me to stop what I'm doing, just say so. Okay? I'm not going to hurt you. I'm only going to make sure you can't distract me." He grinned when I nodded. "I know how you like to take the spotlight off yourself, but I want you to feel every bit of pleasure I can give you."

He stood up, crossed the room and locked the door. My stomach tightened and I felt a swell of desire flood my body. He walked back to the bedside, took a sip of his wine and lit the two candles. When he'd done this, he turned out the light, leaving only the circle of our bed framed by the dim orange glow of the flickering candles.

He stood up beside the bed and began to slowly remove his clothes. I watched, fascinated, enjoying the slow seduction of his movements. First the jacket, then the shirt. The firm muscles of his chest rippled as he moved to unfasten the buttons of his jeans. His eyes never left mine. He pulled his pants and boxers down in one fluid movement, leaving me to stare openly at his erection. His body was beautiful and he didn't try to hide it from me. He stood there easily, letting me look, letting me grow more and more aroused.

"Well," I said softly. "Guess you'll have to untie my hands if you want to go further. You tied me up before you could…"

He turned, reached into his pocket and stopped any more conversation. The soft snap of his pocketknife opening froze any further response in my throat.

"Um, what are…"

Jake stood over me, his eyes black pools in the candlelight. "Do you trust me?" he whispered again.

I looked at him, wished I could reach for him, and found myself nodding. I did trust him, completely.

He straddled my hips, laid the knife down by my side and pushed my sweatshirt and turtleneck up over my head until they rested near my wrists. I lay before him wearing Nina's lingerie choice, a black padded bra.

Jake smiled, leaned forward and kissed the side of my neck, running his tongue in a shivery trail of fire down the side of my neck. I moaned as my body began to ache and throb for him.

"Please," I whispered.

He leaned back, taunting me with his smile. "Oh, I don't think so," he murmured. "I'm just getting started."

He picked up the knife, slid the blade between my shoulder and my bra strap, and with a deft move cut the thin ribbon of material. I gasped, helpless to stop him as he moved the blade to slice the filmy fabric away, exposing my breasts to his inspection.

He tossed the knife onto the bedside table and smiled. "Mission accomplished."

He slid back, brought his tongue to my breasts, and gently ran it around my nipples. I arched into him, pulled my knees up, and tried to push him toward me, and he stopped.

"Do I have to tie your legs, too?" he asked. "Maybe I do."

I moaned, frustrated, and watched as he unbuttoned my jeans and slid them down and off. He used the thick fabric against me, tying one leg and securing it to the bed frame. He used his shirt to tie the other leg, trapping me and exposing me to him at the same time.

"My, my," he whispered, sitting back to study the newly revealed parts of my body. "What lovely panties. Nina buy those for you, too?"

I nodded, unable to speak.

He reached across to the bedside table, picked up the knife

and slit the sides of my thong. With a slight tug, the material was gone and I was completely naked before him.

"I'm cold," I said, shivering.

"No, you're not. You're vulnerable. You're exposed and wondering what will come next, but you are most certainly not cold."

He reached for his wineglass, took a large sip and leaned down to kiss me. The Chianti flowing from his mouth to mine felt like fire as it traveled the length of my throat and warmed my chest.

His tongue began to explore my body, sliding its way slowly down my torso, and I lost track of conscious thought. All I wanted was more.

He teased. He played. He brought me to the edge of screaming desire and then backed off. When he reached my hips, he stopped, parted my legs, and sat studying my body as no man had ever done before.

"You're beautiful," he whispered.

"Please," I moaned. "Please make love to me. I want you inside me."

He met my gaze, one finger gently stroking the outside mound, gently dipping deeper and deeper into what seemed to me to be a bottomless well of desire and longing.

"Oh, I will make love to you, all right, all in good time," he answered, and lowered his head.

I bit down hard on my lip, tried not to scream, and felt myself coming closer and closer to a shattering climax. But just before I plummeted over the edge, he stopped, easing me back and building me up, over and over again, until I strained at the ropes in my desperation to make him let me finish.

He stood at one point and pulled my jeans away from my legs, freeing me to move as he slid between them and hovered above me.

"Untie my hands," I whispered, my voice hoarse with the attempts I'd made not to scream.

"No," he said, and plunged deep inside me with a sudden ferocity that brought me up off the bed to join my body with his.

Every sensation, every frustration and stimulated nerve ending came together in an explosion of pleasure. I heard myself call his name, felt his hand over my lips, and rode the crest of my orgasm until I felt his own rocket deep inside me.

We went on, moving together as one, building slowly to another fiery release. He held me to him, his eyes never leaving my own as he insisted I stay with him. I couldn't look away, couldn't hide the passion that overtook me, and willingly gave him all of it, opening myself to him as I had never done with anyone.

When at last we were both spent, he untied my arms, cradled me to his chest, stroked my hair and whispered my name over and over again until I fell asleep. When I awoke, he was still there, his arms wrapped around me, the gray light of departing dawn driving the shadows from the room as he slowly moved to take me again.

Reality came all too quickly to claim us.

Chapter 16

The shrill, insistent ringing of Jake's cell phone brought what might have been a long lazy lovemaking session to a grinding halt. I saw him hesitate, his lips lingering over my breasts, trying to refocus.

"Get it," I whispered. "What if it's important?"

"They'll call back," he murmured, his tongue tracing a fiery circle around my right nipple.

"Go ahead. I'll be here." I pushed him gently and felt him sigh as he got up to answer the call.

It worked for me. I got to watch him move in the early-morning light; studied his body from head to toe, savoring his easy, pantherlike stride toward the dresser. He knew I was watching. He turned and grinned as he flipped open the phone, his hand slowly running the length of his torso, circling his erection and resting there as he said, "Hello?"

His expression changed from taunting playfulness to wary attention in an instant.

"I'm afraid we've come to a dead end," I heard him say.

I sat up, pulling the sheet around my breasts, and listened.

"That's right. We thought we were close but it turns out the man we were looking for isn't your brother. There's really nothing more we can do for you. I'll have my assistant return the unused portion of your retainer to you in today's mail."

I couldn't hear what Tonya May was saying, the words were indistinct, but the tone left no doubt as to her displeasure. She spoke for several moments while Jake turned away from me and stared out the window toward the ocean.

"I hear what you're saying," he said at last, "but there's really nothing more we can do for you." Then, "Right. I know," and, "I thought so, too, but we were wrong."

Tonya protested, Jake held firm, and in the end clicked the phone shut while she was still talking.

"She sounds pissed," I said.

"That would be an understatement. She thinks we've found him. She smells something but was too smart to say so."

The temperature seemed to drop ten degrees in the room. "So what do you think she'll do next?"

Jake shrugged. "I wouldn't put it past her to come down here."

"Come down here? As in come here to the house?"

Jake nodded wearily. "Doesn't matter. We'll probably be gone before she can reach us, and if we're not, I'll send her packing."

Oh, right, like I couldn't handle her, I thought, slightly irritated by his tone. What, did he think because we'd slept together I was suddenly unable to protect myself and my family?

I took a deep breath and tried to calm myself. I was imagining things. Jake wasn't like that, was he?

The aroma of freshly brewed coffee drifted under the door. The sounds of Aunt Lucy's breakfast preparations echoed faintly in the bedroom, and the thoughts of making love with her right below me dimmed my ardor for Jake considerably.

As if he sensed my mood, Jake stepped into sweatpants and threw on his flannel shirt.

"I'll bring you some coffee," he said.

"Good idea." I didn't meet his eyes. I didn't want to know what he was feeling about us, not right now.

The moment after he walked out the door I was up and down the hallway to the bathroom. I locked the door behind me, turned on the shower, and when it was ready, stepped in to lose myself in the hypnotic rhythm of the spray drumming across my shoulders.

Ten minutes later I stepped out, once again in control of my emotions, and found my coffee cooling on the countertop. How had he come and gone without me hearing him? Unlocking the door would have been easy, but to actually enter the room and leave the coffee without me hearing him? I shrugged, picked up the mug and took a cautious sip. Still hot. I toweled off and made a mental to-do list for the day.

Jake thought we should go home. I thought we should address the Joey Smack problem first. But how best to approach that?

I was no closer to an answer by the time I'd finished dressing and started downstairs. I was back to my sensible clothes, having found them clean and folded on my bed, courtesy of Nina.

I shivered as images from the night before flashed through my head in a slide show of increasing intensity. I wanted more and I also wanted to run away. How was I going to face him at breakfast with the others all sitting there? How were we going to make a plan and not have the heat of last night there between us?

I bit down on my lip, stepped into the living room and slowly walked the length of the room to the kitchen. Spike, Nina and Aunt Lucy all looked up when I appeared in the doorway, but Jake was nowhere to be seen.

Nina looked up at me and gave me one of her I've-got-a-secret smiles. "Jake left. He said he was going up to the diner. Are we really going home today?"

Aunt Lucy set her lips in a grim line and shook her head. "Well, I for one can't go. My car's not ready. The shop called and said it won't be good to go before tomorrow morning and we still have the loaner to return. Who's going to take care of that?"

I started to answer her, but she went on. "And I am right in the middle of the most delicate phase of my cream development. If I move it, the entire process may go ka-flooie. You can leave if you want, but I'm not going before tomorrow."

I saw the determined glint in her eyes and knew better than to try taking her on. If she said tomorrow, then tomorrow it would be. It's not as if we had anything but aggravation waiting for us at home. Why rush? We certainly didn't have a case to work on—not when our "client" was probably an assassin and our "missing person" her next victim.

"I'm with you," I said. "I'm fine to go tomorrow."

"Maybe Jake can get some fishing in," Spike said.

I didn't say anything. We needed to make sure Joey Smack didn't become more of an interference, and keep a weather eye out for Tonya May. I doubted there'd be time for surf fishing.

Nina sighed. "You know, we came here for a reason," she said. "And we haven't accomplished our goal. Today might just be our only time to do that. We need to do our team-building exercises. We need to know where we're going from here as an agency. Don't you think we need that, Stel?"

She looked like a Labrador retriever puppy, her huge eyes wide pools of pleading excitement, her face open and expectant, completely hopeful. How was I supposed to turn that down? Who was I to bring such disappointment down on her head?

"You're right, Nina. It's the one thing we haven't done, and when Jake gets back, that's just what we'll do." I stood up, coffee cup in hand and said, "I think I'm going to walk down to the beach for a minute." I saw Nina's eyes narrow suspiciously and added, "I just need to clear my head. I want to be totally open to the process."

Nina relaxed against the back of her chair and smiled. "Totally," she said.

Aunt Lucy shook her head and muttered something in Italian. From the sounds of it, she wasn't buying anything we were selling.

I found my coat, pulled it on and reached in my pocket for my gloves. My Glock rested securely in my right pocket and I found myself patting it gently as I started down the steps to the front yard.

A glint of light caught my eye. I glanced out toward the public parking lot at the end of the street and saw one lone car parked in the space closest to the street. Had I seen something or was it merely the reflection of the car's chrome bumper? My fingers closed around my gun as I walked toward the lot. Possibilities ran through my head as my cop brain took over and I began to run on protective instinct.

Could be Sheila Martin didn't trust us to leave well enough alone and was having the house watched to prevent interference. Could be Joey Smack had sent another team to Surfside Isle in hopes of retrieving something we didn't have. Could be a harmless bird-watcher out for her morning stroll. Could be anything, but I wasn't taking chances.

I played the possible scenarios over and over in my head. What would I do if someone came at me? What if there was more than one? What if they had guns? Where was my protective cover? If I was two-thirds of the way down the street, I could jump behind the garage of the pink house on my right. If I was within close range, I could duck behind the light post and shoot.

I felt my jacket pockets for a reserve cartridge and found

one in my left inside pocket. Good. I walked, apparently ignoring the car, keeping a careful eye out for any signs of movement.

"False alarm, false alarm," the denial fairy sang as I got within fifty feet of the vehicle.

"Rental car, red alert," my paranoid-cop voice barked. "Doesn't belong here. No tourist season."

I kept my steps light, skirted the perimeter of the car and saw the driver's seat reclined back and a balding, middle-aged man asleep behind the steering wheel.

The denial fairy exhaled a giant sigh of relief. "See? It's just a shoe salesman taking a nap. Isn't he just the cutie-wootiest?"

The paranoid cop froze. "Take out your gun," he whispered. "What's that on the back seat?"

I passed within three feet of the vehicle, turned and approached the car from the rear passenger side, skirting the range of the driver's-side rearview mirror. I crept closer and saw a camera with a thick, long-range lens sitting on the back seat, within easy reach of the driver. But it was the lens that held my attention.

From five feet away the familiar print was visible even if the words were not. I'd used that same lens in Garden Beach while doing surveillance at night on the "Needle Nose" Robanski case. It was a Night Watch; night-vision lens. Birdwatchers and tourists don't have those sorts of lenses, they wouldn't need them, couldn't afford them and couldn't easily obtain them without a law-enforcement background.

I saw a flicker of facial movement, withdrew my gun and circled to the driver's side of the car. I reached out, rapped sharply on the back window and held the Glock level with the man's chest.

His eyes flew open, alert, wary and guarded. He jerked upright and tried, almost convincingly, to portray a startled tourist. His hands rose in the air.

"I don't have any money," he cried.

I smiled. "Shut the fuck up and get out of the car," I yelled.

"But you'll shoot me," he answered.

"I'll shoot you anyway if you don't get out. Now do as I say."

His clothes were rumpled. The detritus of fast-food meals littered the floor on the passenger side. When the man opened his door, the distinct, acrid odor of stale cigarette smoke filled the air between us.

He stepped out onto the gravel lot, hands high in the air, and faced me, his expression carefully arranged to look petrified, but his eyes were looking for an opportunity.

"Throw your gun," I said. "Slowly."

"I don't have a gun," he protested.

"You want to do this easy or hard?" I asked. "I know who you are. I know why you're here. So let's just cut the bullshit and get on with it."

The man sighed, reached slowly into his coat and pulled out a small Smith & Wesson .38. I signaled with the Glock and the man dropped the gun and slid it away from his body with one rubber-soled shoe.

"Empty your pockets and turn them inside out so I can see them," I instructed.

A billfold hit the ground, followed by a slimmer leather twin of the wallet. A digital-camera disc, a few dollars and some spare change, a handheld recorder and a set of earphones came next.

"Kick the badge holder over," I said.

He kicked the wallet.

"Nice try, Einstein, now the other one."

Reluctantly he nudged the leather holder toward me. When I stooped to retrieve it, my new friend got stupid. He jumped sideways, lunged forward and attempted to throw me to the ground.

Instead, he found himself flying over my back and landing with a thud on the hard ground behind me. I spun, stuck the business end of my gun to his neck and said, "If you try another stupid move like that, I'll shoot you and tell the police I was being robbed."

I stayed on the ground beside him, one knee crushing his shoulder, and opened his identification.

"Larry Hodges, private investigator, license number 3316."

"Pleased to meet you Larry. Who hired you?"

Larry's lips were sealed. He looked like a fat kid trapped by the playground bully, his beady eyes blinking in the bright morning sunlight as he fought to remain silent.

"Larry, Larry, Larry," I said, shaking my head softly. "What am I gonna do with you? Don't you have any sense of brotherhood? I'm a P.I., just like you. So how's about coming up with a little collegial reciprocity?"

Nope. Nothing doing. He lay on the ground, glaring at me.

"No professional courtesy, huh, Lar?"

I looked around, hoping the street was as deserted as it seemed, and looked back at Larry.

"You work for Joey Smack?"

No answer.

"Okay, buddy. You don't want to play nice, I'll have to take you home and call your mommy."

I stood up, motioned to Larry, and when he didn't move, decided a little reminder of just who held the power was in order. I fired the Glock. The bullet landed six inches away from his head, chipping gravel and spraying small rock fragments into Larry's astonished, and now terrified, face.

"Hey!" he yelled, coming up off the ground. "What are you, nuts?"

I smiled. "Maybe. Start walking."

I slid my coat sleeve down to partially hide the gun and stepped up behind my quarry. We set off slowly, with Larry dabbing at his gravel cuts while we trudged toward home.

266

"I can have you arrested for this," he muttered. "You'll lose your license."

"Don't have one yet, Lar," I answered. "I got nothing to lose."

"I'll charge you with aggravated assault and kidnapping."

I smiled. "I'll charge you with indecent exposure and attempted assault. I guess it'll be my word against yours. A former cop up against a P.I. You know, cops don't always see eye to eye with your type," I said. "What do you think?"

Larry sighed and kept walking. When we reached the beach house, Nina opened the door just as Jake's truck turned onto the street.

"Oh, goodie," I said cheerfully. "You're in time for team building!"

Nina held open the door, smiling uncertainly at our guest. Behind me, I heard Jake's door slam and the crunch of his boots on the gravel.

"Been fishing?" he asked, his voice hot in my ear.

"Trolling. Found him under the metaphorical bridge, in a rental car at the end of the street, with a night-vision camera in the back seat of his car."

Spike joined us all in the living room and heard the last few words.

"I've got my laptop with me," she said. "If it's a digital camera and he's got the cable in the car, I can download the pictures."

"You can't do that," Larry protested.

"Ah," Jake said, "I think thou dost protest too much. Go get the camera, girls."

Nina and Spike vanished, but Aunt Lucy stood just where she was, frozen in the kitchen doorway, a puzzled frown on her face.

"Hey," she said, "you look familiar. Don't I know you?"

Larry froze, looking like a deer caught in Aunt Lucy's headlights. "No, ma'am," he said, swallowing. "I don't believe so."

She advanced a few feet into the living room and studied his face carefully.

"Yes, I'm certain of it. Now let me think."

Aunt Lucy closed her eyes for a long moment, and when they popped open, I knew she'd remembered.

"You were that guy the census bureau sent two months ago. You remember, don't you? You said they'd skipped my house and you were there to ask a few questions."

Her face changed, a look of sadness passing across her features as she seemed to recall the details of Larry's visit.

"You wanted to know when Benny died and how. You asked if I lived alone. You asked all about Stella and Nina."

She looked at me, puzzled. "He's not a census taker is he?"

I shook my head no. Aunt Lucy's eyes darkened.

"Then who are you?" she demanded. "And why were you asking all those questions?"

Larry the P.I. looked miserable. "I'm sorry, Mrs. Valocchi, really I am, but I can't reveal who hired me or why." He appealed to her. "But he doesn't mean you any harm, ma'am, really he doesn't. He's just watching out for you."

Aunt Lucy's face paled. "Then you go back and tell him I don't want anybody hiding in the bushes, watching out for me. I've got family to do that!"

"Yes, ma'am," Larry said, gulping. "Does that mean I can go now?"

"No," Jake and I answered.

Larry sighed and seemed resigned to whatever lay ahead. When Spike and Nina returned, they were carrying a black nylon bag bulging with equipment.

"I believe we hit the mother lode," Spike exclaimed.

"Yeah," Nina said, "his laptop was in the trunk, along with all this other crap Spike thought we needed."

Spike smiled. "Thought we might listen to his tapes, read his reports. You know, read the secret life of a private investigator."

Larry shook his head slowly and closed his eyes.

Spike took the bag into the kitchen, in clear view of us all, and began laying black cylinders and boxes on the table. When she'd emptied the contents of Larry's black bag, she plugged in the computer, turned it on and sighed.

"Password encrypted, Larry?"

He pursed his lips and looked away.

"That's okay, honey," Spike cooed. "I can handle it." She turned to Nina and said, "Baby, would you bring down my floppy case?"

Nina nodded, an excited grin on her face. "Oh, I love it when she does this!" She practically ran up the stairs to their room, returned a moment later with a fawn-colored leather case, and fifteen minutes later she was producing file after file of information and pictures.

"Clever," she said, looking up at Larry. "You give them numbers and not names. Very smart."

Larry shrugged.

Spike worked for a while longer before calling me over to see what she'd uncovered. Photographs of Aunt Lucy's house, of all of us, of Aunt Lucy in the grocery store, at the television studio and in her garden, popped up in a slide show study of my aunt's recent past. Written reports detailing her normal daily routine, down to her grocery-store preferences and shoe size, were filed in chronological order. Nothing indicated her work for the government, nor was there any mention of her concealed lab. There were no pictures of the inside of her house. It was an investigation into an ordinary woman's life, beginning one month after my uncle's death.

Aunt Lucy walked over to stand beside Spike's free shoulder, leaning in to read the details of her movements and activities. As she read, her face grew even more ashen and I could see that her hands shook.

When she'd finished, she looked at Larry and I saw tears glittering in her eyes.

"Who would do such a thing as this?" she whispered. "What kind of person are you to do this thing to a harmless old woman, eh?"

She walked over to him, leaned down and peered into his face. She spoke softly in Italian, but I had no doubt that she was cursing him. She straightened, regarding him with an almost regal disdain and spit on his shoes.

"Release him," she ordered Jake. "Give him his things and let him go."

"Do you want me to erase the files?" Spike asked.

Jake nodded before Aunt Lucy could speak, and Spike turned back to Larry's laptop.

Aunt Lucy spun on her heel and began walking away. Larry followed her departure with his eyes.

"He was worried about you," he said softly. "He wanted to know you were all right after your husband's death. He wanted me to watch out for you."

Aunt Lucy raised her hand dismissively and kept on walking down the hall.

"If you feel so badly about all this," Nina said, "why won't you tell us who *he* is?"

Larry looked at her, his gaze strong and unwavering. "Because I don't know who he is," he said. "He's always paid me in cash and I've never seen him face-to-face."

Jake looked at me, as if to say, "See? It happens all the time."

Well, not to us, I thought. Never again. From now on, we'd know who we worked for, or we wouldn't take their case. Put that in your mission statement, I added silently.

"Stella?" Spike called softly. "Could you come here a sec?"

Her face was carefully neutral, and to an outsider like Larry, her tone was apparently casual, as well. But I knew Spike now and heard the tension creep into her voice.

I crossed into the kitchen, rounded the table to Spike's side and looked down at the computer screen.

It was a picture of the beach house taken probably from Larry's vantage point at the end of the street.

"Watch what happens when I zoom in closer," Spike whispered. "Look at that car on the right side of the screen."

I watched as Spike hit a button and brought the right side of Larry's picture into closer focus. Joey Smack sat in a dark sedan talking to a woman with short, black hair. Even with sunglasses it was easy to identify Tonya May's profile. Now what the hell did this mean?

The date and time were stamped in the lower right-hand corner. Yesterday morning. Joey Smack and Tonya May had been sitting outside our house yesterday morning. Did Sheila Martin know this? Was this why the CIA had been so interested in calling us off the case? What was Joey Smack doing with Tonya May?

I walked into the living room without a word, took the gun from Jake's hand and motioned him toward the kitchen.

Spike showed him the picture. He looked up, met my eye and nodded.

"Erase it?" Spike asked.

"Everything," Jake murmured.

With a few quick keystrokes, Spike cleared Larry's hard drive. She then packed up his case, handed it to Jake and watched as he turned it over to Larry.

"A word to the wise," Jake said.

Larry shook his head. "Don't worry about it. I quit. I didn't mean to cause that old lady any harm."

He seemed to have aged in the short time he'd been with us and I found myself feeling sorry for him more than angry. But just who was looking out for Aunt Lucy? Would he send another replacement? And if he did, what would we do then?

"I'm gonna tell the guy what happened here," Larry said. "I

don't think he had any idea this would ever get back to her, let alone frighten her." Larry looked at us with basset-hound eyes. "I think the guy loves her," he said. "I really think he does."

I raised an eyebrow and reached to open the front door.

"Then tell him I said he's a coward. If he really loves my aunt, he'll come apologize and face her like a man."

Larry nodded and walked out the door. As we watched, he slowly trudged back to his car, slung his equipment bag into the trunk, climbed behind the wheel and drove away.

"Okay," I said, turning back to the others. "That takes care of that. Now, what do we do about Joey Smack?"

Chapter 17

Nina's lower lip stuck out in what Uncle Benny would've described as a "bee runway."

"Better suck that pout back in, little girl," he used to say, "or some bee's gonna come along and take it for a landing strip."

But Uncle Benny was gone and we were all stuck with Nina who didn't want to hear about insects or Joey Smack, not when she was trying to raise our collective consciousness.

"I *thought* we were over that case," she said. "I *thought* we weren't going to go off half-cocked anymore. This is supposed to be my time."

I bit my lower lip in an attempt not to say what I was thinking, which would've gone something like, "Nina, you airhead, Joey Smack wants to kill us. What more of a motivational statement do you need? We have a mission—stay alive and unharmed!"

Of course, wiser heads prevailed. I thought like a rational, sane person. How could I develop a plan to deal with Spagnazi while simultaneously making Nina a happy camper? I snuck a glance at Jake, saw him giving me a dark "fix this mess" scowl, and rolled my eyes.

"Okay, Nina," I said. "Let's use this Joey Smack crisis as an example. How do we, as a team, develop a unified stance to both address the preeminent threat while not compromising our corporate identity?"

Nina gave me a blank look.

"I think she's saying, how do we stay safe, get Joey Smack off our back and still improve our karma?" Spike translated.

"Exactly," Jake added, finally on board with the plan.

Nina closed her eyes, took a deep cleansing breath and seemed to be meditating on our collective problem.

Jake's cell phone rang and Nina cracked one irritated eye.

"Get it and get rid of whoever it is!" I hissed.

He turned away, flipped open the phone and said, "Hello?"

My God, even his voice turned me to mush; two deep and sexy syllables and I was ready to fly up the stairs to bed.

"Well, I don't know," he said softly. "I'm kind of in the middle of something."

Nina opened both eyes and was unabashedly eavesdropping along with Spike and myself.

"Well, I know that, honey, but…"

Honey?

"Well, sure but…" Jake sighed, took three steps farther away from us and attempted to finish his conversation without us hearing him. Too bad for him. We heard every single word.

"Babe, that was two years ago. You can't hold that over my head now." Silence, then, "I know. I know. No, she's not like that."

Who wasn't like that? Me? I felt a slow, burning steam rise from within my body. In another minute I was going to blow my top.

And then we all heard Jake say, "Of course, if it's really that important, I'll be there in about fifteen minutes. What's the room number?"

He hung up, turned around and saw all three of us staring him down.

"I'm sorry," he said. "I have something I need to take care of. I shouldn't be gone more than an hour or so."

I looked at the kitchen clock. It was almost eleven-thirty. We had work to do. We had to make sure Joey Smack was no longer a threat. How could he just walk out on us?

When Jake turned and walked out the door, I followed him.

"What are you doing?"

He stopped, his shoulders stiffening slightly, bracing for what we both knew was coming.

"Sheila said it's important. She needs me."

"Does it have anything to do with Tonya May?"

He didn't meet my eyes, which was a bad sign.

"I don't know. Maybe."

I took a step toward closer. If he was going to walk out on us now, he was going to look me in the eye before he did.

"Why aren't we both going then?"

"She wanted me to come alone, and since we haven't taken care of the Joey Smack issue, that's probably a good idea anyway."

He was blowing me off and we both knew it. True, I should be staying behind, but so should he. Where was his loyalty anyway?

"Jake, what's the deal with you and Sheila?"

He looked at me then. "We worked together once, a few years ago."

That wasn't enough to explain this sudden departure. "And?" I added. We were standing in front of his truck, but it wasn't enough of a buffer to cut the chill wind that blew in off the ocean. I shivered and looked out toward the horizon.

Thick gray clouds gathered, signaling an impending storm. How appropriate, I thought.

"And we had a brief affair. It was a mistake. I was still married to Donna and even though I knew we didn't love each other, that was no excuse for what I did. I'd tell you it happened because Sheila and I came close to dying and somehow making love reminded us we were still alive, but that's an excuse. We all know excuses satisfy only those who make them."

"And so are you satisfied now?" I asked, unable to keep the anger out of my voice.

"Stella, please. She wouldn't have called if it wasn't urgent."

I stared at him. I wanted to say, "Well, what about us? Isn't this urgent, too? If Joey Smack decides to hit the house while you're gone, will that be urgent enough for you?" But I didn't. I could handle Joey Smack or anything else life threw my way. I didn't need Jake Carpenter's help, or his loyalty, or worse, his pity.

I turned away from him and walked back up the stairs and into the house. A moment later I heard the truck's engine roar to life and the spin of tires on gravel as he hit the road.

Nina and Spike looked as if they felt sorry for me and I couldn't stand it. I forced a small smile, walked back to my chair and sat down.

"Where were we?" I asked.

Nina hesitated. "Honey, if you don't feel like doing this, I understand."

Spike pursed her lips and said nothing.

"I'm fine. Let's keep going. I think the fact that Jake left gives us a clear sign of where he stands with the agency and our partnership, don't you?"

Spike frowned. "Well, I wouldn't go that far, Stella," she said. "Maybe he's just trying to do what he feels is right."

"Yeah," Nina added. "After all, he's a Scorpio. They can be obstinate. He wouldn't want to appear wrong, even if he is."

Aunt Lucy walked back into the room, accompanied by Lloyd, and sat down in a wing chair.

"Girls," she said, "I need your help." She looked at Nina when she said this, and seemed to be as apologetic as it was possible for her to be. "I know we were going to do the mission statement today, but I just called the shopping network people. It seems they've been trying to reach me all week. My magic cleanser is a runaway hit!" Her eyes sparkled. "Do you know what this means?"

I did. "You have more orders than you have supply and we need to help you?"

Aunt Lucy nodded. "Oh, yes, that, but our profit is approximately two dollars a bottle. They've had orders for a thousand bottles this week alone! I only have one hundred in stock. If this keeps up, we'll have to develop an assembly system. We could make enough money to support ourselves!" She turned to me. "You wouldn't need to waste your time running around repossessing sleighs and making bad people mad at you."

I could only nod as my heart sank down to my feet. Just what I always wanted, a job with security and safety. A nice boring routine. A job where you didn't matter.

"Girls, I have to deliver a thousand bottles of cleanser to the network by the day after tomorrow. Now, I've made a few phone calls. Nina, there's a supplier in Atlantic City who has the bottles and spray tops we need."

I listened as Aunt Lucy doled out instructions, tuning out the words and nodding dully as she went on and on. Everybody had a job, but I made sure mine included staying close to my aunt. Spike and Nina could travel together. Joey Smack wasn't likely to hit a moving target. I would stay home with Aunt Lucy until Jake returned, then I was going to do something about Joey Smack. I just didn't know exactly what that would be.

The household galvanized into action. Spike and Nina were on their way to Atlantic City within ten minutes and Aunt Lucy had every pot, bowl and container in the house out on top of the counters a mere two minutes later.

There wasn't time to think and after a while, I was grateful for that respite. I could feel my heart like a lead weight inside my chest. I'd been dreaming when I'd thought Jake and I could perhaps have a personal, as well as business relationship. Worse, I'd let my imagination pair up with my hopes, and envisioned a happily-ever-after that was pure fantasy. How gullible was I? Was I just doomed to repeat the same mistakes over and over again?

Spike and Nina returned two hours later, an hour past the time Jake had said he'd return. I glanced at the clock and went back to work, measuring cupfuls of ingredients under Aunt Lucy's watchful eye.

Four hours later we finished the last batch of formula and by 6:00 p.m. it was dispensed into bottles, packed in cardboard boxes and waiting by the door to be loaded onto the back of Jake's truck. He was still gone.

When Lloyd whined at the door, begging for a walk, Spike handed me the leash.

"Take him for a walk," she whispered. "You look like you could use some time alone."

I looked at Aunt Lucy, reluctant to leave her, but Spike patted her sweater pocket and smiled. "I have a gun, you know, and I'm not afraid to use it. Your aunt has a gun, and I'm afraid she will use it! So don't worry about us. Go. Take a nice long walk and see if you don't feel better."

I took the leash, grabbed my coat and headed for the door. I knew I wouldn't feel better, but I might be able to calm down enough to make some decisions.

Once Lloyd and I reached the beach, I took him off the lead and watched him take off. The air was thick with the smell of salt and rain. I looked up at the sky, saw the thick clouds overhead and knew the storm was about to begin. A few fat snowflakes hit my upturned face and as I walked, more began to fall.

Jake was fine. He had to be. He was merely tied up with Sheila what's-her-name. Instead of worrying about Jake's welfare, maybe I needed to be worrying about why Sheila turned to him when she was in trouble instead of to one of her colleagues. What was up with that? What kind of history did Jake have with her anyway? He said it had been a brief affair, but was that just the candy coating he put over it to assuage me?

The snow began in earnest and flakes blew sideways in their hurry to reach the ground. Any other time I might've enjoyed the oddity, but not tonight. Tonight I walked without enjoyment, feeling my life collapse around me in tangles of confusion. I'd thought things were on track again after Pete. I'd dared to hope I could reinvent myself without the mistakes and pain of the past carrying over to hurt me. I was terribly, terribly wrong.

Lloyd barked in the distance and when I looked up I saw Fang running to join him. The two dogs ran in short circles around each other, barking, and then raced in my direction. I watched them and felt even sorrier for myself. Why couldn't my life be that easy? Lloyd was in love with an animal twice his size at least, but that obstacle hadn't stopped him. He'd persisted, sure of himself, and now Fang seemed to be reciprocating. Not like Jake. If running off to save Sheila was reciprocity, I surely didn't need it!

Fang and Lloyd ran closer, circling me in ever closer rings, finally stopping when I did. Fang walked up to me, whined, and when I petted her head, pulled back, grabbing my coat sleeve in her powerful jaws.

"Hey, girl, let go!" I said.

Fang tugged hard, just as she had when she'd led me to Lloyd. Lloyd yipped anxiously and ran several feet ahead of us, toward the houses lining the beachfront. I stared up ahead and saw nothing but long stretches of darkened houses, their ranks broken by the occasional glow of lights from an occupied cottage or a street lamp.

I followed the dogs nonetheless, walking toward the houses, and finally realizing that Fang was returning to Doug Hirshfield's vacant home.

"Girl," I muttered, "what you need is a place to live. You can't keep staying under empty houses and eating God knows what."

Fang let go of my coat, ran forward and looked back to make sure I was following. I walked behind the two dogs, coming to at least one conclusion. Fang was going to come home with us, not just to the beach house for an overnight, but to Glenn Ford. She needed a home.

As we walked between the dunes, Fang shifted abruptly, leading me away from Doug's house and instead, heading toward another boarded-up beach cottage, two houses down. She walked around to the back of the boarded-up building but I stopped, my attention drawn to the faint sound of music, something classical and morose. It was coming from inside the house.

Fang walked around the far side of the cottage and paused briefly beneath a window. I looked up and saw the faint flicker of orange candlelight, and heard the music more clearly.

Fang barked once, startling me, and continued around to the back door. She climbed the steps, looked back at me and whined before pawing the door open and walking inside.

Lloyd followed her.

"Come back here, Lloyd!" I called softly. "Lloyd!"

Fang reappeared in the doorway and barked. It was all the invitation I needed. I slid my hand into my jacket pocket, wrapped my fingers around the Glock and followed my two canine companions into the house.

I closed the door softly behind us and called, "Anybody home?"

I reached for a switch by the door, flipped it and got no response. In the darkness, Fang grabbed my sleeve again and tugged, leading me toward the music and the faint glow of the candlelight.

My heart beat hard against the walls of my chest. This was probably a very stupid move on my part, but Lloyd was inside the house somewhere and I couldn't leave without him.

Fang drew me out of the kitchen and into the dining room. A man sat with his back to me, slumped over onto the table. A green wine bottle had fallen over beside his outstretched left hand, spilling the few remaining drops of red wine onto the white damask tablecloth. A small handgun lay beside his right hand and his head rested on a few sheets of white paper. In front of him sat an ancient, possibly antique, typewriter. Suicide 101, I thought, my cop brain kicking into autopilot.

Fang dropped my sleeve, walked over to her owner and licked the side of his face. The man stirred, brought his left hand up and swiped at his nose.

"Go 'way, Athena," he muttered. "Good girl."

Athena, or Fang, yipped softly and looked with mute appeal in my direction. I studied her master without moving. He had bright red hair, but as I took a step closer, I could see darker roots. I frowned. He dyed his hair? No wonder he was suicidal. The color was terrible.

"Sir?" I called softly. "Sir?"

What kind of threat was a man with dyed red hair? I stepped forward, reached for his gun and yelped as an iron hand closed over mine.

"What the hell are you doing in my house?" he roared.

Lloyd growled, teeth bared. Fang barked, warning him back, and I struggled to pull my hand away.

"Let go of my hand!"

My captor laughed caustically. "Not until you tell me who you are and what the hell you're doing in my house!"

I peered into the bloodshot eyes, took in the badly dyed beard and tried to see Doug Hirshfield. But while the face was somehow familiar, it wasn't Doug's.

"Your dog invited me in. I believe she was worried you were about to hurt yourself."

The stranger looked at Athena, his eyes suddenly filled with some unbearable sadness. He shook his head slowly.

"I should've taken care of her first," he murmured.

A chill went through my body. This man really intended to kill himself. He was entirely too calm, too sure of his plan to be merely distressed.

"Take care of Athena?" I repeated.

The man looked up at me for the first time. His skin was ashen, his eyes devoid of all hope, and his clothes had the rumpled look and smell of dirty laundry. He'd probably been sitting at the table for hours, perhaps even days.

"I should have given her away," he said.

A tiny flicker of relief came to life in my chest. He still cared for his dog.

"You should go now," he said quietly.

I felt his grip begin to ease on my hand and I tried to move, bringing his gun with me.

"Leave it!"

I looked into his eyes again and saw his mother. So Mia hadn't been looking for Doug!

"Fred, what are you doing here?" I said quietly.

Fred May didn't even have the emotional strength to care how I knew or why I knew his identity.

"Go away."

"Fred," I said, leaning down close to him. "Your ex-wife is looking for you. She hired us to find you, but she was using a false name and we think she wants to kill you."

Fred chuckled mirthlessly. "Good. Probably save me the trouble."

I tried again. "Do you have something she wants?" I asked. "Is that why she's looking for you?"

Fred May's eyes filled with unshed tears. "Not anymore. She's taken everything I have, everyone I ever loved."

"Did she kill your brother?" I asked.

Fred nodded. "That's why I'm supposed to be dead," he whispered. "There was a time when we thought it would be best that I stay hidden, until they found Doug's lens." His eyes glittered as he looked up at me. "I was the only one who could've sealed her death sentence. I knew she slept with my brother. I saw her leave his house the afternoon he died. She took what she wanted and killed him so he couldn't stop her. I was going to testify when the feds got their case together, but they wanted the lens first, so I was just waiting. They said they were going to do something to make her go after it, but they never did."

Fred lowered his head, reached for the bottle, and upon finding it empty, threw it against the dining-room wall where it shattered and fell to the ground in a rain of green glass and red wine drops.

"She killed Becca! I know she did. She killed them both."

A sound registered behind me, the soft click of a gun's safety moving from the on to off position. I spun, saw Fang look up, saw her begin to move and heard Tonya say, "Call your dog or I kill her next!"

"Athena! Stay!" Fred ordered. His voice suddenly sharp and focused.

Athena sat, Lloyd beside her, both dogs growling as Athena watched for the signal that would release her.

Tonya May stood in the doorway with Joey Smack right behind her. They were holding ugly, nine-millimeter, semiautomatics. Behind them stood another woman, a slightly younger version of Tonya with short, blond hair.

Tonya looked at me and smiled. "Thank you," she murmured. "Good job."

She looked at Fred, the smile changing to a mocking, derisive grin. "This is the best the witness protection program could do, dye your hair and let you grow a beard?" She shook her head. "I hired private investigators thinking you'd be slick and have plastic surgery. I had them look for Doug to lead me to you. There was no point in letting them get too close to the truth, was there? I thought I'd never find you on my own. That's why I hired *her*. What a waste!" she said, her glance sliding over to encompass me.

"What are you talking about?" I asked.

Tonya shrugged. "I thought if he had plastic surgery and changed the way he looked, he'd recognize me before I could recognize him. He'd get away and I'd miss my opportunity. I knew he'd come to see his mother eventually. I knew he wouldn't stay away. He was too much of a mama's boy! Of course," she said, turning her attention back to her former husband, "it would have saved a lot of time and effort if Rebecca'd just told me where you were, but no, she had to go and die on me!"

Fred started to lunge up from the table, a guttural growl emanating from deep within his body. I grabbed his hand tighter, forcing it down on top of the table, hoping the tiny handgun was still hidden from view. Fred sank back as Tonya raised her gun, positioning it dead center on my chest.

"Want to kill another innocent?" Tonya cooed.

"Can we just get on with this?" Joey demanded.

Up until now, Joey hadn't seen me, his view blocked by Tonya, but when he pushed past her into the dining room, he suddenly realized who I was.

"No kidding," he said, eyes widening. "Two birds with one stone."

I lifted an eyebrow. "I don't have your cocaine, Joey," I said.

"Of course you do," he answered. "Who else could've taken it?"

I made a slight movement, saw Tonya's finger tighten on her trigger and froze.

"Wanna check?" I asked. "Do I look like the type to run off with a kilo of cocaine? Has it occurred to you that one of your loyal goombas might've been on the take, 'cause I assure you, it wasn't us!"

Joey stopped, a strange look crossing his face. He turned slowly around and grabbed Tonya's sister by the arm, yanking her forward into the room.

"You little shit!" he cried. "Why didn't I think of it! You took the money. Why stop there? You took that kilo, didn't you?"

Tonya's sister, Carla, was a pitiful study. Short, scrawny, pockmarked and wasted away by addiction was my guess. She didn't even have the brain cells left to know when to be afraid and keep her mouth shut. She grinned.

"Oh, just put it on my tab," she said. "Right, Toy?"

Tonya regarded her sister with open disgust. "Shut up, Carla. We wouldn't be in this mess if you hadn't been such a fucking junkie!"

Carla didn't seemed fazed by this pronouncement. She still had the idiot grin plastered across her face. "You can afford to spread the wealth," she said. "After all, I helped you out. I was the one found a place for you to stay."

"Yeah, well, now I gotta risk everything by making a move before I was ready to," Tonya complained. "Another year and things wouldn't have been nearly as hot."

Carla shrugged. "Whatever."

"Will you just get the fucking thing so we can go?" Joey said. He twitched nervously, obviously uncomfortable with Tonya's plan.

Tonya looked at him impatiently. "Well, stupid, let's make sure we have their guns. Pat that one down good—she'll have at least one."

I moved slightly, letting go of Fred's hand and shielding him with my body as Joey approached.

"Freeze!" Tonya called.

No one moved. Joey looked over his shoulder to Tonya, clearly puzzled.

"Fred, move your hand away from the gun and leave it where it is!"

There went that plan, I thought. Now what?

Joey patted us down, pulled out my Glock, secured Fred's gun and moved back beside Tonya.

"Cover them," she instructed, and moved over to the table.

While we watched, she took the typewriter, flipped it over and reached into her pocket for a tiny screwdriver.

"What are you doing?" Fred protested. "Put that down!"

Tonya scowled at Fred. "Keep your pants on. It's not like you'll be using it again. I left something here for safekeeping."

Tonya turned her attention back to Fred's typewriter, loosening a few screws, prying a small bar away from beneath the typewriter and reach up to dislodge a small vial.

"Good!" She smiled at Fred. "I knew, no matter what, you'd never be far away from this hunk of crap. Some good-luck symbol this turned out to be, huh?"

She turned away from him, held the vial up to the light and whispered, "See no evil," before pocketing the bottle in her jacket.

"That's it?" Joey asked, clearly not convinced.

Tonya frowned in his direction. "Of course. The plans are on microfilm and the prototype is in this saline solution, where else? It's all right where I left it before Fred here called the cops and I had to take off."

"Awesome," Carla breathed. "Let's get out of here!"

"Yeah," Joey echoed. "Let's get out of here!"

Tonya shook her head. "Not until we take care of these two. You think I want them yapping? You want the feds on your doorstep, Joey? There's rope in the trunk of my car. One of you go get it and we'll tie them up."

Joey hesitated. "Why can't we just shoot them?"

Tonya sighed impatiently. "Because this way buys us more time. They'll have to put out the fire, and then identify the bodies—that is, if there's anything left to identify!"

Joey nodded, mollified, and Carla was sent to get the rope. I thought as hard and fast as I could. Maybe I could overpower them as they tied us up, use whoever I grabbed first as a human shield to reach the others. I looked at Fred and discounted his ability to help me. He seemed miles away, lost in grief and despair.

When the back door slammed, signaling Carla's return, Tonya barely looked up. She had wandered closer to the table and was reading a type-written page that lay atop a stack of others.

"So you had to write it," she murmured.

Fred never got to answer her. Carla appeared in the doorway, pale-faced, with Jake's arm wrapped in a stranglehold around her neck.

"Tonya," Carla squeaked.

She jumped forward to place the muzzle of her gun up against my temple as she realized the danger. Joey turned and faced Jake, his gun still outstretched in his hand.

Jake's face registered shocked surprise.

"What are you doing here?" he asked me.

I regarded him coolly. "I might ask you the same thing."

Sheila walked into the room behind Jake, saw me and swore softly.

"Back at ya," I muttered.

Jake's grip on Tonya's sister tightened painfully and she gasped.

"Why didn't you tell me she was in here?" he snarled.

Carla didn't say a word, the reason obvious.

Tonya gave Jake a playful smile. "Bet I know what you were thinking," she said. "You thought I'd see you had Carla and give up. You were betting I cared." Her face hardened. "But you see, I don't. If she dies, the situation actually gets easier for me."

I doubted this. Why else would she have come to bail her sister out from her troubles with Joey Smack? And what about Joey Smack? Didn't Jake know Joey was just as much of a threat as Tonya? He was holding a semiautomatic. Why weren't Jake and Sheila paying attention to Joey?

I saw Joey exchange a look with Jake and mouth a few quick words. Joey had to know Tonya couldn't see his face from where she stood and I realized this was a setup gone wrong. Joey Smack must be cooperating with the feds and what might have been simple was now all wrong.

I brought my left hand up, stiff-armed Tonya's gun away from my head and moved to grab her gun arm with both hands. The gun fired; I felt something sting my left calf as we wrestled. I brought Tonya's arm down and cracked her forearm over my knee.

The gun dropped. Tonya screamed, and in the ensuing struggle I focused only on subduing my subject. The loud report of a gun discharging close to my ear surprised and deafened me momentarily. Tonya went limp and I looked up to see Fred May standing over us, Tonya's semiautomatic in his hand.

Joey Smack reached him in one quick stride and snatched the weapon from Fred's hand. Athena moved, sensing her owner's impending danger, and lunged for Joey.

"Jesus Christ," he cried. "Holy Mother of God!"

"Athena, here!" Fred commanded. Fang stopped in her tracks and came immediately to her owner's side.

Fred May sank back down into his chair and stared at Tonya's lifeless body. Athena whined and nuzzled his hand insistently with her head until Fred began to scratch the dog softly behind the ears.

When Sheila and Jake continued to ignore Joey Smack and the gun in his hand, I panicked.

"He's got a gun!" I said. "Aren't you going to take it?"

Sheila looked over at Joey and said, "You'd better put that away before the others get here."

"Others?" I said. "What others?"

"Don't worry about it," Jake said. He's working with them."

"Who? Jake, what are you talking about?"

The dead woman's sister began to wail, and all hell broke loose behind her as a storm of government agents invaded the house, weapons drawn, too late to do anything but clean up.

I looked back at Tonya and heard myself say, "She's gone," to no one in particular. Lloyd padded softly up to stand beside me and I wrapped one arm around his soft, furry body, reassuring him, as people dressed in black swarmed the house.

Sheila said, "It was the wrong house. He gave us the wrong address."

Fred seemed to rouse himself at the sound of Sheila's voice. "I told you I'd be at the old house because I didn't want any interference. This is where Becca and I were happiest. As long as I had her here with me, there were no obstacles. We didn't need bodyguards. As far as anybody knew, she was the only one who ever stayed here and we didn't come all that often. I didn't think it mattered."

Fred's face crumpled and he covered his face with his hands.

"It was all my fault. She's dead because of me. I just can't live without her. I just wanted to be close to her when I…"

He didn't finish his sentence, but it wasn't necessary, the distress on his face told the rest of the story.

Jake said something I couldn't make out and I turned back to look at Tonya's lifeless body one more time. A moment later I felt Jake's hands on my shoulders, lifting me away as two men in black fatigues took my place.

"Tell Sheila to check Tonya's pockets," I told him. "She put the prototype for whatever it was in one of her pockets. It's a little clear vial."

Sheila was standing close enough to hear me and knelt to fish through the dead woman's pockets.

Fred watched dispassionately.

"I can't believe she left it there," he muttered. "I can't believe I had it the entire time and never knew. They could've arrested her. She could've been behind bars and Becca would've been alive. You know what it was, don't you?" he said, lifting his head to look at me.

I shook my head.

"My brother developed a contact lens that would enable the wearer to bypass the retinal identification system used at most of our high-security government facilities."

Fred May looked back at Tonya. "The selfish bitch."

Jake's hold on my shoulders tightened as he steered me away, through the kitchen and out into the snow that now had begun to fall in earnest.

Chapter 18

We arrived back at the beach house to find the driveway full of cars. Aunt Lucy's car sat, completely restored, in the driveway. The rental car was gone, but Tom's unmarked police car sat, engine running, in the driveway. A bloodred Toyota Tundra sat beside it, with a license plate that read, CRZYRDHD. Marti.

I hadn't spoken to Jake on the way home. I hadn't wanted to hear the explanation that could only satisfy its maker. Instead, I held on to Lloyd and wished I could be anywhere but where I was.

The door flew open as we started up the steps and this time it was Aunt Lucy who stood glaring out at us.

"Where the hell have you two been?" she demanded. "We called the police, you know."

I nodded, miserable. "I know. I'm sorry. I didn't mean to scare you."

My aunt pulled me into her arms, hugged me tight and said,

"Well you did, baby, you scared me something terrible!" I heard her choke off a sob and clung to her.

"I'm so, so sorry!"

"Well, it's about time!" I heard Marti say. "Now somebody tell us what in the hell this is all about. I left a diner full of customers to come over here, and it was spaghetti night, too."

Marti sat on the sofa between Spike and Nina, a half-empty glass of Chianti in her hand and the almost empty jug of wine on the coffee table in front of her. Nina's and Spike's glasses sat empty beside the jug.

"If it hadn't been for Tom here," Aunt Lucy said, "we might've all lost our minds. All he'd say was Jake called and said everything was going to be all right."

Tom crossed the room to shake Jake's hand and smiled. "Yeah, if I hadn't been here when I got the call, these women might not have made a dent in the Chianti bottle. They'd just called in a missing-person's report on the two of you. If they hadn't started pouring, I would've had to call out the National Guard. They were ready to start their own search."

Marti said, "Well, can you blame them? With all the trouble they've had, it's a wonder they didn't call out the marines."

Spike went to grab more glasses. Nina found a loaf of Italian bread and some cheese, and the rest of us moved back around the fireplace in the living room.

"We're supposed to get eighteen inches of snow tonight," Nina said excitedly. "Can you imagine? We're getting snowed in at the beach."

"Enough about that," Aunt Lucy cried. "I want to know what happened."

I did, too, but I wasn't about to admit it. I wanted to hear Jake's explanation, wanted to know what had convinced him to leave us and go to Sheila. Even more, I wanted to believe his explanation was good enough to restore the beginning flicker of hope I'd felt about starting a relationship with Jake that included more than business.

I took the glass of wine Nina offered me and stared into the fire while Jake began to talk.

"I received a call this morning from a woman I worked with a few years ago," he began. "She needed my help. She knew I still had a top-security clearance so she asked me to come without telling any of you why. I tried to convince her to tell me and to let me tell you, but she was adamant. I know Sheila," he said, "and I knew she wouldn't have called if it hadn't been a true emergency."

"I know Sheila," echoed in my head. Jake certainly knew Sheila, far better apparently, than he knew me.

"Tonya May, Fred May's ex-wife, stole a valuable proto-type and the plans for a device that would enable its user to bypass the retinal screening device used at most of our government's most highly guarded facilities. She seduced her husband's brother, took advantage of the fact that he had never been involved in a serious relationship before, and eventually stole his most important discovery. She killed him using a combination of drugs that would mimic a stroke. She's a registered nurse, and while anyone could've done it, her training almost helped her get away with the murder."

"Why didn't she?" Spike asked.

"Because Fred was suspicious. He didn't know about the theft, he only suspected her of having an affair. They had recently separated, but Fred wanted to know for sure before he finalized the divorce."

"Then why did she hide the lens in his typewriter?" I asked, turning away from the fire.

Jake looked at me, his face still neutral, but his eyes seemed to beg for understanding.

"Fred found her at the house right before the police arrived to notify him of his brother's death. She was taking some of the jewelry he'd given her out of the safe when Fred arrived and accused her of having an affair with his brother. When the police called and Doug had been taken to the hospital and wasn't expected to live, Tonya panicked and fled.

"The feds have been watching her ever since, just waiting for her to try to retrieve the lens and sell it. Once they recovered that, they could arrest Tonya and prosecute her for murder. Fred would've been the government's key witness."

Nina was shaking her head. "No way. I watched that movie. They could've just kidnapped her, given her truth serum and made her tell the truth."

Jake shook his head. "They don't work that way, and even if they did, Tonya retained a very prominent attorney. He would've screamed bloody murder."

Spike nodded. "Absolutely. What a smart cookie."

"And Joey Smack?" I said. "What was he doing?"

Jake chuckled. "He set Tonya's sister up to rip him off so he could force her to call her sister for money. That way old Joey avoids a government racketeering charge. It was a deal he made with the feds and Tonya fell right into it."

"What about those goons of his beating me up? Did the feds sponsor that, too?"

Jake frowned. "No, that was Joey screwing up. He told his men he thought we might have some stolen cocaine, but actually he only wanted them to watch us. He was trying to find Tonya first and be a hero. He thought we'd do the legwork for him. But his men took it upon themselves to go the extra mile. Don't worry, they'll do time for that."

I didn't get it. I still couldn't figure out what was real and what was a government scam to find the stolen lens.

"The sled repo," I began. "Did the feds set that up?" I remembered Jake, unconscious in my car after being shot, and felt myself begin to steam.

"No," Jake said hastily. "Joey hired Carla to do his book-keeping, knowing she'd rip him off—that was part of his deal with the feds. She had a history of ripping off employers. All Joey had to do was give her enough rope, then reel her in. He didn't know she didn't pay the bill for the sleigh. He had no idea Lifetime Novelty had hired us to repossess it. He thought someone was stealing his sled."

I still hadn't heard why Jake had gone to Sheila. Surely she had backup. What did she need him for?

"Sheila called me because she knew we'd been close to finding Doug Hirshfield. She knew Fred had come into town to see his mother every now and then and maintained contact with the nursing home by calling in and saying he was his brother. Sheila wanted to know what we knew. She asked me to come with her to the address Doug had given her and verify that it was the same house. When Sheila spotted Carla coming out of the house two doors down, we moved. I didn't have any idea you were…"

I wasn't about to talk to him in front of everyone, so I changed the subject.

"What about Becca DeWitt?"

Tom's ears pricked up and the moment between Jake and me passed.

"Joey Smack said Tonya told him she knew Fred was in town because she'd run into Becca. She panicked, thinking Becca would tell Fred, so she killed her."

Tom asked a few questions and I turned back to the fire. So Jake was loyal to an old friend in trouble and went to her, thinking he might also find something that would help our case. Okay, was this the end of the world? Wasn't that just the kind of man I'd want in my life? Maybe, just maybe, Jake thought I could handle myself and the protection of my family. Maybe Jake's leaving was a vote of confidence more than abandonment.

I just didn't know. I wouldn't know until we were alone

and I could look into his eyes and read him. I sighed. What good would that do? Had it helped me safeguard myself in the past? It was all so confusing.

The evening wore on. Aunt Lucy brought out more jugs of Chianti, and by the time Tom and Marti left, the snow was covering grass and gravel and making the streets almost too slick for safe driving.

Aunt Lucy and Lloyd wandered off to bed, followed by Spike and Nina, leaving Jake and me alone in an uneasy silence. I sat on the sofa, not knowing how to proceed, and felt strangely relieved when Jake crossed the room, sat down next to me and took the empty wineglass from my hand.

"Stella," he said, cupping my chin in his hand. "Look at me."

Reluctantly I met his gaze.

"I hope you have enough faith left in me to know that I wouldn't leave you in a bind unless I thought it was a real emergency. Stella, whatever you may think of me, I am not someone who abandons those he loves. You are a strong woman, Stella. If I'd thought you couldn't handle Joey Smack, I wouldn't have left you. After all, who drove me away from Joey's ranch with a bullet in my side, eh?"

I felt my heart lighten and tried not to throw myself into his arms with relief.

"Stella," Jake said, his voice husky with emotion, "what we shared last night was a beginning, not an end."

My heart started tap dancing. I reached over and took Jake's hand in mine.

"You think?" I whispered.

"I hope," he murmured, and brought his lips down to meet mine.

I took his hand in mine and stood, pulling him with me.

"Come on," I said. "I want to show you something."

Jake grinned, his eyes sparkling.

"You want to show *me* something?" he asked.

"Oh?" I said, raising an eyebrow. "What, you think you're the only one with a set of handcuffs and a bagful of tricks?" I chuckled. "You know, I was a professional law-enforcement officer," I said. "We are highly skilled professionals. I can show you things civilians only dream about."

And fifteen minutes later, when I'd tied him securely to my bedpost, I did just that.

Epilogue

The snow fell throughout the night, piling and drifting to near-record heights in tiny Surfside Isle, New Jersey. The entire village lay still under its blanket of white; businesses were closed, roads impassable. Even Marti had to concede defeat and stay snug under her covers. It wasn't so bad, really, not with Tom there to warm her body and her heart.

Across town, on Forty-eighth Street, a lone snowplow lumbered slowly down the block that led to the beach, halting with a loud, moaning sigh of brakes in front of a small, gray beach cottage.

Inside the house, Lloyd the dog ran to alert his elderly benefactor, yipping at her heels as she tried to prepare breakfast, tugging at the hem of her black dress, and in general making a pest of himself.

"In a minute, Lloyd," the old woman murmured. "It's coming. What have I told you about your heart and bacon, eh?"

She didn't hear the approaching footsteps, didn't see the

elderly man making his way to the front door bundled in an arctic parka and clutching a small bouquet of violets to his chest to shield them from the cold.

When the doorbell rang, Lucia Valocchi whirled around, grabbed her ancient Colt .45 and crept softly to the door, finger on the trigger. She peered through the peephole, gasped and fumbled quickly to unlock the door.

The heavy door slid open, snow blew in over the threshold and Aunt Lucy faced her visitor for the first time in over fifty years.

"You!" she cried softly. "It was you!"

* * * * *

Books by Nancy Bartholomew

Silhouette Bombshell

Stella, Get Your Gun #13
Stella, Get Your Man #25

eHARLEQUIN.com

The Ultimate Destination for Women's Fiction

For **FREE online reading,** visit www.eHarlequin.com now and enjoy:

Online Reads
Read **Daily** and **Weekly** chapters from
our Internet-exclusive stories by your
favorite authors.

Interactive Novels
Cast your vote to help decide how these
stories unfold...then stay tuned!

Quick Reads
For shorter romantic reads, try our
collection of Poems, Toasts, & More!

Online Read Library
Miss one of our online reads?
Come here to catch up!

Reading Groups
Discuss, share and rave with other
community members!

For great reading online, visit www.eHarlequin.com today!

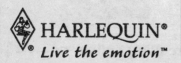

COMING NEXT MONTH

#29 PERSONAL ENEMY—Sylvie Kurtz
When security specialist Adria Caskey's undercover plan to
ruin the man who had destroyed her family went awry, she
found herself protecting the man she loathed most in the
world. But as a cunning stalker drew them into a trap,
her sense of duty battled her desire for revenge....

#30 CONTACT—Evelyn Vaughn
Athena Force
Anonymous police contact Faith Corbett had been a psychic
all her life, but now her undercover work had put her in a serial
killer's sights. As she raced to save innocent lives, she had to
confront the dark secrets about her psychic gift, her family and
the skeptical detective who challenged her at every turn....

#31 THE MEDUSA PROJECT—Cindy Dees
Major Vanessa Blake had the chance to be part of the first
all-female Special Ops team in the U.S. military through
the Medusa Project. Only trouble was, the man charged
with training the women was under orders to make sure
they failed. But when their commander disappeared in
enemy territory, Vanessa and the Medusas were the only
people the government could turn to to retrieve him and
expose a deadly terrorist plot.

#32 THE SPY WORE RED—Wendy Rosnau
Spy Games
When Quest agent Nadja Stefn accepted a mission to
terminate an international assassin and seize his future-kill
files, she had another agenda: finding the child who was
ripped from her at birth. But she hadn't counted on
working with her ex-lover, Bjorn, agent extraordinaire—
and unbeknownst to him, her child's father.